When a lethal traitor threatens to derail the top-secret SPEAR agency, A YEAR OF LOVING DANGEROUSLY continues....

Alex Bok

Tall, virile, potently sexy—lives every moment as if it were his last.

On a deadly mission to bring down a traitor, this hard-edged bachelor is reunited with the only woman who had ever truly touched his heart. Would he pay the ultimate price for passion's sake?

Nora Lowe

She has eyes the color of the pale blue dawn, long, rippling black hair—and is saving all her love for one unforgettable man.

She didn't know what Alex Bok was doing on *her* archeological dig—or why danger shadowed his every move. So she engaged in a sweetly seductive game of kiss and tell....

The man at the helm

Powerful, pragmatic—the shadowed entity no one sees.

Jonah had given Agent Bok direct orders—infiltrate the nearby terrorist compound and ensnare the sinister Simon in a deadly trap. But was one of his own about to be neutralized by *love?*

Dear Reader,

As the Intimate Moments quarter of our yearlong 20th anniversary promotion draws to a close, we offer you a month so full of reading excitement, you'll hardly know where to start. How about with *Night Shield,* the newest NIGHT TALES title from *New York Times* bestselling author Nora Roberts? As always, Nora delivers characters you'll never forget and a plot guaranteed to keep you turning the pages. And don't miss our special NIGHT TALES reissue, also available this month wherever you buy books.

What next? How about *Night of No Return,* rising star Eileen Wilks's contribution to our in-line continuity, A YEAR OF LOVING DANGEROUSLY? This emotional and suspenseful tale will have you on the edge of your seat—and longing for the next book in the series. As an additional treat this month, we offer you an in-line continuation of our extremely popular out-of-series continuity, 36 HOURS. Bestselling author Susan Mallery kicks things off with *Cinderella for a Night.* You'll love this book, along with the three Intimate Moments novels—and one stand-alone Christmas anthology—that follow it.

Rounding out the month, we have a new book from Beverly Bird, one of the authors who helped define Intimate Moments in its very first month of publication. She's joined by Mary McBride and Virginia Kantra, each of whom contributes a top-notch novel to the month.

Next month, look for a special two-in-one volume by Maggie Shayne and Marilyn Pappano, called *Who Do You Love?* And in November, watch for the debut of our stunning new cover design.

Leslie J. Wainger
Executive Senior Editor

Please address questions and book requests to:
Silhouette Reader Service
U.S.: 3010 Walden Ave., P.O. Box 1325, Buffalo, NY 14269
Canadian: P.O. Box 609, Fort Erie, Ont. L2A 5X3

Eileen Wilks

NIGHT OF NO RETURN

Silhouette® INTIMATE™ MOMENTS®

Published by Silhouette Books

America's Publisher of Contemporary Romance

Special thanks and acknowledgment are given to Eileen Wilks for her contribution to the A Year of Loving Dangerously series.

SILHOUETTE BOOKS

ISBN 0-373-27098-4

NIGHT OF NO RETURN

This edition published by arrangement with Harlequin Books S.A.

Printed in U.S.A.

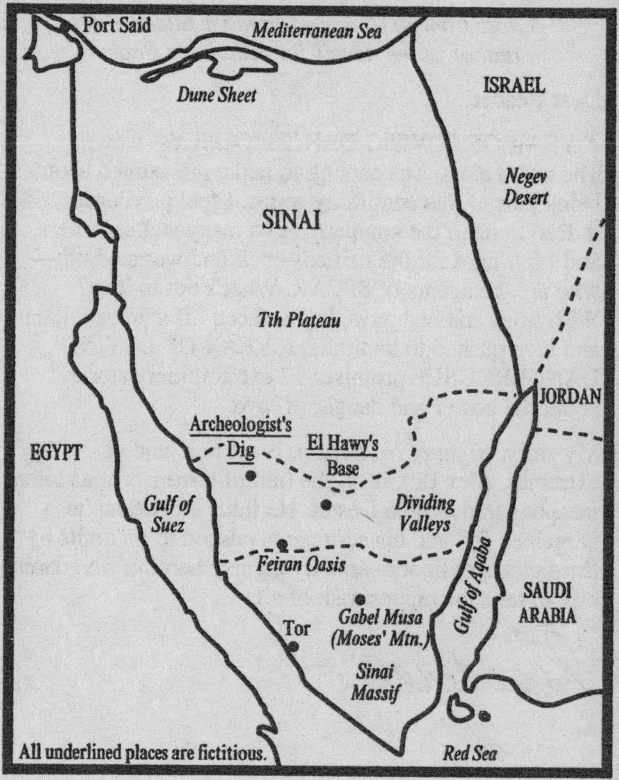
Port Said
Mediterranean Sea
Dune Sheet
ISRAEL
Negev
Desert
SINAI
Tih Plateau
JORDAN
Archeologist's
Dig
El Hawy's
Base
EGYPT
Gulf of
Suez
Dividing
Valleys
Feiran Oasis
Gulf of Aqaba
SAUDI
ARABIA
Gabel Musa
(Moses' Mtn.)
Tor
Sinai
Massif
All underlined places are fictitious.
Red Sea

A note from RITA Award Finalist Eileen Wilks, author of ten novels for Silhouette Books:

Dear Reader,

A YEAR OF LOVING DANGEROUSLY—wow! The name alone was enough to make me excited about being part of this continuity series. I feel privileged indeed to be in the company of so many stellar writers, and I fell hard for the heroes—men and women both—who are the agents of SPEAR. What's not to love? With spies and bad guys, honor faced off against villainy and love pushed to its limits, A YEAR OF LOVING DANGEROUSLY promises 12 extraordinary stories about the power and danger of love.

My story, *Night of No Return,* is set in a land of extremes. Alex Bok is on the trail of terrorists and stolen weapons in the Sinai Desert. He finds more than he bargained for, and his courage is pushed to its limits by the dictates of honor—and by a gutsy heroine who dares him to take the biggest risk of all.

Eileen Wilks

Chapter 1

Southern California, U.S.A., September 7

He didn't want to die.

It was a disconcerting thing for a man like Alex to learn at the age of thirty-four. He sat at one of the wrought-iron tables on the western terrace, dripping with sweat as he watched the southern California sky turn gaudy with sunset over the darkening Pacific Ocean. If the air could have held one dram more of that eye-burning orange, he thought, he'd be able to pluck it like a guitar string.

Color. Life. He drank them both in, relishing the way the muscles in his thighs jumped and the burn in his calves. His heartbeat pleased him. It was almost back to normal, though he'd just finished a five-mile run in the scrubby mountains surrounding the resort. If he wasn't quite at the peak of conditioning yet, he was well enough. His body had done everything he'd asked of it. He was fit again, ready for assignment.

And alive. He was so damned glad to be alive. The depth of his gratitude troubled him because it was rooted in fear, the same fear that shredded his sleep all too often.

He was the only guest on the large flagstone terrace at this hour. The heat was keeping most people inside, or in the pool. A waiter had brought him a glass and a pitcher of ice water when he'd first reached the terrace. The staff here at Condor Mountain Resort and Spa knew him; he'd stayed here before, though never for as long as he'd been here this time.

Too damned long, he thought. He needed to get back into action. Once he did, his fear would lessen. It had to. He couldn't stand to live a timid life.

The glass of ice water he picked up was as sweaty as he was. He held it to his forehead, enjoying the shock of cold. The air was dry, smelling of dust and creosote...yet he could have sworn he smelled lilacs.

That was *her* fragrance. He frowned.

"Brooding again, Alex?"

The voice belonged to another woman—not the one he associated with lilacs. Alex looked over his shoulder and smiled, pleased with the company. He was a man who enjoyed people. Companionship, like sex, came easily to him. If there was a part of him that remained sealed off, untouchable no matter whom he was with, he'd lived with that too long to take much notice of it.

He especially enjoyed tall, slim-hipped women who wore shorts that showed off their legs. That the woman crossing the patio to him now was a fellow agent added to the pleasure of her company. "Hey, I don't brood. I'm enjoying the sunset."

"You do look like you're having a good time melting. You actually like this heat, don't you?"

"Heat is good. Come sit down and we'll talk about it. There's body heat, for example..."

Alicia Kirby pulled out the chair across from him. She was twenty-four, brilliant, and looked, he thought, like a forward on a high school basketball team, with her long, elegant bones and that boyish cap of auburn hair. When she shook her head, that pretty hair bounced with the motion.

Pretty, yes, but it wasn't a long, rippling fall of hair as black as the desert sky, and smelling like lilacs.... Dammit. He had to stop thinking about a woman he'd never see again.

"Life must be painfully dull," Alicia said, "if you have to flirt with me to add a hint of danger to your humdrum existence. No more than a hint, of course. East doesn't take you any more seriously than I do."

He put his hand over his heart. "I live for danger, but flirting with a beautiful woman is a different sort of spice."

The edges of her high cheekbones took on a faint pink tinge, which pleased him. Alicia might not take him seriously—hell, he didn't want her to, she was married to a man he considered a friend—but she enjoyed a compliment as much as the next woman. He had a feeling she hadn't heard enough of them.

"Beautiful?" She managed to look skeptical despite her pink cheeks. "That's laying it on pretty thick. I feel like roadkill."

He straightened, alarmed. "Maybe you should go back inside. In your condition, this heat—"

"Not you, too! What is it about pregnancy that turns halfway sensible men into nervous idiots?"

"The fact that we can't do it, I guess. Is East making a pest of himself again?" He liked the idea that the legendary East Kirby—legendary in some circles, anyway—had been reduced to a nervous wreck by his new wife's pregnancy.

"Why do you think I came out here? I'm escaping." She tilted her head. "Just like you."

"Uh-uh. I might *like* to escape, but I'm stuck here until I hear from our mutual friend. Not that there's anything wrong with your hospitality," he added. Alicia and East ran Condor Mountain Resort and Spa for fun, profit, and the benefit of the occasional SPEAR agent in need of rest and rehab. Like Alex.

Though SPEAR had been founded by Abraham Lincoln, its existence had always been shrouded in such secrecy that few people knew it existed, even at the upper levels of government. Technically, SPEAR stood for Stealth, Perseverance, Endeavor, Attack and Rescue. In a deeper sense, the organization stood for much more. Honor, above all. Sacrifice. Service. Values that a confused, cynical world didn't always recognize, but which the men and women of SPEAR understood and were willing to live for.

Or to die for.

Alicia had a skeptical look on her face. "So all that running you do is purely for the sake of fitness? Not because you're trying like crazy to get away from something?"

Alex fought off a frown. Behind that youthful face of Alicia's was an irritatingly observant woman. He took another drink of water. "Running is a great way to get back in shape. I've been using the gym, too."

"Yes, but you've been running in the afternoons. In temperatures of ninety degrees or better. That seems like an odd thing for a man who nearly died in the desert to do."

But it wasn't heat he feared. It was darkness. Death was

dark. That thick and sticky darkness clung to him still, clogging his dreams...sending him running through the sun-soaked hills. He saluted her with his glass. "Hey, I can take the heat. After all, I grew up in a part of the world that makes southern California seem air-conditioned."

"You nearly died there, too."

She was definitely beginning to get on his nerves. "It was a knife that nearly did me in, not the desert. Have you heard from Jeff lately?"

For a moment he thought she wasn't going to accept the change of subject, but after favoring him with another thoughtful look, she spoke of the young man who was East's adopted son. Jeff was Alicia's age, a decade younger than East or Alex, and he'd recently been through an ordeal much worse than what Alex had endured. Not that Alex knew the details—SPEAR agents might discuss an operation among themselves in a general way, but specifics were shared only on a need-to-know basis. Apparently Jeff had come out of it okay.

The resilience of youth. Alex wanted to think that was why Jeff had rebounded from his experience so quickly. But maybe Jeff was just the better man. Stronger. Not given to waking up in the middle of the night with the icy sweat of terror drying on his skin.

Alex drank his water as he listened to Alicia talk about her new stepson. Jeff was in Los Angeles after spending some R & R time at another SPEAR operation in Arizona. His experience had propelled him to enlist in SPEAR, which was now covering the last of his med school. He'd just started his residency in the ER of a busy Los Angeles hospital.

"I don't expect we'll hear much from him for a while," Alicia said. "He plans on specializing in trauma medicine with an emphasis on on-site treatment." She smiled. "When he isn't working, he'll be sleeping."

"You're probably right." Alex heard the door to the resort open and glanced that way.

A tall man with shaggy brown hair stood in the doorway, one eyebrow raised. "Trying to make time with my wife again, Alex?"

"I do my best," he said cheerfully. "Go away, East. I can't get anywhere with you breathing down my neck."

"*You* go away." East walked over and pulled out a chair. "I just talked to Jonah. You're to call him."

At last. Alex was on his feet instantly. "I'll let you take over with the flirting, then. Be sure to mention her gorgeous legs. I hadn't gotten around to them yet."

"Fickle." Alicia shook her head. "Sadly fickle."

"Come back down after you've talked with him," East said. "I'm supposed to brief you on some background details."

"Will do." Alex was already at the door.

The shock of cold air from the air-conditioning hit him the moment he stepped inside the expensively rustic lobby. He passed the regular elevator, stopping at one that the other guests at the resort couldn't use, and inserted the key required to operate it. His heart was pumping with excitement.

A call from Jonah could mean only one thing—an assignment. He was ready for it physically, and if he still had a way to go emotionally…well, he'd shake down just fine once he got into action again.

Contrary to what his parents believed, Alex had never had a death wish. Nor was he an excitement junky—not anymore, at least. He'd outgrown that years ago. He liked edges, though. A man never felt more alive than when he was challenging his limits. He'd teetered on the slipperiest edge of all more than once while on assignment, but until a month ago he'd never gone over. But when he'd been left for dead in the Negev desert, he'd skidded down that dark slope...until *she* found him. His lady of the lilacs.

It had changed him. For the last month he had been trying to come to terms with that change while strength eased back into his body. He'd hiked or run through the dry mountains that cradled the resort so he could enjoy the slide and flex of thigh muscles, the bunch and release in his calves. Life was good.

Alex's suite was on the top floor. The view was breathtaking—rugged hills falling in sage and dust-colored humps into the vast blue of the ocean. The bed was king-size and comfortable, and the walls were reinforced with steel and an inner layer of sand. They would stand up to anything but a direct hit from a bomb. The steel had the additional property of making it difficult for anyone nearby to pick up the signal from the cell phone he grabbed as soon as the door closed behind him.

This phone, too, had special properties. The signal was digitized and encoded, so that even if someone did manage to intercept part of the transmission it wouldn't do them any good. It wasn't dependent on normal cells, either, but used a system established by orbiting satellites, rendering calls completely untraceable. With this phone, Alex could talk to anyone anywhere on the planet.

He punched in a number he knew well, hung up and waited. A few minutes later, the phone rang, then a cool, dry voice said, "Are you ready to go back to work, Alex?"

Ten minutes later he disconnected. He stood in his air-conditioned room and stared out the reinforced glass of the window, and he tasted the hot, dusty wind of the desert.

No surprise that he was going back to the Middle East. That was where his expertise lay. Among other skills, Alex spoke Arabic and Greek fluently and could make himself understood in Hebrew. He knew smugglers in five countries, and scientists in three. He'd be going in as an archaeologist—a cover he'd used often, since it dovetailed so neatly with reality. Nor was his assignment a surprise; the people who had left him for dead a month ago had ties to the terrorist organization whose base he would be hunting.

No, none of that was unexpected. But the dig he'd be participating in as part of his cover, and the person in charge of that dig—oh, yes, that had surprised him.

The scent of lilacs drifted across his memory again, and Alex smiled slowly. *Never say never,* he thought, his spirits rising. Not only was he going to have a chance to exorcise the fear that clung to him like a bad smell, he would get to work another distracting memory out of his system.

A memory named Nora.

Sinai Peninsula, Egypt, September 9

There were no songbirds in the Sinai. Not in this part of it, not at this time of year. To the north, the land rose in stony leaps to the barren height of the Tie Plateau before slipping down in sandy drifts to the dunes that met the Mediterranean. To the south, ragged mountains heaved themselves high again, bunching up into the gaunt peaks of the Sinai Massif, the range surrounding Gebel Musa—Mount Sinai. Here, in the Dividing Valleys, the land dipped lower. The rare rains of the desert had spent millennia wearing away granite and sandstone, limestone and dolomite, to leave a jumbled confusion of rock cut by canyons and wadis. Here there might be the sound of the occasional caw of a raven or the cooing of quail, but even that was unlikely this early. At this hour, the soft percussion of Nora's footfalls in the sand and gravel was the only sound.

The vague light of dawn canted in steeply from the east, leaving the bottom of the wadi in shadow. It was cool there, cool enough that she'd barely broken a sweat, though she'd been running for ten minutes. The rough terrain kept her from running very fast, but the wadi's course was downward; it would take her ten more minutes to reach the convergence of this wadi with the next, where she'd veer back uphill, toward camp.

Then she could expect to sweat. But now she ran easily, enjoying the flow of cool air over warm muscles, and she dreamed of another run she'd taken. Another desert. And the man she'd found there.

When Nora thought of him, she thought of darkness. The near-dark of the time when she'd found him. Dark, sun-bronzed skin. Hair as black as her own. And the darkness that men create, the darkness of violence and death.

Not that she'd seen the evidence of violence at first. The bloody trail he'd left as he'd staggered across the desert had been hidden by the scrubby growth nearby, and his clothes had been the color of the sand where he'd lain, curled into himself for warmth.

From a distance she'd thought him a heap of sand. As she'd loped closer, he'd looked like a bundle of rags.

Then she'd thought she'd found a corpse.

The blood that had covered his chest and shoulder had heightened that impression. But he'd been alive, alive and conscious...as she'd discovered when she'd touched her fingers to his throat, seeking a pulse.

Again, almost as strong in memory as when it had happened, she felt the shock that had gone through her when he opened his eyes. Amber eyes. She could think of no other word to describe them. Like the petrified resin that people the world over have prized for millennia as a jewel, they had seemed to hold trapped sunlight inside them.

"Hey, Nora!"

She stopped, one foot planted on a tilted granite slab, the other in a drift of sand between rocks, her mind shutting off her reverie as abruptly as her body obeyed her order to stop.

What had gone wrong now?

She looked up at the edge of the wadi, where a man stood—Tim, judging by the gangly outline he made against the pale pewter sky. "What is it this time? I haven't finished my run."

"I can see that. But you'd better head back to camp. Mahmoud just radioed that his truck is fixed and he's nearly here. Looks like you didn't have to send me to the oasis for drinking water yesterday, after all."

"But I didn't know that yesterday. Look, Tim, it's nice to get good news for a change, but it could have waited until I got back to camp. I'll only be another twenty minutes, and if Mahmoud beats me there, you can start unloading without me."

"But he's got something that wasn't on your list. Some*one,* actually—some muckety-muck from the Cairo Museum who wants to look at the cave."

Her eyebrows lifted in surprise. "So soon? Providence and the mills of funding organizations usually grind slower than that." The regret she felt about abandoning her run was quickly swallowed by a surge of excitement. Dr. Ibrahim must have been more interested than she'd realized when she'd reported their cave to him last month.

Or maybe he was hedging his bets. If what they'd found so far turned out to be as important as Nora hoped, he might try to have someone else put in charge of the dig. Someone with one of those dandy Y chromosomes. Damn.

"I'd better be in camp to welcome our colleague when he arrives, then, hadn't I? Be right up."

Typically, Nora didn't bother to look for the easiest path up the side of the wadi, but headed straight up from where she stood. She was a long, leggy woman who moved with the awkward energy of a colt, all sudden starts and stops, yet there was a certain grace to her climb, the ease of a woman comfortable with her body. She reached the top only slightly breathless, and paused to unhook the small water jug on her belt, then downed half the contents in a few greedy gulps.

"Did Mahmoud say who our visitor is?" she asked as she moved past Tim. The path, what there was of it, wound through the knobby outcroppings of rock that made up the sizable hill that lay between them and the camp.

He grimaced. Tim had one of those elastic faces that turn every expression into comical exaggeration. "Probably. I didn't catch it, though. I was concentrating too hard on trying to figure whether he said he'd be here in fifteen minutes, or that his cat was pregnant. Of course, if he'd asked me where the baggage claim was, I would have understood just fine."

"Or the men's room?" She grinned. Her assistant's smattering of Arabic came almost entirely from a phrase book. "I'll never understand how a student of language who's been in Egypt for two years can know so little Arabic."

"Everyone knows we Brits can't cook or remember all those peculiar words some people use instead of a proper language."

"You've managed to learn quite a few peculiar words. At least, Ibrahim seems to think so, or he wouldn't have kept you around."

"Hieroglyphics are different. I don't have to *speak* them."

Tim was totally absorbed by his specialty—the evolution of written language as evinced by the study of hieroglyphics. He was smart, funny and completely lacking in ambition, a trait more foreign to her than any language could be. "Where are Ahmed and Gamal? One of them could have translated for you."

"Praying, I think," he said, vague as usual about anything that didn't interest him. "Do you think we're going to be descended upon by a horde of eager Egyptologists?"

"One person doesn't constitute a horde. Although, if we can impress him with the potential here...." She shrugged, impatient with her own eagerness. "Or her, I should say, though that doesn't seem likely, given Ibrahim's prejudices. I'm surprised he sent anyone at all. I didn't think he was even listening when I talked to him last month."

Nora had tried not to get her hopes up when she'd made the trip to Cairo to present her report in person, but her reception by the director of the museum had been chilly enough to depress Pollyanna. She'd received permission to follow up on her find, but none of the funding or support personnel she required to do the job properly.

Needing advice, she'd made a second stop before returning to the dig—a short trip across the border into Israel, where an old professor of hers lived on a kibbutz in the Negev.

Deep inside, something tugged at her, a feeling sharp and insistent, clearer than memory but less easy to name. *Enough, already,* she told herself. She'd known the man for no more than an hour—oh, it was ridiculous even to say she'd known him. She'd found him, that was all, and she'd done what she could to keep him alive. She didn't even know his name. If she still felt somehow connected to a man she didn't know, that wasn't surprising, was it? Under the circumstances...?

She remembered the shock of his eyes opening and meeting hers, the sense that the world had just tilted, sending her life spinning off in an unplanned direction. Romantic foolishness, but not surprising, really. Under the circumstances.

When Tim sighed she glanced back at him, ready to be distracted. "Wishing for that horde, are you?"

"With hordes, come funding. Another generator would be nice. We could get a new air conditioner. Hey, isn't the path thataway?"

"This way is shorter." The path Tim had indicated was a fairly easy track that went around the rocky hill. Nora preferred a more direct route, up the hill and through a narrow notch between thrusting boulders. "You've been in Egypt long enough for your blue blood to have adjusted to the heat. We already have an air conditioner."

"No, we don't. We have a noisemaker you turn on for a few hours that occasionally coughs up a little cool air."

"It's better than nothing." Which summed up most of their equipment. Theirs was a shoestring operation, and with all the small disasters that had beset them lately, those strings were getting frayed. "Don't get your hopes up," she said, addressing herself as much as Tim as she eased out of the vee-shaped cleft and back onto more nearly horizontal ground. "Even if this fellow gives Ibrahim a good report, we're not going to get any substantial increase in funding. Not unless we make a major find." She started up the hill.

Tim followed slowly. "We'd have a much better chance of that if we had the people and equipment to do the job right."

Didn't she know it. "I could have sworn I gave you my

speech about 'paying our dues' when you signed on, but if you need to hear it again—''

''I know, I know. This is my opportunity to get out of my ivory tower and learn the basics of fieldwork. The problem is, I *like* my ivory tower. It's air-conditioned, and there are no bugs.''

He slipped, grabbing awkwardly at the rock, swore, and finally managed to clamber out and stand beside her. ''And there aren't a lot of mountains to cross to get to my office at the museum, either. Look at this.'' He held out his hand, displaying a scraped palm. ''I'm damned if I know why you have to play mountain goat just so you can find a place to run. Don't you get enough exercise on the dig?''

A smile tugged at her mouth as she turned back to head down the hill. Camp lay below them. ''You like air-conditioning. I like to run.''

''Well, aside from being a blasted nuisance and hard on my epidermis, your runs aren't safe. Especially with everything that's been happening lately.''

''A few petty thefts don't make it unsafe here—as safe as you can be in the desert, anyway.''

''If we stay in camp. But you keep wandering off by yourself.''

Out of consideration for Tim's scraped hand, she chose the easiest way down, circling around a large sandstone outcropping that wind and weather had sculpted into a shape she could only call phallic. ''There's a lot of poverty among the tribes. Not that I mean to accuse the Bedouin, but they're the only people out here other than us.''

''Just them, us, and the occasional terrorist.''

''Are you still harping on that theory? Terrorists blow up things. They don't steal a couple of cases of canned food for the glory of the cause.''

''What about our first generator?''

"We don't know that it was tampered with."

"The mechanic said—"

"I know what he said. I wish he'd kept his dire mutterings to himself, since you seem to have taken them so much to heart. He *also* said it could have been damaged in transport."

"Mahmoud's gas tank didn't get sugar in it by accident."

"Mahmoud isn't exactly Mr. Congeniality. The man collects enemies the way dogs collect fleas. Look, Tim, there are times when I appreciate your stubbornness—"

"You ought to. You could teach a camel the meaning of the word. Hey!" he said as they rounded the outcropping. "Looks like our timing is right on the money."

They had come out on a rise just above the camp, which was located in one of the larger wadis—a much wider channel than the one where she liked to run. A cloud of dust was moving slowly along the dry watercourse, nearly obscuring the truck that caused it.

"If we hurry, we can get there about the same time as Mahmoud," she said, picking up the pace.

"About your morning run—"

"Tim," she said warningly.

"Nora, even if terrorists *aren't* lurking nearby, it isn't safe for you to go running alone. You could turn an ankle or get bitten by something nasty."

"That's why I always run in the same place. If I'm late getting back, you'll know where to come looking for me."

"I don't want to have to come looking for you. Why can't you exercise in camp?"

"Aside from the fact that I enjoy running?"

"Yeah, aside from that."

She shrugged. Her reasons were too private to speak aloud. *Wildness calls to wildness,* she thought. When she was running along a twisting wadi, away from everyone, she could allow herself to dream. Weren't dreams as important to life as safety? Yet maybe...maybe she'd been dreaming too much lately. Dreaming about one thing, the same thing, over and over. The man. The one she would never see again.

The truck pulled up in a cloud of dust just as Nora reached level ground, and every member of her small crew descended upon it. The small crowd wasn't enough to block her view, but the truck itself kept her from seeing who climbed out of the passenger side. She lengthened her stride, as curious as the others were about their visitor.

Mahmoud headed straight for the cookstove in front of the main tent, where a pot of coffee was perfuming the air. Nora greeted him briefly.

Their guest was speaking to Gamal in fluent Arabic, his back to her, when she rounded the front of the truck. *He's Egyptian, then,* she thought. Not surprising, if he came from the museum. His clothing, however, spoke of the West—khaki shorts much like her own, a plain pullover shirt and Nikes. A lot of Egyptians did wear western clothing, though the more devout would have disapproved of his shorts.

He wore no hat, which made her frown, but she would hold off on the lecture until she saw if he was foolish enough to do that in the heat of the day. His short hair was as black as her own, and his body told her he was younger than she'd expected—young and attractive, with a lean, muscular body.

The sight of those masculine shoulders, slim hips and strong legs made her hormones kick in with a pleasant little rush, but Nora didn't doubt her ability to keep any tickle of desire under control. She'd been doing it for years.

DeLaney, however, was another story. The youthful college student might start mooning after their guest instead of Tim.

Of course, Tim would probably be relieved if she did. Nora was smiling when she spoke. "Welcome to the dig. I'm Dr. Nora Lowe."

"Yes," he said, in a low, pleasant voice as he turned to face her. "I know."

His eyes met hers. Amber eyes. Clear as sunlight trapped in time, smiling down at her.

Chapter 2

Alex looked at the astonished face of the woman he'd crossed an ocean to deceive, and his mind emptied of all but scattered impressions. Smooth skin, tanned to honey. Unpainted lips. Eyes the color of the dawn sky overhead, startling pale in that tanned face...soft blue eyes that looked as dazed as he felt.

A single thought appeared from nowhere: *It couldn't really happen like this, could it?*

Immediately, he was irritated, and the irritation cleared his mind. What kind of question was that? *What* couldn't happen? Because the question made no sense, he shoved it away.

Long habit had him smoothing his features into an amused grin. "We weren't properly introduced the last time we met, were we? I'm Alex Bok." He held out his hand.

The dazed look hadn't cleared from her eyes. "Alex." She took his hand and he felt a second shock, but this one was purely sensual. Understandable, and distinctly pleasant. "Alex Bok?" Her gaze sharpened, and he knew she'd recognized the name. "Any relation to Franklin and Elizabeth Bok?"

He smiled crookedly. "You could say that. They're my parents."

She laughed. "Good heavens, you're an archaeologist! If you knew what all I had imagined..."

He hadn't released her hand after shaking it. Nora Lowe had narrow palms, with the callouses of a woman who works with her hands. She wore no rings. Her skin was warm...and she smelled of lilacs. "Why, what did you think I was?"

"Oh, all sorts of things—a smuggler, a reporter, a pilgrim. Archaeologist never made the list." She tilted her head. "I think we have a friend in common. Myrna Lancaster."

It took him a moment to place the name. "Myrna. Of course. We got to know each other on a dig in the Eastern Desert two years ago." He'd been on the trail of a particularly bloody assassin, and Myrna had provided welcome relief from the grim hunt. A delightfully energetic young woman, he recalled, and no more interested in permanent entanglements than he had been.

A short, curvy young woman with glasses that wouldn't stay up on her dot of a nose tugged at Nora's sleeve to get her attention. "So who is he?"

"The son of the couple who wrote the book on Old Kingdom pottery. Literally." That came from the man Alex had seen returning to camp with Nora when he arrived. "You must have studied it in one of your classes." He didn't sound excited. More like suspicious.

Or jealous?

"He's also the man I found in the Negev," Nora said.

Then, apparently realizing Alex still held her hand, she flushed and pulled it away.

"The one who was *stabbed?*" The young woman's eyes widened behind her glasses in delicious horror. "By bandits? The one you stumbled over when you were visiting your old professor?"

Nora glanced at Alex apologetically. "The story was too good not to share."

He'd counted on it. "That was inevitable, I suppose." He reached back inside the truck, taking out an olive-colored duffel bag, and bent to pull an envelope from its side pocket. "This is from Dr. Ibrahim. I gather it introduces me and explains why he sent me."

She took the letter, but didn't open it. "Let me introduce you more formally—now that I know your name." A quick, shy grin lit her face. "This is DeLaney Brown, our resident cheerleader."

The young woman with the slippery glasses made a face. "Just think of me as part of the cheap labor."

"Glad to meet you, DeLaney." He already knew who she was, of course. Jonah had supplied him with backgrounds for the Americans and the single Englishman at the dig. DeLaney Brown was a twenty-three-year-old graduate student at the university where Nora Lowe taught. Her father was a successful surgeon; her mother was deeply involved in charity work. No siblings. She was bright, impulsive, and prone to throw herself at political causes of all sorts, though there were no known ties to any of the Arabic fringe groups. He held out his hand.

DeLaney's palm was sweaty. She gave his hand a single quick squeeze before pulling her hand back so she could push her glasses up again. "What on earth did you do to make someone stab you, anyway?"

"Good God, DeLaney, you have the manners of a small

child sometimes. I'm Lisa.'' The third woman present held out a broad, blunt-nailed hand. ''More cheap labor.''

Lisa was also a graduate student, Alex knew, but she was more than twenty years older than DeLaney, having returned to college after a messy divorce. She had dark skin, grizzled dark hair cut very short, three earrings in each ear, and an ex-husband with gambling debts. Her handshake was firm.

''Welcome to the dig,'' she said. ''I can't place your accent. You American?''

''Yes, but I grew up in this part of the world.''

''That would explain it. You sound almost like Tim.''

''Speaking of whom,'' Nora said, ''this is Timothy Gaines, my assistant—Dr. Gaines, actually—but we don't bother much with titles out here. But maybe the two of you have met? Tim is with the British Museum, but he's currently attached to the Cairo Museum.''

Alex held out his hand again. ''I'm not on staff at either museum, so I haven't had the pleasure.''

''Technically, I'm not on staff in Cairo, either, but they do give me office space. Good to have you here, Bok.'' At twenty-eight, Timothy Gaines had the bony, stretched-out frame of Abraham Lincoln, a basketball player's hands, and the suspicious manner of a dog whose territory has been invaded. Gaines didn't play any childish games with the handshake, though, keeping it brief and business-like.

''Dr. Ibrahim sends his regards.'' Alex hadn't actually spoken to the museum's director, but it seemed a safe thing to say.

''Tactful bloke, aren't you? I can just imagine what he really said. Ibrahim tends to forget I'm around, and when he does remember, he doesn't like me above half.''

Nora gave Tim a puzzled glance, as if she sensed his

hostility but didn't understand it, and then went on to introduce the last two members of her crew. Alex knew less about Gamal and Ahmed than he knew about the westerners. He needed to learn more, fast. He was hoping one of these people was connected to the terrorist group that called themselves El Hawy. It would make finding the boss a lot simpler. Not easier, necessarily, but simpler. The Egyptians were the likeliest plants.

Ahmed was in his twenties, a quiet young man with a formal manner. Educated, judging by his accent, which made Alex wonder what he was doing here, rather than in one of the cities. Gamal was older and more talkative, with a wide, gap-toothed grin.

And then, of course, there was Nora Lowe, the woman who had saved his life. He'd been too out of it to retain a clear image of her face, but her voice—that had stayed with him. Her voice, her scent, the feel of her hair, her warmth. Most of all, he remembered the warmth of her. He'd been so very cold, when she'd found him.

Alex tried to look at her objectively, as she laughed at something DeLaney said. He knew quite a bit about Nora Lowe. He hadn't been able to fit the dry facts in the report to his memory of soft hands, warmth, and clouds of dark hair. He was having trouble now, fitting either facts or memory to reality.

According to the report, Dr. Lowe was thirty, unmarried and brilliant. Also determined. She came from poverty, yet had put herself through college and graduate school with the help of scholarships, loans and grants. Her mother was dead, her father unknown; she had two sisters, both older than her. One of her sisters had been married twice, the first time while still in high school. The other sister had earned her GED from a jail cell, where she'd served time for passing hot checks.

The woman standing in front of him had a quick smile and a sexy mouth, wide and fluid. Her nose was slightly crooked, and her face was too narrow for real beauty. The clouds of midnight-dark hair that he remembered were pulled back today in a braid that hung halfway down her back.

Her pale-blue eyes, fringed in black, were nothing short of stunning.

"I imagine you're tired," she was saying. "The drive from Feiron Oasis isn't that long, but the last stretch is pretty rough, and Mahmoud's insistence on driving at night means you haven't had much sleep. What would you rather have first—breakfast, a nap or a look at the dig?"

You. "All of the above, except for the nap. I don't need much sleep. But first, maybe you could show me where to put my things until I can get my tent up?"

"Sure." That mobile mouth turned up in a smile. "I'm glad you brought your own tent. We're a bit crowded."

"I'll be glad to show him around," DeLaney said eagerly.

"Nope. You need to help unload. Okay, everyone—" Nora waved her hands in a shooing motion "—make like good little worker ants. The faster we get the supplies unloaded and stored, the faster we can get some real work done. Alex, I'll show you where to set up."

With a measure of good-natured grumbling, the others headed for the back of the truck. Except for Tim. "So, are you really here on Ibrahim's behalf," he asked, "or did your parents send you?"

"Tim!" Nora sounded half-amused, half-appalled. "What's with you this morning? Have you been eating your own cooking or something?"

"Am I being rude? Sorry. I haven't had my coffee yet." He spoke to Nora, but he watched Alex.

"For heaven's sake, then, grab a cup. You can drink it while you help unload."

"All right, all right. I can take a hint." The younger man tossed her a salute and moved off to join the rest.

Nora's clear blue eyes looked puzzled when they met his. "I am sorry about that. It isn't like Tim to take pot shots at someone else's professional background. He's usually so laid-back it's hard to be sure he's awake."

"I'm used to it. With my parents being who they are, I've had opportunities that others haven't." Not all of those opportunities were part of his public record, of course.

"But it isn't up to him to question your credentials, is it? This is my dig." Her faint emphasis on the possessive pronoun suggested she thought there might be some doubt in his mind about that.

"Of course." Alex had no intention of challenging her authority. "Dr. Ibrahim didn't send me here to look over your shoulder. I'm here to work, not just to watch."

She nodded thoughtfully, as if she were considering taking him at his word but hadn't made up her mind. "We can go into all that later, maybe over breakfast. Right now, why don't we take care of your things?"

Alex noticed the way Tim kept track of them when Nora showed him where to put up his tent. Definitely jealous, he decided. Was there something going on between Nora and her long, tall assistant?

He didn't like the quick snap of temper that idea brought.

"This is the guys' side of camp," she was saying. "The latrine is on this side, too, about fifteen feet further down the wadi. We've got a shower, too. It's on the other side of the main tent."

"So the men get the latrine on our side of camp, while you ladies get the shower?"

Her eyes brightened with humor. "It wasn't intentional. Honest. We situated the shower as close to the well as possible."

"You have a well, then?"

"It was here before we were, and needed only a pump to be useful. The water is too brackish too drink, but it washes the dust off. That tent is Tim's," she said, nodding at the nearest one. "You can probably guess that the goat hair tent belongs to Gamal. He shares with Ahmed."

"I noticed a small green tent on the other side of the big one."

"That one's mine. Lisa and DeLaney bunk in the main tent. They used to have their own, but..." She shrugged. "Someone has decided we're here to increase their standard of living."

"It was stolen?"

"I'm afraid so." A small, worried vee appeared between her brows. "We've had a problem with theft."

Their problem was a lot more serious than she realized, but he couldn't tell her that. Alex put his folded tent down in the space she'd indicated. "I can put this up later. Why don't I help unload?" It was best if the others thought of him as one of them, part of the close community that usually formed on a dig. He was aware of a tug of impatience, though. He wanted to get Nora Lowe alone.

"We don't put our guests to work right away," she said. "Wouldn't you like some breakfast first? I can even offer fresh eggs. I saw Lisa carrying some in."

"Think of me as an extra pair of hands, not as a guest."

"I do usually throw a crust or two of bread at my workers before I hustle them out to the dig."

"As appealing as that sounds, I ate before I left Feiron.

I'm not hungry yet. How about taking a couple of cups of coffee out to the site? I'd like to get a look at the cave."

"I wouldn't mind a cup myself. I usually have some after my run."

"Is that where you were? I, ah, saw you and Gaines coming into camp about the same time I did."

"I run most mornings." She started toward the main tent, where the cookstove was set up. "Partly to stay fit. Partly because I just like to. Tim came to get me this morning when Mahmoud radioed that he was bringing a visitor to camp."

"Me."

"Yes." Her gaze flicked to his and a smile touched those full, unpainted lips. "Though I didn't know it."

He wanted to taste that smile. The urge was strong and troubling—and it was shared, he could tell. Their gazes held for another second before she turned away to kneel beside a large plastic box that sat near the stove.

It was the memories, he knew. He'd gotten her tangled up in his mind with nearly dying. After all, Nora Lowe had been the one to find him, to save him. He could sort out his reaction to her objectively, but he couldn't seem to stop reacting. He wondered how much of a problem that was going to be. When pretense and reality blurred, it was easy to make a misstep. And when a man in his line of work made a misstep, people died.

"You take anything in your coffee? It's strong," she warned, taking two mugs out of the box and snapping the lid back on. "Not quite as stiff as the stuff the Bedouin make, but stronger than most Americans are used to."

"I like it strong. And hot."

"Good," she said briskly, standing. "Getting things hot is no problem around here." If she noticed any innuendo in his words or her own, she didn't show it.

"Does Gaines run with you?" Or did they go just far enough away from camp to be alone?

"Are you kidding?" She chuckled and handed him his mug. "Tim's idea of morning exercise is getting out of bed. He thinks I'm crazy." Again that slightly shy smile flickered. "But that's how I found you, you know. I was visiting a former professor of mine at a dig near Kibbutz Nir Am, and I'd gone out for my morning run."

He knew that—now. At the time, he'd thought her appearance a miracle. "Funny. I like to run myself, but I never realized quite how important it was to my health before."

She laughed.

A loud yelp hit the air a second before an even louder crash. Alex spun around, and saw Timothy Gaines lying flat on the ground near one of the tent ropes. Plastic bottles of Gatorade had spilled from the box he'd been carrying, and were rolling merrily around on the dusty ground.

Alex grinned. He suspected Tim had been trying so hard to keep an eye on him and Nora that he'd tripped.

His grin slipped away after a second, though. Everything was falling into place perfectly. Tim was jealous...and Nora was fascinated. Everyone was going to think exactly what he wanted them to think.

Pity it made him feel like such a heel.

Alex took a mug of coffee with him as he and Nora walked along the dry wadi toward the quarry. Nora had brought a mug along, too, as well as a thick slice of the grainy native bread smeared with the soft cheese the Bedouin made from goat's milk. Alex enjoyed the strongly flavored cheese himself, having eaten it innumerable times as a child, but most westerners considered it, at best, an acquired taste.

There was a clarity about the desert that appealed to

Alex, the raw virtue of extremes. The land was badly broken, the earth's cracked bones thrusting up through its thin skin, their nakedness dusted in places with sand and spotted with the tough, bleached vegetation of the desert. Overhead, the sky was vast and cloudless. The dry air stirred against his cheeks in a baby breeze. Alex looked over the rugged landscape, and thought about death.

It wasn't his own death that preyed on his mind this time. It was the death that others—one man in particular—wanted to carry across the ocean to the U.S. The many deaths he was here to prevent, and the traitor he needed to catch, a man they knew only as Simon—a man determined to bring down Jonah and the entire SPEAR agency.

Alex walked beside the woman he needed to charm in order to maintain his cover, sipping coffee as he considered means and ends, and when one justified the other. The coffee was exactly what she had claimed it would be—hot and strong. He glanced at Nora.

Heat and strength there, too, he thought. The strength showed physically, in the lean lines of her body. Lord, about half of the woman was legs—long, honey-gold and gorgeous. But she wasn't just physically strong. Not many people tested themselves against the desert every morning and called it fun.

The heat didn't show, but he sensed it. "You're very quiet."

"I was taught not to speak with my mouth full." She popped the last bite of bread into the mouth in question and dusted her hands without looking at him.

In fact, she'd scarcely looked at him directly since the moment he'd turned around, seen her, and their gazes had locked. "I was expecting you to have more questions about why I'm here, what my qualifications are."

"Isn't that what you're here for? To ask questions?"

"I'm here because you've found a burial chamber where there shouldn't be a burial chamber. But that isn't the only reason."

"No?"

"Nora." He stopped her with his hand on her arm. "Are you uncomfortable with me?"

She sighed and, at last, faced him directly. "Yes. Yes, I guess I am, silly as that sounds. I never thought I'd see you again, you see. After our, ah, dramatic first encounter, you took on this larger-than-life quality in my mind. Not quite real. Now here you are, sent by Dr. Ibrahim to check us out. Real as can be." Her mouth quirked up. "It's disconcerting. Life is certainly full of coincidences, isn't it?"

Her honesty made things easy for him. Too damned easy. "My arrival isn't entirely a coincidence."

"What do you mean?" A few wisps of hair had worked loose from her braid, and that breeze tossed them against her cheek.

"Dr. Ibrahim did send me here, but it was at my request." He turned away, running his hand over the top of his head. Reality and pretense were blurring in an uneasy alliance. "I'm at loose ends right now. I...the attack changed things. Once I recovered physically, I flew to Cairo to see my parents, and while I was there, they had Dr. Ibrahim to dinner. He mentioned your dig. I was interested professionally...and personally. I talked him into sending me instead of the man he'd had in mind. He wasn't hard to persuade." He grinned. "Like DeLaney and Lisa, I work cheap."

She looked at him steadily for a long moment. "I've heard of you. You have the reputation of being something of a dilettante."

"I'm lucky enough to have a private income, which lets me work when and where I choose. If that makes me a dilettante, or a dabbler—'' He shrugged. ''I suppose to some it does.''

''I read your paper in the *Archaeological Review.* It wasn't the work of a dabbler.''

He felt a small, absurd warmth at her words. He'd been proud of that paper. For a moment, pretense and reality merged. ''I love what I do.''

She nodded, and he knew she was considering him, thinking over what he'd told her. He wished he could get inside her head and find out what those thoughts were.

She started walking again. ''Working on a dig is physically hard. You know that, of course. Are you fully recovered?''

''The doctors think so.''

''I never knew...I couldn't find out anything about you. I knew you'd been airlifted to Tel Aviv, but when I went there the people at the hospital wouldn't tell me anything except that you were alive and couldn't have visitors. I guess I can't blame them. I didn't even know your name.''

He hadn't known she'd come to the hospital; it disconcerted him. ''I was pretty much out of it. I'm told that they pumped me up with other people's blood, operated, and then shipped me back to the States.''

''You don't remember?''

''Only snatches.'' Snatches of cold and pain and fear, no soft voice to anchor him, no one there at all...not even himself, after a while. ''They tell me I died on the operating table.''

''What?'' She stopped and stared at him.

''My heart stopped.'' He didn't know why he'd told her that. *Too much truth. What's wrong with me?* He forced the grimness back behind a grin. ''Death proved temporary, I'm happy to say. They got my heart started again, finished what they were doing, and sewed me back up. Not that I remember any of it."

"You actually died?" She shivered. "I've wondered so often...you'd lost a lot of blood by the time I found you, I couldn't believe you were still alive. Then you opened your eyes."

He'd thought he'd heard someone calling him. It had been a hallucination, of course, created by a mind fooled by blood loss and shock. Nora hadn't known his name, so she couldn't have called him, could she?

Yet he had heard it, or thought he had. Somehow he'd swum up from the murky place where the cold had driven him, and found that he wasn't alone. She had been there, and she'd lain down with him, loaning him the heat of her body to hold the cold at bay. And talking to him. Her quiet voice had given him something to hold onto as he fought the sucking darkness.

As always, those memories made him restless. He started walking again, intending to turn the conversation to the dig, to the thefts, to anything that would move him forward instead of back.

Instead, he heard himself say, "I was a bloody mess when you found me." He'd made it to within a handful of kilometers of the kibbutz, first staggering, then dragging himself onward. But he'd lost too much blood. By the time Nora had stumbled across him, he'd been going into shock. "Why did you stay instead of going for help?"

"Fear," she said wryly. "I was more afraid to leave you than to stay with you. I knew someone would come looking for me when I didn't return from my run on time, and they'd be able to follow my tracks in the sand. What I didn't know was how long I'd have to wait." She shook her head. "I'd taken some first aid courses before I came out here, since I knew there wouldn't be a doctor or a nurse close enough to count on in an emergency. So I was pretty sure you were in shock. Your skin was cold to the touch. But I was scared stiff I'd made the wrong decision.''

Scared, she might well have been. But not stiff. She'd been supple and very much alive. ''You were right.'' It came out husky. Too damned *real* again. He jerked his mind back to his purpose, only to discover that it had changed slightly while he wasn't watching.

He had to have a good reason to stay here for a couple weeks, and part of that reason was walking beside him now. No one would wonder if he lingered here, dabbling in archaeology while he pursued a woman. He'd spent years cultivating the reputation of a man likely to do just that. A dilettante, just as she'd said, who enjoyed both archaeology and women with the same temporary enthusiasm.

But this time he would pursue without catching. Nora didn't deserve to be used as a means to an end, no matter how important that end. ''I never got a chance to thank you,'' he said more lightly. ''That's part of my reason for being here.''

She slid him a curious glance. ''And the rest of it is professional?''

Keep her charmed, he told himself, keep her interested—but keep your hands to yourself. If he didn't touch her, maybe he wouldn't hurt her. ''Not entirely.'' Because looking at her made him want her, he looked ahead without giving her the smile or the slow, appraising glance that would have made his meaning obviously personal. He forced himself to change the subject. ''That's the quarry up ahead, isn't it? Tell me about the cave you found.''

Chapter 3

Alex had been right, Nora thought as they closed the distance to the quarry. She did have questions. Lots of them.

But it wasn't professional matters she wanted to ask him about.

She wanted to know if his wound still troubled him, whether he had any brothers or sisters, and why a man with his background *wasn't* working for the Cairo Museum or some similar, prestigious institution. She wondered if he preferred dawn or sunset, classical music or rock, and what he thought about before falling asleep at night.

Most of all, she wanted to know what he thought of her, and if he had really wanted to kiss her earlier. She was almost sure he had. But just because she'd helped save his life didn't mean he owed her answers to the highly personal questions buzzing in her brain, so Nora let him steer the talk back to safer shores.

It was better this way. Nora knew how to handle herself

professionally. She relaxed as they discussed the dig. The quarry they were headed for had supplied copper to one of the dawn kingdoms of the Bronze Age—Egypt's Old Kingdom—over four thousand years ago. The period fascinated Nora, and was her particular specialty. In many ways, civilization had been invented then, with all its banes and blessings.

They weren't here to excavate the quarry itself, however. That had been done long ago. Recently, a cave had been discovered after being blocked by a rockfall for many years, and preliminary investigation indicated that it had been used as temporary living quarters by the overseers and slaves sent to work the quarry. That cave was Nora's objective.

Or it had been—until she found the second cave. And the tunnel leading off it.

"An unlooted burial," she said now. "Think of it! Admittedly, it won't be a rich find—the provincial governors were still being interred near the pharaoh at the time the tunnel was blocked, so whoever ended up here couldn't be terribly important."

"Are you sure it *is* a burial?" he asked. "I've never heard of a tomb so far from the central kingdom."

"What else could it be? The tunnel started out as a natural one, but it's been shaped. No mistake about that. The marks from the tools are easy to read. And the debris used to block it is typical of the fill used in burials for later Dynasties of the period."

He grinned suddenly. "I hope you're right. I'd love to be part of a dig that uncovers an unlooted burial, even if it does belong to some minor official. The puzzle of why anyone would have been entombed so far from the Nile is enough to get your blood pumping all by itself, isn't it?"

"If only I could get Ibrahim's blood pumping, too.

Without his backing, the Ministry won't approve bringing in more equipment or workers. We're doing the best we can, but we're damnably limited."

They'd reached the quarry. It wasn't deep at this end, and the side was sandy and sloping. Nora automatically started to take her usual headlong route down, stopping in mid-stride when she realized she ought to at least point out the easier path to Alex.

She looked back up at him. "Most everyone goes down over there." She gestured at a more gradual slope, where the tramping of many feet had formed a discernible trail.

"You don't, though."

Something about the way he stood, with the morning sky behind him gathering brightness as the fleeting colors of dawn faded into day, made her breath catch.

He looked so very solid. Strong. It was hard to believe he'd nearly died—actually *had* died, for a few minutes—just a month ago. "I don't see much point in taking the long way around if I don't have to." Oddly flustered, she turned away and took the slope in long, sliding strides.

He came down right behind her. "Are you impatient," he said when he reached the bottom, "or just fond of taking the most difficult route to your goal?"

"I save my patience for when it matters—like over there." She nodded at the other end of the small quarry, where scaffolding had been erected to make it easier to reach the cave she'd discovered last month. The cave's entry was a narrow crevice nearly twenty feet above the floor of the quarry. "Do you want to go inside?"

"Definitely." He started walking, and she fell in step beside him. "I don't see how you spotted it. The entry is almost invisible from down here. Unless you're a caver?" He gave her another of those charming smiles he seemed well-stocked with. A personal sort of smile that invited her to move closer, to share space and thoughts. "I have a friend who climbs, walks or crawls into every hole in the ground he can find. He considers it great fun."

"Not me." Small, dark spaces spooked her, they always had. There was no particular reason for it. Nora hadn't mentioned her minor phobia to anyone on her crew, and didn't intend to. As long as she had light and something to occupy her mind, she was okay. "But I think my brain was permanently warped towards spotting them the last time I was in the Sinai."

"That must be when you learned to like goat cheese."

She grinned. "As a matter of fact, it was."

"What were you doing here?"

"I wasn't here, exactly. I was farther south, at Gebel Musa. That's Mount Sinai—but you know that, of course." She kept her attention on where they were going. It was easier than looking at him to see if he was smiling in that personal way again.

"How did working at Gebel Musa warp your brain?"

"I spent the summer before my senior year in college mapping and cataloging the tiny caves used as cells by religious hermits in the Byzantine period. One of my professors was keen on tying some theories of his about the period to the hermitage movement."

"Students do make good cheap labor."

"Exactly. Let me tell you, I got very good at spotting caves. Put me anywhere near a good-sized heap of rock and dirt, and I automatically look for caves."

"What made you decide to investigate this one, once you spotted it? Especially if you aren't into caving. It would have been a difficult climb."

"A dream." She laughed at the faint skepticism that crossed his face. "I'm not claiming psychic powers, but the unconscious mind does notice things the waking mind misses. See along here?''

They'd reached the scaffolding at the base of the cliff. She pointed up at the cave's entrance. ''There used to be a path along there, a ledge. It came down recently—maybe only two or three hundred years ago. You can see that the edges of the rock where it broke away aren't worn, and there's a lot of the rubble here at the base. I didn't notice all of this consciously, but some corner of my mind did. I dreamed about finding a cave here, so naturally the next day I checked to see if my dream had any basis in reality.''

''Not everyone has such confidence in their dreams.''

She shrugged. ''It made me curious, that's all. We knew they'd used one cave as living quarters, so it seemed possible they might have used this one for something, too.''

''I should have known you'd be a dreamer.''

''What do you mean?''

''Aren't all archaeologists dreamers?'' His eyes were opaque now, the light blocked. It made them unreadable. ''Caught in the romance of the past, more fascinated by the traces left by people who lived and died long ago than by the lives being lived around them in the present.''

''That sounds more like criticism than a compliment. I could have sworn you were an archaeologist yourself.''

''I don't claim to be immune to the disease. Don't look so worried,'' he said, reaching out to tug lightly on her braid. ''Archaeology may not be curable, but it's seldom fatal. It just causes those of us afflicted to do strange things...like live in a tent in the Sinai during *Al-kez*.''

She grinned, recognizing the Bedouin name for the hottest of their five seasons: *Al-kez*, 'the terrible summer.' ''Since you're among the afflicted, you're probably eager to have a look at my hole in the ground.''

She turned, grabbed the ladder that led to the top of the scaffold, and started up.

"I don't see a generator." His voice told her he was following, several rungs below her. "Is it inside the cave?"

"Yes. I thought it best to move it after the thefts started. It was a real pain getting it in there, too." She was halfway up, moving automatically. "We had to—hey!"

With a quiet crack, one rung of the ladder gave way beneath her. Off balance, she tightened her grip on the rails and got that foot down onto the lower rung, where her other foot rested.

It broke, too.

She slid. The rough wood of the rails shredded her palms, slowing but not stopping her. Acting instinctively, she swung her feet up, connected with something solid—and pushed off. The world whistled by.

She landed hard.

Years ago, Nora had had the breath knocked out of her during her one and only attempt to ride a horse. She'd forgotten how terrifying it felt. She lay on her back, darkness fluttering at the edges of her vision, and tried desperately to breathe.

She couldn't. Stunned muscles refused to work, her lungs refused to inflate, and panic flooded her, breaking the next few moments into disjointed impressions.

Alex's grim face appeared over hers. He was speaking, but she couldn't hear him for the roaring in her ears. The light was getting dim. Hands ran over her arms, her legs, her sides. At last, just as she was sure she had killed herself, that her body was broken too badly for breath, things started working again.

Her chest heaved. That first lungful of air tasted sweeter

than any she'd ever had. She sucked it in gratefully, then gulped down another.

"Where do you hurt?" That was Alex's voice.

Her own voice was more of a gasp. "Everywhere."

Even as she spoke, the pain came flooding in—her chest, her shoulders, her back. But her legs moved easily enough when she shifted them slightly. "I don't think anything is broken," she managed to say, her voice rising all the way to a whisper. "But my chest hurts. And my hands."

"You had the breath knocked out of you. No, stay flat." His hands on her shoulders kept her from sitting up when she tried. "I didn't feel any broken ribs," he said, but he ran his hands along her sides again, then moved them to her front.

He was feeling the front of her rib cage now—right below her breasts. She wanted to protest, but something about his expression stopped her. Or maybe it was his lack of expression. His face was hard. His eyes were...strange. Dark. Focused. Empty. "I'm okay."

If he heard her, he ignored it. His hands continued their businesslike exploration, moving now to her collarbone and shoulder. He pressed here and there, then manipulated her arm. "I don't think you've dislocated anything, but you shouldn't move. Your back—"

"I really am all right." She summoned the energy to push his hands away and tried again to sit up. This time he helped, sliding an arm behind her back. The position left his face very close to hers.

His gaze flickered to her mouth, but his expression didn't change. Her heart was beating hard—which was only natural, she told herself. Under the circumstances.

"What in the hell," he said in a low, controlled voice,

"did you think you were doing? Why did you shove off into thin air like that?"

Her eyebrows went up. "In case you didn't notice, the ladder broke."

"So you pushed yourself backward." Now there was something in his eyes. Anger. It made them lighter, the color of dark honey.

Her tongue came out to lick her lips nervously. "I didn't want to slam into you and knock you off, too."

"Hell." He pulled away. "Stay there. Don't move."

She didn't much feel like moving yet, so she didn't argue. She watched as he went up the ladder quickly. "Be careful. If any of the other rungs are loose—"

"Shut up."

Her eyebrows went up again. The man had an annoying way of reacting to an accident.

Alex stopped just below the broken rungs. After a quick inspection, he came back down just as fast as he'd gone up. "The rungs weren't loose," he said tersely. "They were cut."

On the third morning after Alex's arrival, Nora woke up much as she had on the first two. Aching. Restless. With the edges of a dream slipping away the moment her eyes opened, and the evidence of that dream still throbbing in her body.

Alex had been naked in her dream. So had she. That much she remembered.

No point in trying to recall the details, she thought as she blinked at the darkness in the tent. Her subconscious couldn't conjure up more for her in the way of experience than she'd actually had.

She glanced at the luminous dial of the battery-operated clock on the folding table near her cot. Thank goodness.

It would be light enough to run in another fifteen minutes or so. She threw back her covers and sat up, sliding her feet onto the canvas floor. Various bruises protested, but not as severely as they had for the last two mornings.

She would stretch out thoroughly, she decided. But by damn, she'd have her morning run. She needed it.

Nora hadn't been able to run since her fall. She'd missed it. Sexual frustration, she reflected wryly, was an excellent reason to enjoy running. And a woman who was still a virgin at twenty-nine years, eleven months and twenty-eight days of age might not know a lot about sex, but she knew a great deal about sexual frustration.

She stretched, yawned, and lit the small oil lamp next to the clock. The main tent had electricity, but none of the others did.

Her bare arms and legs were chilly. Though the temperature didn't dip much below seventy at night at this time of year, that was a drop of forty degrees or so from the daytime temperature. To Nora's heat-adjusted body, anything under seventy degrees felt pretty nippy.

And to a body whose systems were faltering due to loss of blood, sixty-some degrees could be cold enough to kill. Alex's skin had been cold to the touch when she had found him in the Negev. He'd been suffering from exposure, and blood loss had driven his body into shock.

She shivered, pulled off her T-shirt and kicked off the baggy boxer shorts she wore with it. Her clean things were already set out, waiting. She grabbed the panties first.

Alex. Blast the man. He'd invaded her thoughts as well as her dreams, and she couldn't decide what to do about it. Or even if she should do something.

Last night after supper she'd offered oh-so-casually to walk back to the quarry with him. He'd pitched his tent there rather than in camp, saying he wanted to discourage further vandalism. He'd turned her down flat, and lectured her on safety.

Nora uncapped the large plastic bottle that held the lilac-scented lotion she loved, and that the dry climate demanded. It was just as well he'd turned her down. She didn't have any business encouraging him. She remembered what Myrna had told her about Alex and their brief affair all too well.

Perfect for a fling, Myrna had said. According to her, Alex was a wonderful lover—charming, fun, and sexy enough to melt a woman's bones with a glance.

And temporary. He'd made that clear to Myrna. Apparently, Alex was one of those commitment-shy males who preferred quantity to quality in his relationships. It was an attitude Nora despised. How many men with the same attitude had she seen waltz through her mother's life?

Yet, for some reason, she didn't despise Alex.

He puzzled her. His reaction to her casual suggestion that she walk back to his tent with him had been weird. You'd think she had offered to go strolling through Central Park with him at midnight. If he thought walking to the quarry at night was that dangerous, he shouldn't be there.

Nora frowned as she pulled on her running shorts. She didn't like the idea of his being out there alone every night. She didn't know why anyone would have wanted to sabotage the ladder, but the act had been intended to cause harm. That was disquieting.

She didn't like having her authority undermined, either. He hadn't asked for permission to pitch his tent there. He'd just done it. Admittedly, Alex wasn't exactly her subordinate. He'd been sent by Ibrahim. But she was in charge at this dig, and she didn't like the way he forgot that when it was convenient.

He had come in handy, though. With Nora stiff and sore

from her fall, Alex's strong back had been as welcome as his expertise. He'd repaired the ladder and had spent hours digging into the hard-packed fill in the tunnel, and they were making real progress.

Professionally, they were making progress. Personally, they were stuck in a dance where he called the steps—and he was making some very mixed moves. He seemed interested in her, giving her those special smiles, sitting with her at meals, talking. He had a way of getting her to talk about herself, but he didn't say that much about himself.

And he didn't *do* anything. Like try to get her alone. Or let her get him alone.

Or kiss her. Her mind veered to that thought and got stuck. She wondered what his kiss would be like. Not gentle, she thought, though she wasn't sure why. He acted perfectly civilized.

Yet he didn't *look* civilized. Maybe it was those hard, sharp cheekbones, maybe the odd color of his eyes, but she had the sense that there was something wild about him. Power, she decided, dragging a brush through her hair. He felt like leashed power.

He came from money, she knew. Not on any grand scale, but his parents had private incomes, long pedigrees and two permanent homes, one in Cairo and one in New England. Perhaps she was simply picking up on the confidence that came from growing up wealthy and assured of his place in the world.

It was a type of confidence she'd never know. But real self-worth came from actions, not heritage, she assured herself as she fastened a band at the end of her braid. She knew she could take care of herself, that she wasn't dependent on the whim of a man or the grinding, inadequate charity of the system. That was what counted.

Whatever the basis for the impression Alex gave of being a wild thing that had somehow wandered into camp, he behaved well enough. In fact, he was so darned pleasant and polite she couldn't tell if he shared any of the feelings that assaulted her around him—shivery, excited feelings that were part physical need, part something else. Maybe imagination. Heaven knew she had plenty of that.

She sat on the cot to tug on her socks. She picked up a pair of athletic shoes and thunked the heels against the ground to dislodge any creepy crawlies that might have curled up inside for a snooze overnight.

It was entirely possible that she'd fantasized about him so much before he showed up that she now imagined some sort of connection between them that didn't really exist. She was a romantic. Nora admitted that, made no bones about it. And she'd been waiting a long time for the one man, the special man, to come along. The man she could give her heart and her body to.

Maybe she had persuaded herself there was something special about Alex just because she wanted him so badly.

In the dune-rippled Negev desert, dawn is a sudden arrival. Not so in the broken land of the southern Sinai. Although the tumbled hills Alex walked now were every bit as much a desert as the one that had soaked up his blood last month, here dawn seeped in more gradually, announcing itself in graying skies before the sun peeked over the crags that had hidden its first appearance at the rim of the world.

The dim light now blending night into day told Alex he'd stayed out too long and would have to hurry to get back to camp before he was missed.

Distances and directions were hard to gauge in such rough country. He had a map, of course. It had been built by combining the twenty-first century digital wizardry of computers and satellite and reconnaissance photographs with the only detailed on-ground survey of the Sinai's interior in existence—the maps drawn by Professor Edward Henry Potter of the British Ordnance Survey Expedition to the Sinai in 1868.

Alex knew that the terrorist base was close to the dig. He knew it was underground. That much he'd managed to learn before someone took exception to his questions and left him for dead in the Negev. But that was all he knew. Using the map, he'd selected the likeliest locations and had begun a methodical search, heading out in a different direction every night once the moon was up.

He hadn't found the base, but last night he'd found evidence that someone had been camped on a bluff overlooking the camp. A watcher, he thought, which might mean that El Hawy didn't have anyone planted with Nora's crew, after all.

Alex wasn't depending entirely on his own wanderings to find the base. He'd left word in Feiron Oasis for a man he'd worked with before to come here to the dig. Farid Ibn Kareem was a smuggler, a businessman, a thief—a canny scoundrel with an unrivaled information network, and good reason to hate El Hawy.

In the meantime, Alex would search, and he would keep track of the comings and goings of the others at the dig. Just in case. Alex hoped there was a plant. He or she would have to make contact with El Hawy at some point. Following one of the terrorists to their base would be the easiest way to locate it.

He had more than one reason now to find the base quickly.

Apparently, the mild discouragement of petty thefts was no longer enough. The damaged ladder was meant to cause an accident—an accident that, added to the other misfortunes, might cause the nosy foreigners to pack up and leave. It wouldn't matter to the terrorists if someone died or was badly hurt—not if it accomplished their goal.

It hadn't, of course. Nora had no intention of leaving her tunnel unexcavated.

Alex paused at the crest of a ridge, scowling at the burning sliver of sun nudging itself above a knobby hill to the west. He was not in a good mood.

He should have been. Though he hadn't found the base, he was in a good position to search for it. With the moon nearly full, he had had decent light for his search, and his biggest problem had been solved the day he arrived. The vandalized ladder had given him a reason to pitch his tent in the quarry. He could come and go at night without anyone knowing.

From a professional standpoint, the sabotage had been a stroke of good luck. From a personal standpoint… He had no business having a personal standpoint.

He paused. That narrow slice of sun told him he'd better hurry. He had been following one of the smaller wadis, using it as a guide to get back to the quarry, but moving alongside it rather than at the bottom. He briefly considered moving to the bottom of the wadi, where he could make much better time, but the idea made the nape of his neck prickle. This particular wadi was too narrow and too exposed. A perfect place for an ambush.

He continued along the top of the wadi, his thoughts much darker than the gradually brightening air around him.

Nora was in danger. She didn't realize that there were people who didn't want her here routinely used mutilation or death to express their opinions. The thefts that worried Nora had reassured Alex. They had indicated that El Hawy hadn't wanted to draw attention with anything as overt as murder.

But the open act of sabotage was a warning. The terrorists were getting nervous. The arms were on their way, and the buyer of those arms—the traitor named Simon—would be arriving once they did. El Hawy didn't want outsiders nearby.

It was not healthy to be camped near a bunch of nervous terrorists.

The worst of it was that he couldn't tell Nora she was in danger. He couldn't even mention the watcher, much less tell her what was going on. He couldn't afford for her to become too frightened or discouraged, because he needed her to continue to work the dig. He had to have a reason to be here, where few outsiders came.

Tourists didn't venture into the Sinai's interior. Religious pilgrims visited Mount Sinai and St. Catherine's Monastery, while pleasure seekers stayed at resorts scattered along the coasts. Foreigners weren't even allowed to leave the few main roads without special permits.

No, he couldn't say anything, couldn't even—

Alex's thoughts stopped as suddenly as his body. He froze, head up, listening. Footfalls, coming this way down the wadi. Fast.

He moved quickly behind a boulder that overhung the dry waterbed. A perfect spot for an ambush, yes. Which was fine—as long as he was doing the ambushing.

Nora had finally managed to run her mind blank, free of all the problems that had beset the dig—and free of the man who kept invading her dreams. Her whole being was focused on the challenge and exhilaration of moving swiftly over rough terrain, in spite of the aches that still plagued her from her fall.

She was breathing hard and sweating lightly. A tight curve loomed ahead where the wadi narrowed drastically, banked by a huge boulder on one side and crumbling rock on the other.

The ground was littered with gravel and loose stones. She slowed, not wanting the complication of a turned ankle.

Something hit the ground, hard, right behind her.

She stopped dead.

A hard voice demanded, "Why the hell didn't you keep running?"

She spun around.

Alex. He stood four feet from her. There was no mistaking him now for civilized. From the savage readiness of his stance to the beard stubble on his cheeks to the glittering anger in his eyes, he was everything wild and unpredictable.

Her hand went to her throat. "Good grief! Where did you *come* from?"

"You're a fool, you know. I could have slit your throat before you turned around. You would have been dead before you hit the ground."

Chapter 4

Nora took a step back, fear balling up in her stomach. "You need a new line, Alex. That one won't impress many women."

"You think I'm trying to impress you?" He closed the distance between them, stopping close to her. Too close. "That's as stupid as coming out here alone."

She licked suddenly dry lips. "I've been out here alone almost every morning ever since we set up camp. So far, you're the only thing that has happened to worry me."

His mouth twisted in what looked more like a threat than a smile. "At least you've got the sense to be worried now."

Should she try to get away? Somehow, in spite of the way he was acting, she couldn't believe Alex meant to hurt her. But fools seldom recognized their folly while they were busy committing it, did they? "What are you doing out here, anyway? Did you follow me?"

He hesitated. "I was following someone, but not you. I must have lost him."

"Did someone come messing around the quarry? And you took off after him!" Anger licked in, freeing her from the fear. "And you've got the gall to call me stupid! I *knew* I shouldn't have let you camp away from the rest of us, but I didn't realize you'd turn into a one-man vigilante squad!"

"I wasn't in any danger."

"But I am?" She shook her head, disgusted. "You went chasing after someone who is either a thief or a vandal or both. I'm out here by myself, yes, but I'm no threat to anyone."

"You could be, if you see something you're not supposed to see. The Sinai is a major drug smuggling route."

And he had been nearly killed—by bandits, maybe, as she'd first guessed. Or maybe by drug smugglers. That might explain his odd behavior. "Is that what happened to you?" she asked more quietly. "Did you see something you weren't supposed to?"

He turned away abruptly and started down the wadi, heading back the way she'd just come. "I'm not supposed to talk about it."

Nora fell into step beside him. She supposed that talking about whatever he'd seen might be dangerous. The authorities wouldn't want their investigation jeopardized, either. "Look, I appreciate your concern, even if I don't like the way you went about expressing it. But most smugglers aren't as bloody-minded as the ones who stabbed you." A grin flickered. "Take Mahmoud, for example."

He frowned. "Your driver? You think he's connected to smuggling?"

"Probably. This odd quirk he has about driving at night—he claims he doesn't like the heat, but I suspect it's habit. He's used to driving after dark to avoid patrols. Smuggling is an old, honored tradition among many of the Bedouin, you know. They don't consider it wrong."

"It's a tradition that has become tainted by the drug trade."

She sighed. "I suppose so. So many of their ways have been changed, and often not for the better, by what passes for modernization. But that's another subject." She reached out to stop him, laying a hand on his arm.

He was warm to the touch. And hard. She pulled her hand back quickly, because her blasted heart started thumping again. "Alex, I'm not claiming that I'm perfectly safe, but I'm probably safer on my dawn runs here than a lot of joggers are in big cities. I do take precautions."

"Precautions." One lifted eyebrow loaded the word with a wealth of skepticism. "Such as—?"

"Why do you think I always run in the same place at the same time?"

"Do you?"

"Yes. If I'm predictable, I'm less likely to surprise someone who wouldn't appreciate it. So I run at the same time, along the same route, every day. I made sure Mahmoud knows this, just in case, and I've mentioned it to people in Feiron Oasis, too."

Grudgingly he nodded. "That's not a bad idea. But..." His glance slid down her body, then back up to her face. "Let's keep moving. You could use some cool-down time."

Nora bit her lip. She ought to ignore him and finish her run.

She went with Alex instead. "We've talked about my safety. Now let's talk about yours."

"My safety isn't your concern."

"Not personally, no. But professionally—"

"Let's not pretend, Nora. You and I will never have a truly professional relationship." He said that coolly, as if he were mentioning the weather. "There's too much heat between us."

That messed up her breathing, even as it infuriated her. She got both breath and temper under control after a moment. "Still, the last time I checked, I was in charge of the dig. You may only be here temporarily, but while you are here you are under my authority."

"You're in charge of the dig, yes. You're not in charge of me."

"You're quibbling. I assume you went chasing off after this intruder you spotted because of the vandalism at the site, which makes your actions my business. I don't want you doing such a foolish thing again. Is that clear?"

"We don't always get what we want, though, do we? I don't want you taking these blasted solo runs of yours."

She wanted to kick something. Maybe him. "You sound like Tim. He's always nagging me to give up my runs, but it's terrorists he's got on the brain, not smugglers."

A pause. "Terrorists?"

"Ridiculous, isn't it? I've tried to tell him that terrorists are interested in headlines—big, splashy acts that will draw attention to them and their cause. Pestering a handful of archaeologists in the middle of the Sinai isn't going to do that."

"Americans are targeted for kidnapping sometimes."

Good grief. He sounded as paranoid on the subject as Tim was. "What good would it do anyone to grab me? I'm not connected to the government or to any big, rich corporation that might pay to get me back. And though there's always tension in this area, there isn't anything going on right now that has people especially stirred up against the U.S." She shook her head. "They'd have to be pretty stupid to waste time on me."

"There's no rule that says terrorists have to be smart."

"Oh, come on. Do you really think there's a danger of some under-bright terrorists snatching me on my morning run?"

"Are you willing to bet your life that there isn't?"

She thought about it. "There are risks in everything," she said at last. "I'm from Houston originally. Have you ever seen the traffic there? People risk their lives on the way to work every day, taking the chance that they won't become a statistic, the victim of road rage or another driver's inattention. Or their own."

"That's not risk taking. It's habit, coupled with the comforting conviction that the bad stuff only happens to other people."

She nodded. "Partly. But I think people do automatically take risks when we feel the outcome is important—whether that outcome is a good job, a new house, or time alone in the desert. I'm not going to give up my morning runs unless I can see that the risks outweigh the benefits."

"I take it I haven't persuaded you of that."

"No."

The silence that fell between them then wasn't entirely comfortable. In spite of her confident words, Nora had to wonder if she *was* being foolish. Ibrahim had included a professional bio of Alex with the letter he'd sent her. Not only had Alex Bok spent large parts of his childhood in this region, he'd spent a fair portion of his adult life here, too, on various digs. He was much more familiar with the area than she was.

She glanced at him. According to Myrna, he was a great deal more familiar with other things than she was, as well.

Sex. Any woman would think about that around a man

like Alex. It wasn't any pleasant, pastel version of romance he conjured up, either, but the raw, blunt side of passion. Tangled sheets and straining bodies. Sweat and need and urgency.

Plenty of women had done more than think about sex with Alex. She needed to remember that. A woman who fell for a commitment-shy man, thinking she could change him, was begging for trouble.

Nora wasn't one to look for trouble. Still, she stole another glance at him. He looked tough and unapproachable, nothing like the dilettante he was reputed to be. His eyes were shadowed by thoughts she couldn't guess. His cheeks were lean and unshaven, somewhat hollow beneath the high cheekbones. He wore shorts, as she did, and the muscles in his thighs were hard. And fascinating. They flexed with each step he took, the smooth, muscular action drawing her unwilling attention.

He excited her. She wasn't happy about that admission, but it was true. Everything about him fascinated her, excited her, even the forbidding expression on his face right now. He looked as unyielding as the stone around them.

She wanted to ask him what kind of thoughts put that look on his face. She wanted to test the roughness of those cheeks with her fingertips.

How much of a risk was Alex?

Nora hated being confused. Their relationship—if she could even call it that—was ambiguous. Not truly professional, as he'd said. But it wasn't truly personal, either. He kept changing the beat in mid-step.

She had been letting him play the tune for this uncertain dance of theirs for too long, she decided. It was her turn to call out the next step.

If she could just figure out what that should be.

* * *

Alex was thinking about edges. And color. And sex.

The land around them was all edges—some worn, some sharp, all naked. Unblunted by the soil and growth that softened the greener parts of the world. A barren land, some would say.

But the colors of the land, as revealed by the growing light, were subtle. The rocks were dun, pale gray, rusty gray, clay. Just ahead, a stubby acacia tree perched halfway up the slope of the wadi, the colors of its dusty trunk and leaves drawn from the same palette as the rocks and dirt around it.

The scattered tufts of shaggy grass were as bleached of color and life as the rocks and sand. The Bedouin called that species of grass *mitnan*. Even the tough, black goats wouldn't eat it, but the nomads found other uses for the grass, weaving the tough strands into baskets. At this season, the grass looked dead. It wasn't. It waited for the winter rains that might or might not come this year, just as the acacia waited, its roots dug deep into the dry ground.

Life is persistent, he thought. Fragile in some ways, yet stubborn. That was one of the lessons the desert had taught him when he was still quite young. All his life, he'd been fascinated by the extremes of the land.

And all his life, he'd been fascinated by edges. They tested his limits. But he'd never felt tested, challenged, by a woman before.

It was a matter of risk and priorities, he thought. Just as Nora had said. The work he did for SPEAR was his priority. Because he couldn't risk that work, he'd been careful not to leave any important pieces of himself in a woman's hands. Sex had always been pleasant, simple. Never edgy and important.

Alex didn't look at the woman walking quietly beside

him, but he was deeply aware of her. Sex with Nora would be more than pleasant, and anything but simple. It would be a mistake. He was sure of that, but he couldn't stop wanting her.

He broke the silence abruptly. "Your hair was down. When you found me in the Negev, you didn't have it pulled back the way you do now, yet you'd been running then, too."

She looked startled. "I...you needed warmth. I'd braided it like usual before I went for my run, but I undid the braid when I found you."

And spread her hair over the two of them. He remembered that, the feel of a silky, shifting blanket covering his chest and shoulders. "I'd like to see it down again." See it, feel it against his skin, take it in his hands.

"Would you?" She stopped and turned to face him directly. "I don't know if I believe that. You've been giving off some pretty mixed signals, Alex."

He stopped, too. "Have I? Maybe I'm not sure myself what I want." Another lie. He knew what he wanted. He just couldn't have it. "Dying has a way of changing a man's perspective, even when death turns out to be less than permanent." And that was more truth than he'd intended to speak.

"It would, of course." She hesitated. "It must be difficult, being back in the desert, so near where the attack took place."

Her perception annoyed him. "I don't blame the desert for what happened."

"No, but it must have some unpleasant associations."

He had no intention of sharing those associations. Not with her, not with anyone. "You like it out here, don't you?"

"I don't know if 'like' is the right word. This is..." She

swept her hand out widely. "Well, it's like no place else on earth."

"There are a lot of other deserts."

"But they aren't in the Sinai, are they? Here, Africa meets Europe and Asia, and three of the world's major religions touch. This is where Isis sought Osiris, and Moses and the children of Israel wandered here for forty years in the wilderness." Her eyes took on a dreamy cast. "It's been called by many names—Paran, the way to Hejaz, Shibh Jazirat Sinai."

"It's also been called the bloodiest desert in the world." Much of the blood was ancient. Some was all too recent.

She nodded. "True. It's a hard place, equal parts grandeur and grit."

"And you're in love with it."

She gave a quick, startled laugh. "I wouldn't put it that way, but how can I not be compelled by such a place? It's so wild here, so extreme. There's an honesty to that."

It was disconcerting to hear her use the same word he'd often applied to the desert. Extreme. "It takes a fierce sort of independence to withstand the solitude of the desert. Look at the Bedouin." Are you a fiercely independent woman, Nora? he wondered.

"I like that phrase—'the solitude of the desert.' Maybe that's part of the fascination. I always felt crowded as a child. Even the air I breathed was shared with a couple of million strangers." She smiled shyly. "I grew up in Houston, you see. And I spent my childhood feeling crowded."

"Big family?" He already knew, of course. But he wanted to hear about them from her.

"Just my mom and my sisters—two sisters, both older, and we always had to share a bedroom. There never seemed to be room for me." She grimaced. "Oh, I sound like a poor-me. I had a happy childhood in lots of ways. My sisters and I are still close."

Most people wouldn't call a childhood spent in public housing, supported by food stamps and a series of temporary "fathers," happy. "Your mother?"

"She died three years ago. Heart attack. She was only sixty-two. Oh, we knew she'd had some heart problems, but..." Her voice trailed off sadly.

"Death is always a shock."

She nodded.

The inward look of her spoke of grief eased but not erased by the passage of time. He wondered at that. "She must have been, what—about thirty-five when you were born?"

"If you're trying to figure out how old I am, just ask."

He chuckled. "I would never ask a woman her age. No, I was surprised by the coincidence. I was a fairly late arrival, too. I astonished my folks by showing up when my mother was thirty-six and my father was forty."

"Really?" She seemed to like the connection. "Both of them are still alive, I know. I read one of your mother's papers in *Archaeology Today* recently."

He chuckled. "Still alive, and still mucking around in the dirt whenever they get a chance. Archaeology has always been their passion. That was sometimes convenient when I was growing up."

"What do you mean?"

"When we were on a dig, they didn't pay much attention to what I did. I took advantage of that. I had a taste for adventure." He grinned, remembering some of his early exploits. "Poor old dears. They never could figure out how they'd hatched such a changeling."

"Poor old dears?" Her eyebrows went up. "You sound rather condescending."

"I don't mean to be. I'm very fond of them both." Even when he'd been young and angry about all the things his dear, dotty parents were too wrapped up in the past to notice, he'd known there was little point to his anger. They simply couldn't be any different than they were.

"They certainly gave you a childhood any archaeologist might dream of." She was silent a moment. "Will you answer honestly if I ask you something?"

"Either honestly or not at all." Another lie.

"You've got far more field experience than I do, and I can't help wondering about Dr. Ibrahim's purpose in sending you here. He's not comfortable having a woman in charge. He may want you to take over the dig."

"No. Ibrahim knows me better than that. I'm a restless soul, Nora." It was a warning, if she had the sense to realize it. "I've got the patience to be a good excavator, but I'm not much on follow-through. I don't stay in one place long enough."

A slight frown tightened her face. She didn't answer.

Her silence and her expression told Alex that she was thinking over what he'd said...and what he had implied. If Myrna had told her anything about him, Nora already knew he wasn't a settling-down type of man.

Maybe, though, what she'd heard about him had made her curious. She might be considering a fling with a restless man.

And he might be a wishful fool. There was an innocence about this woman, something shining and rare. And vulnerable. She wasn't the type for a quick affair, and he knew it. However much he wanted to persuade himself differently.

They reached the place where this smaller wadi converged with the larger one where the camp was sited, and turned together to make their way up it, still without speaking.

She was chewing on her lip—bothered, he decided, by his silence and her own confusion. Alex knew Nora had feelings for him. He saw them shimmering in her eyes when she glanced at him sideways, sensed them in her smile. She wanted him, but she wanted sex wrapped up in a romantic glow. Not so different, he thought, from the way she romanticized this blasted desert.

He chose an impersonal subject to break the silence. "You aren't planning on making the current campsite permanent, are you? Wadis are water channels, even if it doesn't seem like it right now. Flash floods aren't unknown."

"Only in the winter, and only if the rains come." She looked preoccupied. "We may have to move camp later, but it's convenient to stay close to the well for as long as we can. I do like being able to take a shower every night."

He knew. He'd sat outside the main tent last night, waiting for his own turn to wash up while the sky faded to lavender and the evening star came out. He hadn't been able to see the shower from there, of course. They'd had to site it where the water could drain out without dampening the ground near the tents, which put it on the far side of Nora's tent.

But he'd heard it.

Alex had listened to the sound of water splashing in the desert and had known it was running over her naked body. He'd heard her humming some old rock and roll tune, and pictured her glorious hair sleek and wet, her body gleaming, with water running in shiny rivulets between her breasts, down her legs.

Then she'd come back to the tent. Her hair had been wet, but hidden in the towel she'd wrapped around it. He hadn't been able to see much more of her body than usual, either—but enough to know that she'd been braless beneath her T-shirt. Which she'd worn with Mickey Mouse boxer shorts.

He smiled, remembering. "You're a fan of Mickey?"

"Of—oh." To his delight, she blushed. "My, uh, sleep clothes. One of the rules of the camp is that no one is allowed to make fun of my Mickey shorts. They have sentimental value."

Jealousy stabbed, quick and unexpected. "Fond memories of an old boyfriend?"

"Oh, no. I bought them myself when I went to Disney World last year. I always wanted to go there—well, what child doesn't? But there was never money for that sort of thing when I was little, so I took myself there as an adult. It was my first just-for-fun vacation."

"Was it fun?" It must have been a letdown, he thought. The blissful escape a child had yearned for wouldn't be what the adult woman had experienced.

"I had a blast. It was like walking inside a fantasy and just living there for days."

That she could step so easily into fantasy irritated him. "Why boxers for a souvenir, instead of a watch or T-shirt?"

"I did get a watch, actually, but I forget to wear it. There isn't much need out here, is there? But boxers are very practical on a dig, where privacy can be a hit-or-miss proposition."

"Oh, very practical. I sleep in them myself." He'd stopped sleeping nude after the time he'd been rudely awakened by a man with a knife, and had ended up chasing his would-be attacker across an inn's courtyard in the buff. He'd caught the bastard—but he'd attracted a fair amount of attention in the process.

The difference between her idea of what was practical and his deepened his irritation. His preoccupation with this woman was foolish. Although they walked the same ground at the moment, he and she lived in different worlds. He could dabble in hers for a time, but she would never know or understand his.

And why would he even want her to? Irritation darkened into anger.

"I've been thinking," she said abruptly. "You really believe it isn't safe for me to run alone out here?"

"Yes." His voice was clipped, frustrated. He wished he could tell her exactly how unsafe it was.

"Why don't you join me, then?"

He stopped. She did, too, legs braced, shoulders straight, blue eyes bright with challenge—though whether it was him or herself she was challenging, he wasn't sure.

Whichever one of them she meant that challenge for, he was tempted to take her up on it. "I don't think that would be a good idea."

She shrugged, carefully casual, her eyes falling away from his. "Never mind, then. I didn't mean to impose. I just thought...you said you liked to run, too. But it doesn't matter." She started to turn.

He stopped her with a hand on her shoulder. "I didn't say I wouldn't like to do it. I said it wouldn't be a good idea. Neither is this." Then Alex did what he'd told himself he wouldn't do, and touched her. Just her hair, sliding his fingertips along the side of her head. Cool silk.

He wanted to take the braid out. "You don't want to give me the wrong idea, Nora."

The pulse pounded visibly in her throat. "What idea?"

"That you're interested in me...the same way I'm interested in you." He teased his fingertips down the elegant line of her cheek, pausing to test the rapid thrumming of her heart in the vulnerable place beneath her jaw. "Maybe I'm wrong. Maybe you'd like to find out how hot we can burn together before I leave. Because it would be hot, no doubt about that. Sand-scalding, mind-blowing hot. And I *will* leave."

Her chin came up. Her eyes narrowed. "Maybe. And maybe you don't know as much as you think you do."

"I know you want me."

Alex expected her to pull away, to stamp back up the wadi to camp, leaving him before he could leave her. It was only sensible. Just what he intended her to do.

He didn't expect the hand that slid around his neck, the long fingers brushing the ends of his hair, or the warm, calloused palm that pulled his head down. Or the lips that met his a second later.

Soft lips. For all the authority of that hand, urging him firmly to her, her mouth was achingly soft and uncertain.

His pulse went wild. He felt it drumming in his ears, felt his blood pooling lower down. Need, sweet and sudden, fisted in his belly.

And then she pulled back. Too soon, much too soon, her mouth left his. That demanding hand slipped away, leaving the nape of his neck cool and bare again.

She stared up at him, her eyes wide with shock, the pupils big with pleasure.

"Ah, Nora," he whispered. "Big mistake." And pulled her to him.

The second that Alex's arms went around her, Nora knew he was right. This was a big mistake. A huge, colossal, incredible mistake.

Absolutely incredible.

Surprise, not design, kept Nora's eyes open when he pulled her hard against him. She saw a tiny white scar shaped like a crescent high on the blade of his cheek, glimpsed the flare of his nostrils and the amber glow of his eyes, open like hers, in the second before his mouth claimed her own.

She'd been right, too. Alex didn't kiss like a civilized man. He kissed like music—primitive, fluid, jarring. His tongue swept over her lips, then stole inside, and the taste of him made colors swirl through her body.

His clever, restless mouth hurried on, eager to play other notes against her skin. It drew quick, hungry beats of pleasure everywhere it touched, pausing to nibble on her ear, then speeding over her jaw to linger at her throat.

Had she thought this kiss was her idea, her way of taking control of their dance? He had ideas of his own, a huge, crashing chord of notions played out in silence and movement—his hands smoothing her shoulders, her back, her hips. His breath warm on her throat, mingling with the dampness from his mouth.

There was no control here, not in her. His body was hard and steady, his mouth hasty. One arm bound her to him, like warm, unyielding iron clamped around her waist. The other arm left her back while his tongue teased the corner of her mouth.

His hand lifted to stroke her hair. And trembled.

That small tremor finished her. Her knees went weak and her mind went white—no colors now, no thought, no sound.

Only sensation. Only him.

Her hands, suddenly avid, sped up his back, then down, one forcing a path between them so she could feel his heart drumming out the same primitive rhythm as hers. Her other hand cupped his head, holding him to her, drinking in the wild music of his kiss.

And somewhere in that white, dizzy place a thought

floated, one drifting shape of coherence in the silent world of sensation.

This is different.

Though she was a virgin, Nora wasn't completely without experience. She'd kissed plenty of frogs and a few nice guys, always hoping this time it would be different, that at last she would feel the spark, the connection she longed for.

This time was different. Oh, yes. This was unlike any kiss she'd ever shared. But this was no simple spark. And the connection, the draw, was carrying her into an abyss of strangeness.

She didn't know this man. That thought formed, icy in the midst of heat, bringing a rush of fear.

Instinctively she pulled back.

For a moment it didn't seem that he would release her. Then his arm loosened, his body straightened, and she was free.

And alone. Her heart clamored in her chest and her breath came fast and shallow. Her body hummed with need and regretted the loss of his. She considered speech, but had no idea what to say. If she blurted out the thoughts swirling in her head, he'd think she was crazy.

Alex was as aroused as she was. She could tell that much. His eyes were heavy, their focus distorted by heat. His lips were damp. But he found it damnably easy to pull himself together, his voice husky but steady when he spoke. "I've decided to take you up on your offer."

Her own voice was annoyingly weak. "My offer?"

"I'll join you on your morning runs if you'll agree not to go into the desert without me."

She found herself nodding without having the least notion what she was agreeing to.

Chapter 5

Sifting the fill they removed from the tunnel was the most tedious part of excavating. Necessary, of course; even the tiniest of artifacts could be significant. The shards they'd used to date the tunnel's blockage had been found in just this way. Samples of the sand itself would be analyzed. But, Lord, it was tedious.

Hot, too. Nora dragged the back of her hand across her forehead, smearing dust and sweat together. It was well past noon, and the temperature was over a hundred—slightly less here in the shade of the canopy, but still muscle-sapping hot.

Beside her, Lisa was just as sweaty, her dark skin damp from her efforts as she poured and sifted, sifted and sorted. Tim was doing the same on the other side of Lisa. They each had a small pile beside them of what looked like, and in most cases were, hardened clumps of sand.

But sometimes beneath the sand was something else: a bit of pottery or metal; a flake of paint. It all mattered.

Nora loved to dream big dreams, but her practical nature also thrived on detail. Archaeology combined the two needs beautifully. But there were times when the sheer grittiness of tending to the details involved in pursuing her dreams made her cross.

Like now. When all she really wanted to think about was him. And that kiss.

"Is it time to go collapse yet?" Tim asked.

"Soon." They didn't work in the hottest part of the day, save for what chores could be done in the relative coolness provided by the asthmatic air conditioner back at the main tent.

She reached for the bucket and poured more sand and gravel into her sifting tray, set the bucket down and paused, her gaze drawn to the dark opening of the cave.

Gamal came out onto the wooden platform as she watched, two buckets fastened to a yoke balanced across his shoulders. He would lower the buckets to Ahmed, who waited below to bring them to the foreigners who were so absurdly interested in buckets of sand.

Alex had filled those buckets. He was inside the tunnel now.

For a moment, she experienced a weird division as her thoughts tried simultaneously to dwell on Alex and what had happened between them, and to shy away. It was not a comfortable feeling.

Funny. She had always thought love would bring peace, not nerves and chaos.

Her knuckles turned white where she gripped the frame. She was *not* in love. That was absurd. This—this *whatever* it was she felt, call it a connection or a compulsion—was not love. She couldn't love someone she didn't know and wasn't sure she trusted.

"Did you find something?" Lisa asked.

For a second Nora's mind refused to sort meaning from the words. "Oh...no. It's nothing." Nothing at all, she told herself firmly, and started shaking the frame again.

Lisa set down her frame and stood. "I'm dry. Anyone else want a drink while I'm up?"

"I want a swimming pool," Tim said. "I can't get enough liquid on the inside of me to make up for how hot it is on the outside of me."

It would be cooler inside the cave, Nora thought. She had already taken her turn in the tunnel that morning, for the first time since her fall. The shoveling had made her back ache, but it hadn't been really painful, just a message from stressed muscles.

Worse, to her, had been the closeness of the air inside the tunnel. It had seemed to stick in her lungs, dry and dead, making her feel she couldn't draw a full breath. She'd finished her self-assigned shift, though. She wasn't about to give in to her stupid fears. The person in charge of the dig had to be able to follow where the excavation led. No matter how much it scared her.

Nora frowned and tried not to believe there was any more significance to that thought than what lay, plain and obvious, on the surface.

There was no connection between her silly phobia and her reasonable caution about these feelings she had for Alex. He wasn't a mystery to be solved, the way the tunnel was. He was a man. She didn't have any fear of men, or of relationships, not anymore. She'd worked all that out years ago. She was cautious, that was all. There was no reason to—

"Nora! Wake up, will you?"

She blinked and saw that Lisa was holding out a glass of water. "Oh. Thanks." She took it and gulped some down.

"One will get you ten she's been daydreaming about *him* again," Tim said, his voice uncharacteristically sharp.

"What are you talking about?"

"The glassy-eyed stare that keeps overtaking you. Ever since you had your little rendezvous with your boyfriend outside of camp this morning, you've been slipping off into wonderland every five minutes."

"Oh, for crying out loud! Boyfriend? You make me sound like a misty-eyed teenager. And you're way off the mark. Alex and I didn't have any rendezvous. I told you that. We met out there because he took off like a macho idiot when he saw someone messing around here."

Lisa had a husky chuckle, almost mannish, that Nora usually found charming. For some reason it grated this time.

"Well, honey, you did go out on your run alone, and you did come back with Alex. And if that isn't whisker burn I see on your cheek, I need glasses."

Her hand flew to her cheek, betraying her as readily as the blush that heated her face. "I, um..."

"*Ilehnisa* Nora!" Gamal called from the top of the scaffolding. "*Isayyid* Alex say come here now. He find problems."

Entry to the cave was through a narrow crevice that admitted little daylight. They'd had quite a time getting the generator inside, ending up disassembling it and putting it back together in the first chamber. The crevice was tight enough to give Nora a twinge as she slipped sideways through, but it widened quickly into a small stone room, the limestone chalky gray in color, with a high ceiling.

Nora was comfortable enough here. Her annoying phobia didn't trouble her until she ducked beneath a low arch at the back of the chamber to stand with the stony ceiling of the second chamber only inches from her head.

Alex stood at the entry to that stony wormhole, his expression grim.

"Bad news?" she said as lightly as she could.

"I'm afraid so. The roof's come down at the end of the tunnel."

The blood drained from her head so suddenly she went dizzy. *"What?"*

"Not recently," he said reassuringly, coming up to her. "Sometime in the last few thousand years, though, the end of the tunnel caved in. We're looking at digging out some pretty large boulders instead of fill, however tightly packed. And it will have to be done right, or we'll have more rock shifting and settling where we don't want it."

She wanted to curse, but couldn't think of any words vile enough. Her clenched jaw made her words come out tight. "Show me."

She would have moved past him then, but his hand on her arm stopped her. "You don't have to go in there."

Her eyebrows went up. "Of course I do. It isn't a matter of questioning your judgment. I have to see it for myself, that's all. If you're right..." If he was right, they would need more expertise than any of them possessed to get safely past the blockage. Her jaw tightened again.

"That's not what I meant." His voice was gentle. He didn't let go of her arm. "I know how uncomfortable you get in the tunnel, and with the ceiling caved in—"

"I'm fine in the tunnel." She tried to pull her arm away, but his fingers tightened.

"You aren't fine, but you handle it well. For someone with claustrophobia."

"I don't have claustrophobia. I just don't like being

crowded. Like you're doing right now," she added pointedly.

His eyes had an odd, angry glitter. "It goes beyond dislike."

"Discomfort, then." What was his problem? He didn't have any reason to be upset. She never let her silly fears interfere with what she needed to do. And how had he guessed that the tunnel bothered her, anyway? No one else had. "It doesn't matter."

"Discomfort wouldn't turn your face fish-belly pale. Why insist on digging in here yourself? It's so damned unnecessary! You've got four men with strong backs who can dig and haul the fill out twice as fast as you can."

"That's why I take a shorter shift than you big, brawny men. But I'm in charge. I have to keep track of our progress." Stiff with resentment, she tried again to get past him.

This time he caught both of her arms, turning her to face him. "You could keep track of our progress without spending an hour in here every day, sick with fear and too bloody damned stubborn to admit it!"

"It's none of your business!" Anger lent her the force to wrench herself free. "Unless, of course, you consider it your duty to report to Ibrahim that my fears are interfering with my performance here, in which case—"

"Dammit, that's not what this is about! It's personal, not professional!"

His raised voice sounded very loud in the small chamber. As if the muffled echo of his words surprised him when it bounced off the stone around them, his eyes widened. He looked away.

Her own voice was soft and a little unsteady when she repeated what he'd said to her earlier…just before she had kissed him. "Careful. You don't want to give me the wrong idea, Alex.'' *Or I might start thinking you're interested in me, the same way I'm interested in you.*

''I just don't like it.'' He glanced at the rocky floor, then at the wall where the unshielded glow of a forty-watt bulb hung from its electrical umbilical. ''I don't like the way you push yourself—or punish yourself—every day by going in there.''

''I don't do it to punish myself. I do it so the fear won't win. I can't let the fear keep me out. This...'' She gestured around her at the closed, cramped space of the chamber, her arm ending stretched out toward the place where it dwindled off into the tunnel. ''*This* is why I'm here.''

His mouth was turned up in a smile that looked somehow sad when at last he looked at her again. His eyes were dark, the spark of light she usually saw trapped in their depths invisible in the poor lighting. ''I do understand. God help us both.''

With that puzzling statement, he moved away, stooping where the ceiling dropped at the entrance to the tunnel. He stopped there, looking over his shoulder and holding out his hand. ''I don't think it counts as letting the fear win if you take a hand now and then.''

She swallowed. ''No, I don't suppose it does.''

The walls of the tunnel were close, about as far apart as the sides of a doorway back home. But that wasn't what bothered Nora the most. It was the way she had to stoop beneath that low, uneven ceiling. All the rock of the small mountain seemed to press down on her, sucking out the air, the moment she bent beneath that low ceiling.

But Alex's hand was warm, his grip reassuringly firm. He went ahead of her, bending even lower than she did to avoid bashing his head as he navigated the uneven floor.

The first few feet of the tunnel were just as they had been when Nora first found the cave. Then, she'd come to a dead end abruptly where the tunnel snaked around an outcropping of harder rock. Long-dead hands had packed the tunnel with fill from that point on.

Today she was able to move around the tight turn into the section of tunnel they'd excavated. But she only went a few feet, stopping short of the tunnel's end. Her breath escaped in a sigh.

Behind her, the generator chugged reassuringly, keeping light burning steadily in the bare bulbs strung along the left wall.

In front of her lay disaster. "I can't argue with your conclusion," she said grimly, forcing herself to move forward the last few feet—which meant she crowded up against Alex, their bodies brushing in the narrow corridor.

She pulled her flashlight from the loop that held it to her belt. The small additional light added little to what was obvious from the first glance. There was the gravel and fill she was used to seeing, but it was backed up against rock. Not worked stone, either, such as she'd seen used to seal the entrances of some crypts.

No, it was as Alex had said. The roof of the tunnel had come down at some point in the past. A huge slab of stone blocked the upper half of the tunnel; it rested on smaller pieces. There was a cavity at the top, but even with the assistance of her flashlight she couldn't see how far it extended. "We can't get the smaller pieces out without moving the slab, and I don't see how..." She had to stop and swallow. "I haven't the foggiest idea how to remove that without bringing the rest of the ceiling down."

That gave her another unwelcome thought. She glanced up uneasily. "Maybe it was the support from the fill that kept the cave-in from taking down the entire tunnel."

"That's possible."

"It may not be safe here now that we've removed the

fill, then.'' Her heart was pounding too hard, and she tightened her grip on the flashlight.

''I don't think there's any immediate danger. That slab broke away from the rest of the ceiling when it fell—that would have relieved the pressure. Come on, Nora. Let's head back.''

Unhappy, she straightened as much as she could, reluctant in spite of her fear to leave, as if staring at the boulder would give her a clue how to remove it. ''You know what's driving me crazy? If this stretch came down because it was free of fill, that might mean the chamber is just on the other side of this slab.''

''It might also mean that the chamber got buried when part of the mountain slipped.''

She hadn't thought of that. For one terrible moment, she was afraid she was going to cry. He held out his hand again. Silently, she took it and followed him back to the larger of the two outer chambers.

Once she was out from under the worst of that low, breath-stealing press of stone, her mind started working again. Dammit, she wasn't going to give up, even though she hadn't a clue how to proceed. ''I don't know where to start. I'm not qualified for this.'' She grimaced. ''Tim won't be any help.''

''Not unless he finds instructions on removing boulders from tunnels written in hieroglyphics,'' Alex agreed. ''But it *can* be done.''

''How?'' She shoved a strand of hair back out of her face. ''Do you have some experience with this sort of thing?''

He shook his head. ''I've helped build supports, but I wouldn't know how to go about clearing that slab safely. No, you'll need an expert for this.''

''Well, I don't have one,'' she said bitterly. ''The university would send someone. I'm sure of it. But unless Ibrahim suddenly changes his mind about the value of this dig and my qualifications, I'm not going to get permission to bring anyone else in."

"Why not use an Egyptian engineer?"

"I'd think that was obvious. Money."

"I might be able to help you there."

"How?"

"I do have some connections. Maybe I can find someone who would be willing to give you a week or so, gratis." His smile didn't look entirely happy. "If I can't, I know people who can."

She hesitated. "Your parents?"

"They've got plenty of strings to pull."

"I get the feeling you don't like asking them for favors."

He shrugged. "We don't see eye to eye on some of my choices. It doesn't matter."

A smile tugged at her mouth. "That's what I said about my, ah, discomfort in the tunnel."

"So it is." Though a smile lingered on his mouth, his eyes had forgotten it. She saw clouds there, but couldn't name them. Reluctance? Regret? He put his hands on her shoulders. "This is a setback, Nora, but it isn't the end of the line."

The blasted man was always touching her—stopping her one minute, pulling her with him the next. "Don't worry. I'm not giving up."

"No, you wouldn't be very good at that, would you?" He spoke lightly, but his eyes were saying something else. Something, maybe, about her mouth, because that's where his gaze had drifted, making her suddenly very aware of her lips, her breath, the few inches of air between her face and his.

He was going to kiss her again. She knew that as clearly as if he'd said it, as clearly as she knew that she wouldn't stop him. A thrill of heat sped through her to pool, thick and enticing, where she felt her pulse pounding.

His hands fell away. He turned. "I guess you'll need to tell the others. And I'd better get on the radio and see what kind of strings I can find to tug on."

Disappointment crashed, followed by a lively spark of temper. She watched him walk out of the cave, her eyes narrowed.

She was getting sick and tired of his mixed signals. One second he wanted her, the next he was moving away. Just what was Alex Bok up to?

Nora followed him out of the cave, her brain a jumble of questions. Too many of them were questions about him, rather than how to deal with the blocked passage. One question, though, she wanted answered. Now.

She stepped out onto the wooden scaffolding and blinked at the brightness of the day.

Alex stood at the edge by the ladder. She didn't see Gamal and Ahmed, who should have been nearby—they carried the buckets of fill to the shaded area where the others sorted and sifted. But at the moment she didn't care where they were. "I'd like to know what's going on," she said abruptly.

Alex stood with his back to her. "Right now, that would be visitors."

Visitors? She followed his gaze. There, at the edge of the quarry, stood three bearded men, each wearing the flowing *galabiyya* of the Bedouin. Two of them held rifles; the man in the middle was empty-handed. Ahmed was making his way up the side of the quarry toward them.

Normally, Nora would have had to repress a twinge of resentment over having to stop work in the middle of the day. Desert hospitality demanded that she do so, and offer food and water. She would have to throw on the robe she kept for such occasions so her bare legs wouldn't offend the men.

Normally, she would have had work to do, though. Now all she had were questions—including the one she had been about to blurt out: *Do you want me, or not?*

Saved by the Bedouin, she thought, heading for the ladder. For now.

Nora quickly realized that at least one of their visitors was accustomed to western ways. Farid Ibn Kareem was not a typical tribesman. He was educated and well-off, judging by the questions he asked about the dig and the late-model SUV he'd used to get here. He was an older man with white in his beard and clever black eyes tucked into the wrinkles that time and the harsh desert sun had drawn in his face. The other two men were much younger, and silent—his sons, he said.

He was here to see Alex. Though he didn't say so, that was obvious the moment she and Alex climbed out of the quarry and the older man grabbed Alex by the shoulders, pouring out a torrent of Arabic Nora only partially understood, then embracing him.

Nora's eyebrows went up. Obviously the man knew Alex well.

She had to wonder why he was here. He made a passing reference to business in Tor, but that was some distance to the south, along the coast. Had he come just to see Alex?

She saved that question for later, as she was saving her announcement about the blocked tunnel. Time enough to present the others with the news of their latest problem when their visitors left.

Either courtesy or curiosity made Farid accept Nora's offer to show him around the dig. He wasn't uncomfortable speaking directly to a woman, she noticed—another indication that he was used to westerners, or at least to the more relaxed ways of Cairo and Alexandria. After showing him and his two silent sons around the quarry, Nora offered them the use of the shower and the comfort of the main tent, where they could wait while a meal was prepared. Farid accepted for all three of them.

They ate at two tables, with the men outside and the women inside. Nora suspected it wouldn't have shocked Farid to sit down to a meal with females, but he didn't suggest it, and she thought it would be discourteous for her to do so.

Afterward, Farid thanked her elaborately for her hospitality, then went back to the quarry with Alex, with the other two men trailing silently after them—leaving the dishes still to be done, Nora thought wryly as she helped collect the plates from the tables. Some masculine habits were the same in every culture.

Where had Alex met Farid? she wondered. In Cairo, maybe? Alex's parents had a home there, she knew. He came from a world vastly different from hers. A world of servants, heirlooms and traditions. A world where you knew not only your father's name, but the names of your ancestors for generations back.

Nora sighed as she scraped the scraps from one plate into the garbage. Alex seemed so at home here that it was easy to forget that he had no doubt been equally at home at Princeton. Another world, indeed. She glanced around. "That's the last of it, Tim. You can bury the scraps now."

"In a minute. I'm on a winning streak here."

He and Lisa were sitting at the table inside the tent, absorbed in one of their hard-fought games of gin rummy.

This was supposed to have been Tim's night to cook, but none of them wanted to subject guests to his hit-or-miss ideas of cuisine. He'd been given garbage duty instead, while Lisa had done most of the cooking. Nora and DeLaney were left with the clean-up chores, since she'd excused Alex so he could visit with his friend. The two of them had removed the caftans they'd donned for their guests to keep from dipping the sleeves in the dishwater.

"Don't wait too long," Nora said. "The sun's on its way down."

"I'm not afraid of the dark."

"Neither are jackals. If any of them are close enough to smell our leftovers, you might not like the way they bargain for a bite." Actually, jackals were pretty timid. But so was Tim.

"All right, all right." Tim pushed his chair back. "Don't let Lisa peek at my cards while I'm gone. DeLaney, you look very womanly with your hands in dishwater. I like it."

That, of course, set DeLaney off. She treated him to a short, impassioned speech about women's rights that made him chuck her under the chin and tell her she was cute when she was mad.

When he left, whistling cheerfully, his shirt was wet from the dishrag she'd thrown at him.

"You know he just says things like that to get a rise out of you," Lisa said.

"Of course it gets to me. Especially after having to wear that stupid caftan and eat at separate tables so as not to offend our visitors. I really hated that." DeLaney bent to pick up the dishrag she'd flung at Tim.

"I noticed," Nora said dryly, adding what she had said many times before. "We are in their country. It's only polite to respect their customs."

"No, it's dishonest. *We* don't believe that women are supposed to be covered from head to toe so they don't tempt some poor, weak man. I don't understand you, Nora. You're one of the most independent people I know, male or female. If someone like you caves in to sexist pressures—"

Lisa made a rude noise. "Try thinking of clothes as clothes instead of political symbols. In case you didn't notice, Alex put a robe on, too. And even Tim changed into pants."

"But in Cairo—"

"We aren't in Cairo." Nora reached for a dish towel and started drying the plates DeLaney had washed. "Here, neither men nor women appear in public with their arms and legs exposed. Imagine how you would feel if some of the foreign exchange students back at the university insisted on attending classes naked because they didn't wear clothes back home."

DeLaney made a face. "I suppose you're trying to tell me my attitude is not professional."

"Crammed full of cultural bias," Nora agreed, reaching for another plate.

"Here, give me that. This was supposed to be your night off." She grabbed the towel from Nora. "So why don't you make us cover up to keep from offending Ahmed and Gamal? Do their feelings not count?"

"They're employees, not guests. The degree of courtesy owed is different." She glanced out the tent's open flap. The shadows were growing long, but were still distinct. Darkness wouldn't fall for another half hour or so. "I'd better hurry if I'm going to get a shower tonight."

"Like you just told Tim, it's going to be dark soon," Lisa said. "Maybe you should wait until morning."

"I'll hurry," she repeated.

Nora smiled as soon as she stepped outside. The steady chugging of the generator was the only sound, a mildly irritating intrusion on the silence. The air was still and warm, comfortable on her bare arms. Crimson splashed the western sky, marking the sun's descent, and the evening star hung a hand's span above the eastern horizon, where the sky was gathering night closer in shades of purple and blue.

Oh, I do love it here, she thought, breathing deeply as she ambled past her tent. How lucky Alex was, to have spent so much of his childhood in this part of the world. She fought back a pang of envy. It would be easy to envy him his childhood, and not just for the time he'd spent here.

You would know yourself differently, she mused, when your family's heritage was over two centuries thick. She didn't even know who her father—

"Oh!"

A man had stepped out in front of her. "Pardon, Miss Nora. I wish to speak to you."

"Ahmed! You startled me." She pressed her hand to her chest, where her heart was bounding around like a wild thing. Ahmed and Gamal usually kept to themselves, especially at mealtimes. The western habit of conversation at the supper table was as foreign to them as the idea of sharing a table with unmarried women. It was unusual for one of them to seek her out this way. "Is something wrong?"

"I wish to warn you."

Ahmed's English was decent, but heavily accented. "What about?"

He stepped closer, lowering his voice. "You should know about that man, *Ilehnisa* Nora. That Farid Ibn Kareem."

"What do you mean?"

"He is a criminal. A smuggler and a thief. This is well known in Port Said, where my uncle lives. Farid is a very important man there, a wealthy man, but he is feared, too."

Her heart was still beating hard, but now the fear wasn't for herself. "He's out there with Alex. Alone, except for those two men of his."

Ahmed shrugged. "I think Mr. Bok knows this man well. If he sees no danger, I think there is no danger to *him*."

"But..." But Alex had been left for dead by smugglers. He wouldn't be friends with one. Would he? "If you're not worried that Farid is a danger, why did you tell me about him?"

"What if he has heard about the treasure you seek? He may be here to steal it."

She shook her head. "Ahmed, we're not likely to find any treasure, not in the sense you mean." There was always a market for stolen artifacts, but she didn't expect to turn up anything that would tempt a knowledgeable crook...if that's what Farid was. "I do hope to find some interesting objects, but they will be valuable because of where they're found—here, where there shouldn't be a burial. Not because they will be worth a lot of money."

"Still, I will keep an eye on him for you."

"We do not spy on our guests, Ahmed," she said firmly. "Besides, he couldn't steal anything tonight if he wanted to. The tunnel is blocked."

"You do not understand, *Ilehnisa*." His eyes were dark and intense. "I will keep an eye on Alex Bok, who is such good friends with a smuggler. Maybe Alex Bok will do the stealing, later, when Farid is gone."

"Don't be ridiculous. Alex is no thief."

"I will watch," he said stubbornly, and ended the discussion by walking away.

Frustrated, she frowned at the gaudy sky. How absurd. Just because Alex knew Farid didn't mean he had some unethical connection with the man. Shoot, she knew a couple of convicted criminals herself. At least, she'd known them several years ago. Her sister Mary hadn't always had good taste in men. That didn't make Nora a criminal.

Still, it bothered her. It bothered her, too, that Alex had never explained exactly what had happened to him last month in the Negev. For the first time she wondered why he'd been in the Negev in the first place.

What had he been doing so far from any settlement?

Unbidden and unwelcome, a more recent memory rose and she thought of the way he had looked that morning when he'd surprised her on her run—and of what he'd said. *"I could have slit your throat before you turned around."*

He had sounded damnably sure of that. As if he knew himself capable of such an act.

Could the attack in the Negev have been the result of a falling-out among thieves?

Nora shook her head, impatient with herself. Too much imagination, that was her problem. Just this morning she'd thought—feared—she might be falling in love with the man. Now she was fancying him as some sort of sinister figure because of a few unanswered questions.

Questions that probably weren't any of her business. The dig, she reminded herself, was her business. And the Lord knew there was enough to concern her about that.

She started forward, but took only one step before stopping in disgust. While she'd been locked up in a private world of worry, the shadows had slid up on each other, joining their edges in the long quiet of approaching night. She'd missed her chance for a shower tonight.

From far off came the siren-like howl of a jackal, an eerie noise like nothing else on earth. Goose bumps popped out on Nora's bare arms. The moon wasn't up yet, and the gaunt tumble of rocks around her were losing their shapes in the growing darkness. The land seemed suddenly alien. Threatening.

Too much imagination, she reminded herself, and started back towards the yellow glow of artificial light spilling from the main tent.

All the same, it wouldn't hurt to ask Alex a couple of questions tomorrow. About his connection to Farid, and just why he'd been alone in the Negev in the first place.

Chapter 6

Alex was in a foul mood. It didn't show, of course. He knew how to counterfeit whatever emotion would get the job done. But the need for pretense only made his mood worse.

"Excuse the cramped quarters, *ya beyh,*" Alex said. He and Farid sat cross-legged on the canvas floor of his tent. He'd had to fold up the legs to his cot and stand it on its side to make room for them both.

Farid made a dismissive gesture. "Am I city-bred, that I would weaken at a night spent away from walls? You have all that a man needs in the desert. I thank you for sharing the comfort of your tent with me. Although," he added with a twinkle, "there is one comfort you possess that I do not expect you to share. A most pleasant example of Allah's gifts."

The words spoken were Arabic, though Farid Ibn Kareem was almost as fluent in English as Alex was in Farid's tongue. They each held steaming cups of the syrupy tea of the Bedouin. One of Farid's sons had made it by boiling water with equal parts sugar and tea over a dung fire he'd built in front of Alex's tent. He and his brother were out there now, enjoying their own cups of tea while dusk faded into night.

Alex took a sip from the small porcelain cup. The tea was strong enough to give a camel a buzz. "I am glad you find my tent pleasant. I know you are fond of the desert, but you are also fond of the comforts of your house in Port Said."

Farid chuckled. "I refer to the young woman who so courteously donned a *galabiyya* to spare my blushes. She looks well able to ensure your pleasure while you are here."

"Western women do not regard their purpose in life the same way you do," Alex said dryly. He thought of the kiss Nora had surprised him with earlier that day…and the one he had taken from her.

Damn her. Why hadn't she slapped him, shoved him away, made it clear she wouldn't let him use her?

"But I saw the way this woman watches you, my friend. If she isn't pleasuring you yet, it will take little effort on your part to change this. Then, too, there was the small, plump woman who glared at me so often. She also watches you." He smiled. "You are young enough to enjoy both, if you are careful."

Alex didn't feel young; he hadn't for a long time. "It takes a more clever man than I am—or one more brave—to juggle two women." He held up his cup in a salute. Farid had two wives.

Farid laughed, open-mouthed. His teeth were strong and yellow. "Now you flatter me, and deftly, too." He took one last sip from his cup, then set it down. "I was sorry to hear of your accident last month."

Alex wasn't surprised that Farid knew about the attack. The man had an efficient information network. "I do not think that rather pointed rebuke to my curiosity was an accident."

"Then I will say I am pleased that Allah decided you should live in spite of your enemies' intentions. You are well now, I hope?"

"Quite well. It was a clumsy attempt. I very nearly lived through it."

Farid chuckled. "I am glad to learn your sense of humor did not drain away along with your blood. And now, I am curious as to the reason for my being summoned."

Alex lifted his eyebrows. "Perhaps my message was garbled. I would not dream of summoning you, *ya beyh.*" He gave the old scoundrel the courtesy title his age deserved.

"Your request was phrased most politely. But it was a summons, nonetheless." The black eyes couched in their network of wrinkles were as shrewd as they were dark. "As you see, I am here. But wondering why."

"El Hawy."

All traces of humor fled. Only one thing took priority over business with Farid al Kareem: revenge. Three years ago, his oldest son had been killed in a bomb blast that had been planned and executed by four fanatics. Only one of the men who had killed Farid's son was still alive, the others having died violently—two of them, to Alex's certain knowledge, at the hand of Farid or one of his remaining sons.

The man who still lived called himself Jawhar Ibn el Hawy these days—Jawhar, the bloody-minded leader of El Hawy.

The older man leaned forward. "You have learned where he is."

"Not exactly. I have learned that El Hawy has a shipment of arms coming. It should arrive in the next two weeks."

His eyebrows lifted slightly. "Your sources are better than mine, then. I have heard nothing of this."

"I am sure you heard about the shipment of Russian weapons that was intercepted before it reached Iran last month, however."

"Ah. That I have. This did not happen in Israel, where you received such pointed objection to your curiosity. There is a connection?"

"I overheard a conversation last month. El Hawy objected." Alex took another sip of the sweet brew. "Jawhar has a buyer for the shipment. I take as great an interest in this buyer as you do in Jawhar."

"I must, of course, deplore anything which profits those sons of jackals, but this does not seem closely connected to my own concerns. Except, of course, for your very interesting presence on this dig." He paused. "You have found their base?"

"The general area where it is located, yes. Not the base itself."

"And so you summon me to help you search." A smile spread over his face, slow and pleased by the prospect of murder. "Good."

Alex chuckled. "I am not such a trusting soul. If you found the base before I did, you might forget to mention it until your business with Jawhar was finished. I ask two things of you. First, leave the area. He'll know of your visit to me—that can't be helped. But he would be much more wary of your continued presence here than he will be of mine."

"He knows who you are?"

"He has some idea, I'm sure. He will assume that I am

in league with you to take possession of the arms shipment.''

"I cannot find the dung-eating offspring of jackals if I leave the area.''

"I'll find him when I locate the base. I'll either let you know where he is, or make sure you have no further need to seek revenge.''

His eyebrows went up again. "You ask a great deal.''

"You said once that you owed me a great deal.''

Farid fell silent, scowling.

Alex waited. It was risky to call in his favor this way. Farid was as likely to take offense as he was to agree, and the man made a much better friend than he did an enemy. But Alex couldn't have Farid going in, guns blazing, and scaring away his main target—Simon—the traitor who was trying to take down SPEAR.

Farid broke the silence by giving a demonstration of the rich possibilities Arabic afforded for cursing. "I pay my debts,'' he said at last. "I do not like it, but I will wait. Not long, but I will wait.''

"Thank you.'' Alex inclined his head. "That part is the favor. The rest is business. While you are waiting to hear from me, I want you to locate and track the arms shipment—and resist the urge to appropriate it for yourself. The people I work for will see that you do not suffer for your forbearance.''

"I continue to puzzle over just who you work for, my young friend.''

In some circles, Alex was known as his parents' less-than-satisfactory son—bright enough, knowledgeable enough, but lacking in the ambition or discipline to make a name for himself in the field where they shone. In other circles he was known as a man connected to a large, anonymous criminal organization—a man who could arrange the sale of all sorts of stolen goods quickly and quietly. Farid—and Jawhar—belonged to the second group.

"Does it matter?" Alex asked blandly.

"You are a loyal man. I have often noted this. A commendable trait, but it could present problems if your employer's goals diverge from mine. There is much about your purpose here you have not told me."

"Of course." Alex smiled and put down his cup. "Come, we both know our purposes overlap in some places, but not all. It has not kept us from working together in the past. I would be a fool to tell you everything, but I do not lie to you. I have a good chance of reaching your son's killer while I pursue my own goal, and will do what I can to either offer him up to you...or see that he is beyond the reach of any judgment save Allah's."

"And if you fail?"

"I will be dead and beyond your reproaches."

Farid laughed. They had another cup of tea, bargained over the amount of the "finder's fee" Farid could expect if he located the shipment, and discussed Farid's numerous remaining progeny—two of whom were putting up Farid's own, much larger, tent while they talked.

Farid objected to one part of Alex's plan. "You warn them of your presence, and put them on the alert against you."

"My goal is to put them on alert against you. They will assume you arranged it."

"Which will, indeed, be the case. But why would I do such a thing?"

"To delay the arrival of the arms so you can find them."

"Which is, again, alarmingly true. I see no wisdom in allowing my enemy to predict my actions."

"While Jawhar is watching you, he will pay less attention to me. And he will not guess at my real goal—the destruction of El Hawy." Nor would Jawhar—or, Alex hoped, Farid—guess at Alex's other goal: to make sure the terrorist leader didn't resume his increasingly dangerous harassment of the archaeologists.

Alex knew his presence here might increase the danger. He couldn't let that happen.

Farid considered that in silence a moment. "Very well," he said at last, rising to his feet. "My youngest son will remain behind to handle this for you. But it will make matters more difficult for me. Jawhar will not want me to locate the shipment."

"I have confidence in you, *ya beyh.*" Finding the arms was the least vital of his goals—but it wouldn't do to let Farid become aware of that.

Alex felt reasonably sure Farid would abide by their agreement when he bid his guest good-night. That was the only thing he felt good about.

Earlier he'd allowed worry and anger to push him into trying to frighten Nora. He'd been thinking only of keeping her safe, not of his mission. *Big mistake,* he'd whispered to her when she kissed him, but the biggest mistake had been his. He had let her see a side of him that didn't mesh with the man he was supposed to be.

Alex couldn't afford mistakes, and he couldn't allow himself the distraction of worrying about one woman's safety.

But he couldn't seem to stop.

He'd done what he could to lessen her danger, he told himself as he unfolded his cot and spread his sleeping bag on it. It would have to be enough.

Tonight he wouldn't go wandering the desert. He trusted Farid only so far. If Alex went out, Farid would undoubtedly send one of his sons to follow him—and Farid's sons could track a mouse across the desert without the mouse knowing. If Alex did run across the base and Farid learned its location, nothing would stop the old man from pursuing his vengeance.

He couldn't let that happen. Timing was critical, if he was to have a chance of accomplishing his main goals—find the arms shipment, destroy El Hawy and take out a traitor known only as Simon. The man who wanted to ruin SPEAR.

Which meant that tonight Alex would sleep, not search.

God, how he dreaded it. He wanted to move. His muscles twitched with the need to be up and about, acting with purpose.

Alex's sleeping bag was down-filled, too warm, really, on a September night in the Sinai. Being too warm was better than being cold, though. He stretched out between the layers and felt weariness dragging at him, a gut-deep tiredness that was only partly physical.

Exhaustion was so much better than dreams.

Darkness had once been Alex's friend, a comforting veil to draw across activities he couldn't afford to have seen. No more. Now he lay awake, sweating lightly under the weight of his sleeping bag, and silently cursed the darkness.

The sky had been a rare, complete black on the night he'd been stabbed, a skein of clouds having hidden the stars. That blackness, combined with his attackers' laziness, had been his salvation at first. Though he'd taken a wound in the fight, he'd managed to get away. They hadn't pursued him long, convinced his wound would kill him without their help.

He'd been determined, so blindly determined, to prove them wrong.

He remembered first walking, then stumbling, across the desert. The pain had dragged at him, but he hadn't let it defeat him. How many other times had he been hurt, yet prevailed? How many other times had he used mind, body and will to beat the odds? He'd been convinced he could beat them again.

Even when he'd no longer been able to stay upright, he'd forced himself on. He'd crawled. Then he'd dragged himself one bloody inch at a time.

He remembered, too, his vague astonishment at the final betrayal of his body. It had simply stopped moving. He'd ended in a heap on the ground, one arm bent uncomfortably beneath him, unable to shift even slightly to straighten that arm. And all around him, nothing but darkness—vast, cold, indifferent. Darkness draining him out of himself, leaching his thoughts and his will until only a small, shivering animal remained in the dying body. So cold…

Alex expected to dream that night. He didn't fear giving himself away to Farid, camped so close by. His dreams never made him cry out.

No, what visited him all too often in his sleep was worse than pain—though there was pain. Worse than fear, though there was fear. It was the *comfort,* the damned, hideous, luring comfort of the darkness. That was what made him as fearful now as a child longing for a night-light.

Because in the end, before warm hands and a soft voice had somehow called him back, the cold had won. Not because he'd taken a fatal wound. Not because of the loss of blood, though that was what the doctors believed.

But Alex knew the truth. He hadn't passed out. No, for all the hours that he'd lain there, unmoving, beneath the chilly black vault of the sky, he'd been conscious. And so he remembered…much more than he wanted to.

The cold had won because it had been inside him as well as outside. Because he'd given up.

* * *

Nora awoke the next morning to a feeling of anticipation. She couldn't account for it. Lord knew she ought to be worrying over how to remove a half ton of rock without bringing the mountain down on the tunnel: yet little bubbles of excitement kept welling up and bursting out in smiles while she attended to the usual morning rituals of dressing and brushing her teeth and hair.

She was humming the whistle-while-you-work song when she unzipped her tent flap and stepped out into a pink-and-gold morning, carrying her towels and her robe. It was early yet, but later than she usually got up. Last night Alex had told her he wouldn't be able to join her for a run this morning, and her promise kept her from enjoying a solo run.

Missing her run should have made her irritable. Instead, she paused just outside her tent to savor the delicacy of the morning sky, then was charmed by the greed of a small brown bird that hopped across her path, its attention fixed on a shiny black beetle.

From the other side of the camp rose the quiet chant of Ahmed at his morning prayers, a newly familiar sound. Nora smiled at the dawn, the bird and the prayer, and added a wordless one of her own, thankful for the day and the moment.

A few seconds later, the bird snatched the beetle and flew off, Ahmed's prayer ended and Nora started for the shower.

Why shouldn't she feel good? she asked herself. She was where she wanted to be, doing work she loved. The aches from her fall were gone. That, and the luxury of having spent a good thirty minutes of extra snuggle-time beneath her covers, no doubt explained this rising sense of well-being.

And Alex had promised to help them find an expert who

could tackle the blocked tunnel. He might even contact his parents on their behalf. If the Boks chose to use their influence, Nora was sure that Ibrahim's attitude would undergo a major reversal.

Who knows? Like her mom used to say, today's problems sometimes turn into tomorrow's blessings—if you work hard enough.

Anticipation followed Nora like a wag-tailed puppy to the shower, where it even survived the spluttering chill of water that had cooled overnight in its overhead tank. She washed quickly, dried herself, then pulled underwear, shorts and shirt on over goose-bumped flesh before brushing her towel-dried hair and putting it in a hasty braid.

It wasn't until she slid her arms into the sleeves of the robe she'd worn yesterday that the giddy feelings took a hit from reality. The robe was necessary in case Farid and his men joined them for breakfast this morning.

Farid, the man Ahmed said was a smuggler...and Alex claimed as a friend.

She was going to ask Alex about that, she reminded herself, as she stepped out of the canvas walls of the shower to a day with some of its luster dimmed. About that, and the mystery of his presence in the Negev last month. No doubt he would be able to explain both things easily.

Though he might be insulted by her asking. She frowned as she fastened her damp towels to the line strung up near the shower. Well, if he didn't like being questioned, then he didn't. Tact was not her strong suit. She really only knew one way to introduce a delicate subject—straight on. The same way she approached everything else.

Lisa and DeLaney hadn't yet stirred outside, but to her surprise, Tim was already up. He sat on a camp stool near the stove, sipping from a mug.

"You made coffee," she said, pleased. The pot sat in the middle of the flat heating surface of the stove, perking gently. She headed straight for it.

He stood and handed her an empty mug. "I want to talk to you."

"You sound serious." She poured coffee, dark and bitter, into her cup. "Is there something wrong?"

"I don't know. I think so. I learned something from Ahmed last night that's worrying me."

"I should have known Ahmed might feel the need to confide his worries in a man. He told you about Farid, I suppose."

"And Bok." He set his mug on the table. "Look, I know you're dazzled by the man, but—"

"I am not dazzled," she snapped. She took a too-hasty sip of coffee and burned her tongue. "Damn. You've let it boil again, haven't you? It tastes burnt." Like her tongue.

"Never mind about the stupid coffee. Nora, aren't you concerned about Bok's connection to a known smuggler?"

"For heaven's sake, Tim, Farid isn't a 'known smuggler' just because Ahmed says he is." She moved the coffeepot farther over to the edge of the stove.

"He has no reason to lie."

"No reason we know of, maybe. But there could be all sorts of reasons we don't know about. Or he might simply be wrong." She took a more cautious sip from her mug, looked at Tim's determined faced and sighed. "Go ahead. Say what you have to, then I'll tell you what I intend to do."

"You do mean to take some action, then. Good. Ahmed didn't think you took his warning seriously, and I was afraid you were too besotted with Bok to consider the implications."

"Besotted." Her temper was simmering hotter than Tim's burned coffee. "Do you have any clue how insulting you're being?"

He stood. "Maybe I'm not choosing my words well, but hell, Nora, I've seen the way you look at him. And I've watched him doing his damnedest to charm you. He's bloody good at it, too. The man's obviously had plenty of experience getting what he wants from women. So maybe it's no wonder—but I don't trust him."

Best, she thought, to ignore his comment about the way she looked at Alex, and get to the meat of the matter. "Guilt by association doesn't work for me. Maybe Farid is a smuggler. That doesn't make Alex a thief."

"Bok knows him awfully bloody well, though, if Farid came all the way out here to see him! I suppose you think I'm prejudiced because I'm jealous, but—"

She was jolted. "Jealous?"

"Oh, hell." He turned away, running his hand over his already-messy hair. "You haven't even noticed, have you? Never mind. Forget I said that. The thing is, Nora, even if Bok's connection with Farid is entirely innocent, he isn't the kind of man you want to get involved with."

She didn't know what to say—or, rather, there was too much she wanted to say, much of it contradictory. "Dazzled" and "besotted" still rankled. And what made Tim think he knew what sort of man she wanted to be involved with? And she *wasn't* involved with Alex…exactly. But Tim's confession of jealousy had thrown her. True, when they first met, he had let her know he was interested, but he'd taken her gentle rebuff good-naturedly. He'd seemed satisfied with being friends.

"Tim," she said at last, "I know you mean well. But for whatever reason, you were ready to dislike Alex the moment you met him. I don't think you're seeing him clearly."

"And you are?" Tim faced her again, his long face creased with worry. "Just...be careful, Nora. I don't want you to be hurt."

"There. We do agree on something. I don't want to be hurt, either." She tried for a reassuring smile, but it felt stiff. "Really, Tim, you're doing a great deal of worrying based on very few facts. I do plan to ask Alex about Farid, if that makes you feel any better."

"Now *that's* a useful idea. I suppose you think that if he's here to steal from us, he'll mention it when you bring up the subject."

"And I suppose you want me to kick him off the dig—a man sent by the director of the museum that authorized our project—based on gossip repeated by one of our workers! Tim, be reasonable. Alex doesn't have any need to steal from us or anyone else. He comes from a wealthy family."

"And does he have money of his own? Stock, bonds, coupons to clip?"

She hadn't thought of that. "Well, I don't know, but—"

"Maybe you should find out. Because from what I can tell, he doesn't work for a living. And if that doesn't tell you something about the kind of man he is—"

"What kind of man who is?" That voice came from inside the main tent. A second later DeLaney pushed aside the flap to the tent and came out, smiling at both of them curiously. "Are you two arguing?"

Tim flushed.

"Yes, we were," Nora said coolly. "I'm surprised you didn't hear us."

"I did, actually," DeLaney said cheerfully. "But I couldn't hear very well. Your voices were too low. Who were you arguing about? I heard something about someone stealing. Has something else been taken?''

''No. It's your turn to fix breakfast, DeLaney.''

''But who were you talking about?''

Nora shook her head, exasperated and amused. ''My comment about breakfast was a hint that I wanted to change the subject, in case you couldn't tell.'' She paused. The low murmur of male voices carried clearly in the dry air. ''You'd better get your robe. I think I hear our visitors coming.''

DeLaney grimaced and ducked back inside the tent.

Tim stepped closer and said in a low voice. ''Be careful, Nora. I'm worried about you.''

She couldn't think of anything to say, so she nodded stiffly and turned to look down the wadi.

The visitors were indeed headed their way. So was Alex. It was an oddly stirring sight, the four tall men in their desert robes walking side by side, dust rising at their feet with each step.

One of the younger men was talking to Alex. They looked very much alike to her in that moment, two dark, serious men, both of them a little too good-looking for comfort. Both quite foreign to her experience.

Then Alex laughed at something the other man said. Nora saw the white flash of his teeth. She couldn't see his expression clearly from this distance, but she didn't have to. She knew exactly how his eyes crinkled up at the corners when something amused him.

She put a hand on her stomach and smiled, too. In spite of everything, the bubbles were back.

Chapter 7

Nora's eyes were shining. Alex couldn't help noticing that, just as he had noticed the quick grace of her movements earlier, when she had politely insisted on serving Farid and his sons a simple breakfast before they left. Just as he always noticed the faint scent of lilacs that followed her.

Yesterday, she'd taken the news of the blocked tunnel hard. Today she was calm and unemotional as she broke that news to her crew after their guests had left. Not surprisingly, her listeners didn't respond well. Groans, questions and lamentations rose in a sudden babble.

She wrapped her knuckles on the table to get their attention. "Okay, I know you're disappointed. I am, too. Most of your questions I can't answer. I think—I hope—we'll be able to get additional funding for any extra equipment needed to clear the tunnel, but I don't know yet what that might be. Also, we can't bring in more personnel or heavy equipment without permission from the authorities here. Alex has offered to try to find someone local with the expertise we'll need, which would get us over one major hurdle. But for the time being, work on the tunnel is suspended."

Not surprisingly, that brought another round of exclamations. DeLaney's voice rose above the others. "But what are we supposed to *do?*"

"Oh, we've got plenty to do. Don't worry about staying busy. There's fill to be sifted, and we have a lot of bits and pieces that need to be washed so we can see what, if anything, we've got."

They had to discuss it, of course. Over a quick meal of bread, cheese and coffee, they talked out their disappointment, made unlikely suggestions, and more or less accepted the changed plans.

Tim amused Alex by darting suspicious glances at him, as if he thought Alex were somehow responsible for the setback.

"Are you sure this cave-in happened a long time ago?" Tim asked Nora. "It isn't recent?"

"There's no weathering to speak of inside the tunnel, of course, so I really can't say. If you're worried about whether the tunnel is as safe as we thought it was—well, so am I. That's why the tunnel is off-limits until we get an expert appraisal."

"So." Tim leaned back, his voice fraught with significance. "The only reason you think the roof caved in a long time ago is that Bok says it did."

Did the man think Alex had somehow arranged for the roof to cave in? "It was an educated guess, Tim, nothing more. We know of two periods of earthquake activity in this region—it makes sense that the collapse happened during one of them."

Tim had the grace to look abashed. "I guess so."

"So what's our illustrious leader going to be doing while the rest of us are sifting, washing and sorting?" DeLaney asked. "Are you going to go to Cairo to talk with Dr. Ibrahim?"

"I may have to. We'll see. This morning I'll be trying to patch through some calls from our radio."

That didn't suit Alex's plans. He needed everyone to be away from the camp this morning. "Wouldn't you rather use my cell phone?"

Nora's eyebrows lifted in polite surprise. "Alex, I hate to tell you this, but there isn't any cellular service out here."

"It's not a regular cell phone. The signal is bounced off a satellite. I'm supposed to be able to call anywhere in the world from anywhere in the world." Such a system had recently become available commercially, so Alex's possession of the phone wouldn't give away his connection to SPEAR. Especially since no one but him could access the phone's more unusual features.

"It sounds expensive."

He shrugged. "You know what they say about men and our toys. This is my newest toy. I haven't had a chance to use it much yet—this would give me a good excuse to see how well it works."

Her mouth quirked up. "So I would really be doing you a favor by running up an enormous bill."

"Exactly."

Their eyes held for a moment in shared amusement. "Far be it from me to withhold a favor from a friend," she said, pushing back from the table. "Now, if everyone has finished eating, we've got work to do."

There was the usual good-natured bustle involved in clearing the table and setting off towards the quarry. Nora didn't start out with the rest of them, however. Her face wore an oddly determined look when she stopped Alex from leaving with the others. "Alex, before we start running up your phone bill, I need to talk to you about something."

DeLaney, who had started for the quarry, stopped. "What?" she asked.

Lisa took her arm. "Never mind, child. Come on."

"But I just wanted to know..." DeLaney's voice trailed off as Lisa dragged her away.

Alex grinned. "That one is an Elephant's Child if ever I've seen one."

"Full of 'satiable curiosity,' you mean?" She smiled. "I loved those stories when I was little. Especially the one about 'the Cat who walks by Himself.'"

He finished the quote: "'...and all places are alike to him.'"

"That's it! You must have enjoyed them, too."

"My parents believed in stimulating a child's intellect. Besides, there wasn't much else to do at night on a dig. They took turns reading aloud every night. Kipling was a big favorite of mine. In fact, when my copy of *Just So Stories* went overboard into the Nile one day, I dived in after it."

"You *what?*"

"It wasn't one of my brighter impulses. The book never was the same after its dunking. And boy, did I get in trouble." He shook his head, smiling at the memory.

"It's a wonder you didn't drown or get hit by another boat! Your parents must have been scared to death."

"Now, I really *would* have been in trouble if I'd waited for them to find out I'd gone overboard and get all worked up about it. No, once I reached the shore I made my way to a village and persuaded the authorities there to contact the nearest U.S. Consulate, who notified my folks that they needed to come pick me up.'' He grinned. ''They were certainly surprised.''

''They didn't even know you were gone?'' She looked more aghast than amused. ''How old were you?''

''Ten, I think. Maybe eleven. Rather old to be so attached to a child's storybook, you're thinking, but—''

''No, I'm thinking you were awfully young to be left to fend for yourself that way.''

''I wasn't neglected, if that's what you're thinking. I liked fending for myself—liked it a little too much, maybe. Kind of like that cat who walks by himself.'' He cocked his head to one side. ''Seems to me you're bent somewhat in that direction yourself.''

''Maybe.'' She started walking—a habit of hers, he'd noticed, when she was nervous or troubled. ''I certainly don't have any business criticizing your parents. I'm sorry for that.''

''Forgiven. I guess my childhood looks a little peculiar from the outside, but on the whole I enjoyed it tremendously. I had a taste for adventure, and found chances to indulge it—partly because my folks were so vague about present-day reality.'' He chuckled. ''I wasn't an easy child for them, you know. Think of Huck Finn being raised by a couple of absented-minded professors.''

Her smile flickered. ''I can feel some sympathy for them.'' After a moment she cleared her throat. ''I guess you didn't outgrow your habit of falling into adventures when you grew up. I mean...look at what happened to you in the Negev. And at your friend Farid. He's, ah, not exactly the sort of person an absent-minded professor would know well, is he?''

His eyebrows went up. ''Is that what you wanted to talk to me about? Farid? I knew people would be curious about him, but I'd expected to be cross-examined by DeLaney, not you."

She grimaced. "No doubt you will be, but I...the thing is—well, to put it bluntly, I was told that Farid is a smuggler and a thief."

"That's blunt, all right." He kept pace with her, his mind turning over possibilities rapidly. "Was it Tim? I couldn't help noticing that he seems to suspect me of something dire."

"Oh, no. But the person who told me this also told Tim. I'm afraid he considered it rather...incriminating."

"In what way?" He put just enough frustration in his voice to sound innocent. "I'd like to know who's trying to make trouble for me."

"I don't think that's relevant."

It was damned relevant, since there was a good chance that the person who had told Nora about Farid was acting on behalf of the El Hawy terrorists. But of course he couldn't mention that. "I'd also like to know where they got their supposed facts."

"This person said Farid's activities are common knowledge in Port Said."

Farid's less-than-legal operations were hardly common knowledge. It sounded as if El Hawy was trying to discredit Alex, maybe get him kicked off the dig. He wondered if the next step would be to plant drugs in his tent. "Let's see. You said it wasn't Tim. Obviously it wasn't DeLaney or Lisa, which leaves either Gamal or Ahmed as the tale-bearer."

She gave him a quick glance. "What makes you so sure it wasn't Lisa or DeLaney?"

"Where would they have heard that sort of gossip? They've only been in the country a couple months. Besides, DeLaney would have told everyone, not just you and

Tim. And while Lisa might have passed gossip on to you if she thought it was important, she wouldn't have run to Tim with it, too."

"You've gotten to know us pretty well in such a short time." She walked on in silence a moment, chewing her lip. "So...is it true?"

"I've heard stories about Farid," he admitted, with his best semblance of candor. "I don't know if they're true or not. He's a wealthy man and he lives in Port Said, which is probably enough to start a rumor or two about his being involved in smuggling. I don't know if you're familiar with the situation there."

She nodded. "It's a free port, but Egyptian citizens aren't allowed to bring duty-free goods back with them, so there's a lot of smuggling. I'm not so concerned about that, Alex. I know smuggling is a time-honored custom here. The authorities may take it seriously, but a lot of the ordinary citizens don't. But the, ah, person I talked to seems to think Farid also deals in stolen antiquities."

That was a nice touch, Alex thought grimly. Associating with a smuggler might not seem all that suspicious to an archaeologist. But if the man was also a dealer in stolen antiquities... "If you're asking me whether I plan to steal whatever we find at the end of that blasted tunnel—"

"No, of course not. For one thing, I doubt very much if we'll find anything worth stealing. I tried to explain that to, ah, the person I spoke with, but I don't think he understood the difference between intellectual treasure and monetary treasure."

"Thanks for the vote of confidence." He was angry, he realized. How absurd. Why should she trust him, after all? He'd lied to her several times, and intended to go right on lying.

But not because he was a thief.

"I'm not accusing you of anything, Alex. Once the question was raised, though, it seemed only fair to give you a chance to respond."

"Is that what you're doing? Giving me a fair hearing? I don't see what you expect me to say. I can't very well prove that Farid doesn't dabble in that trade. Or that I don't."

She sighed. "I guess, since I've already offended you, I may as well go ahead and finish the job."

"That sounds ominous."

"What were you doing in the Negev last month, so far away from any settlements?"

That was actually a very good question. He ran a hand over the top of his head. "I wish you hadn't asked that."

The look she darted his way was almost as suspicious as the ones Tim had been giving him earlier. "Why?"

"Because it's embarrassing. I was lost."

She stopped moving. "Lost?"

He gave her a rueful smile. "Thoroughly. I was visiting friends, and I couldn't sleep. That happens to me a lot. I've never needed as much sleep as most people seem to. I didn't want to wake them up, so I did what I often do when I get restless at night. I went for a walk."

She stared at him incredulously. "That must have been quite a walk. The nearest settlement was Kibbutz Nir Am, but you came from the opposite direction. And I was staying in Nir Am. I asked around afterwards. No one there knew who you were."

"I like going out into the desert at night. Sometimes I walk for hours." Alex was a good liar. He knew well how to mix truth into his stories to give them the flavor of reality. So why did it leave a foul taste in his mouth this time?

He looked away, uneasy, knowing she would see his

reaction—knowing, too, that she would put it down to what had happened to him that night. "I normally use the stars as a compass, but it was cloudy that night. I got turned around. When I thought I was headed back, I was really moving deeper into the desert. And then..."

"Then you ran across some people who didn't want to be seen." Impulsively she put her hand on his arm. "Alex, I'm sorry. I didn't mean to bring back difficult memories."

"They're never that far away, anyway." Damn. Why had he said that? "Look, if I've satisfied your curiosity, I'd just as soon drop the subject."

"Of course." She walked beside him in silence until they came to the rim of the quarry, where she paused to look at him. "Um...how insulted are you?"

He stopped to look at her. *She belongs here,* he thought. It was an odd thing to believe about a woman who had grown up in one of the largest cities in the United States, but it was true. Even her colors seemed to blend with the land around them—skin tanned to a dusty brown, eyes the hot blue of the noon sky, hair as black as a desert night. "I'll get over it."

Those eyes smiled at him mischievously. "In time to find us an engineer?"

"Oh, by the time I get to my tent, I imagine." He cocked an eyebrow at her. "You could speed the process up. Want to race?"

"Race? Here?" She glanced at the steep slope down into the quarry.

"You seem to like plunging off edges."

She grinned. "And I'm good at it, too. I hope your ego is healthy enough to let you handle being beaten by a woman."

"Worry about your own ego, woman. On your mark, get set—"

"Go!" she cried, and took off.

* * *

Nora won the race—or so she claimed. She did reach the bottom of the quarry a second ahead of Alex, but he beat her to his tent. They argued over which spot had been the real finish line while he fastened the tent flap open, then bowed and gestured her inside.

"I definitely won," she said as she ducked and stepped inside. "I'm sure the others will back me up on that, as soon as they get their eyeballs tucked back in their heads." Her crew had shown various versions of the same expression when she and Alex pelted down the slope and on to his tent: pure astonishment.

He chuckled. "I think you shocked DeLaney."

"I must have been acting terribly stuffy, if she could be shocked by a foot race." She glanced around the tiny interior of his tent. There wasn't much to see—the cot, his duffle bag and backpack, a small, square wooden table set low to the floor that held a laptop computer, a couple of books, a canteen and a compass.

Had he bought the compass after getting lost last month?

"I can't see you as stuffy. Professorial, maybe."

She grimaced. "That's almost as bad." Curious, she lowered herself to sit, cross-legged, on the floor beside the table and picked up the top book. A popular thriller, she saw, about spies and bad guys. The other book was more of a surprise. It was a slim, leather-bound volume with gold-embossed printing. Unfortunately, the printing was in Arabic script, which she couldn't read.

"Is it teachers or teaching you don't approve of?"

"Oh, I like teaching, and I've had some great professors. That part of the academic life is fine. It's the rest of it that makes me nuts—the egos and petty politics, everyone jockeying for tenure."

"Spoken like an honest, straightforward person who doesn't have tenure."

She grinned. "True. But believe it or not—and this would sound like heresy to most of my colleagues back home—I wouldn't care about tenure if it weren't tied to the things I really want to do."

"Let me guess. Field work?" He hadn't moved away from the entry, but stood quietly, watching her closely. As if there was something fascinating about the sight of her in his tent.

It put a delicious flutter in her pulse. *Like some silly teenager,* she told herself, trying to stay on the reasoning side of her brain. "Good guess." She held up the book. "You read Arabic as well as speak it, apparently. I'm impressed."

"No. You're nosy." He moved the two steps that took him to his duffel bag and sat, cross-legged like her. In the crowded space of the small tent, this put him less than an arm's length away. "If you want to know what the book is, just ask."

"What is it?"

"The Rubáiyát of Omar Khayyám."

"Good heavens." She glanced at the slim book. "In Arabic?"

"My Farsi is too limited to read it in the original language, I'm afraid. But the quatrains are lovely in Arabic." He took his cell phone out of his bag, along with a small notebook. "You want to call first, or shall I?"

She waved the phone away. "You. If you can find an engineer willing to work for free, that might make a difference when I start begging Ibrahim to use his influence to get us whatever permits we'll need."

While he dialed, she opened the book and glanced at

the flowing, unreadable script. "I suppose reading the English translation would be too easy?"

He chuckled and leaned forward, holding the phone to his ear with one hand. She could faintly hear the phone ringing on the other end. "'Ah! my Beloved,'" he quoted softly, "'fill the Cup that clears To-day of past Regrets and future Fears; Tomorrow?—Why, Tomorrow I may be Myself with Yesterday's Sev'n Thousand Years.'"

Oh, God, the man was quoting poetry to her.

Nora's mouth went dry, and she wanted, badly, to take his hand and hold it to her cheek. "You, ah, do know the English version well, obviously. That reminds me of the old 'eat, drink and be merry' bit."

"I mentioned that my mother liked to read Kipling in the evenings. My father preferred Omar Khayyám or Louis L'Amour."

She smiled, delighted. "That's quite a combination. My mother read to me when I was little, too. But it was usually Dr. Seuss."

"Nothing wrong with Seuss." He shifted positions, bringing one knee up and resting his forearm on it so he could keep the phone held to his ear.

This left him with one hand free. He used it to tuck a strand of hair behind her ear while his eyes smiled at her in a most unfair way. "I can just see you as a little girl. I'll bet you were very serious—when you weren't racing the boys and beating them."

She couldn't think of what to say, not when he looked at her like that. "I, ah, was on the track team in high school."

"I'm not surprised. I—oh, hi, Mom," he said into the phone.

While Alex talked to his mother, Nora fought to get her hormones back under control. She gave herself a stiff mental lecture about duty and responsibility and not allowing a simple case of lust to overwhelm her good sense. She even listened to herself. In fact, she was paying so much attention to getting herself back under control she nearly missed the important part of Alex's conversation.

"Whose phone number did you ask her for?" she demanded.

"Rashi al Hammad. I'm sure you've heard of him."

"Oh, just once or twice. Good grief, Alex, the man's practically a legend! And he must be over seventy. You're not going to ask *him* to come out here, are you?"

"Sure I am," he said cheerfully, punching in a new set of numbers. "Why not start at the top? Besides, Rashi can't stand Ibrahim."

"Is that supposed to reassure me? Alex, I thought you were going to find us an engineer, or someone with comparable experience. Asking Rashi al Hammad to clear our tunnel is like—oh, like asking Thomas Edison to fix our generator."

"Not exactly. Edison's dead, so you'd have to channel him."

"I may have to hurt you."

"No violence, please." He looked amused, not frightened. "Trust me, Nora. I usually know what I'm doing. When I don't, I can fake it pretty well."

She didn't have any more time to argue. Alex started speaking in Arabic into the phone, the words flowing too quickly and colloquially for her to follow. She caught snatches, though.

"You gave him directions out here," she said levelly, trying to keep hope from bursting out and making her do something silly. "And your phone number."

"The directions weren't for him. Rashi is interested,

though. Especially since he hadn't heard anything about your cave.''

''Well—why would he have?''

''There's precious little he doesn't hear. He's good and mad about it, too,'' Alex said, sounding satisfied. ''He's going to call Ibrahim.''

She groaned. ''Oh, that's just what I need, to get Ibrahim upset with me because I went behind his back and talked to one of the biggest names in the field. The man already dislikes me.''

''Actually, that *is* what you need. Nora, you asked me once if I came here to take over the dig. I didn't, but I think you're right about Ibrahim's prejudice. He doesn't want you to succeed. He wants to make things difficult enough that you'll quit or run out of time—your leave from the university can't be extended forever—and then he can put a man of his own choosing in charge. In the meantime, he'd rather the archaeological community here in Egypt didn't know much about what you've found. He'll want your replacement—a man—to take the lion's share of the credit.''

She chewed on that for a moment. ''You mean you sicced al Hammad on him on purpose, to put pressure on him?'' When he nodded, she frowned. ''But why would he send you out here, then?''

''I more or less sent myself. Ibrahim can't stop everyone from talking. I heard about your dig and made it difficult for him to refuse to send me. Of course, he probably thought it wouldn't matter that much. My reputation as a dilettante, you know.''

''Dilettantes don't call up Rashi al Hammad and get him to put pressure on the director of the Cairo Museum.''

''Sure we do.'' His smile was lopsided. ''I may be more of a dabbler than a true professional, but I do know the system and the people, and how to rattle cages when needed. I know what you need to do next, too."

"Oh, you do, do you?"

"You need to wait at least half an hour to give Rashi time to talk to Ibrahim, then call him yourself."

She sighed. "Waiting isn't my favorite thing. It hits my list in the same general area as root canals and politics. But I guess I can do it. Are you going to call some more people while I'm practicing patience? We still need an engineer."

"No, we don't. Rashi may not be able to come out here himself, but he offered to get us someone from the Department of Mines."

"You mean you did it? You got someone already and you didn't tell me right away?" Happiness bubbled up, quick and fizzy. Impulsively, she leaned forward and pressed a big, smacking kiss to his cheek. "That's wonderful! When will he get here?"

"I won't know that until Rashi calls me back. That was much too quick, you know. We've got half an hour to pass. Want to try again?"

"What?"

"The kiss. Some things," he said, reaching for her hand, "deserve to be lingered over."

He didn't just hold her hand. He turned it palm-up and drew his fingers along the center. It tingled. Her eyes widened. She hadn't known such a simple touch could be so...evocative. "All right, this is my fault. I shouldn't have kissed you. I was—" *Excited,* she thought, but that was not the right word to use right now. "We need to keep things professional."

"I think I told you that we didn't have an entirely professional relationship." He lifted her hand, and this time it was his lips she felt on the soft center of her palm, bringing another quick rush of sensation. This time, she shivered.

"Cold?" He cocked an eyebrow at her, his eyes wicked.

Then it was his tongue she felt, wet and warm, in the sensitized flesh of her palm.

Nora wanted to say something clever or enticing or at least sensible. She wanted to pull away, to leave him and his tent and his laughing eyes. But the sheer wonder of what she felt caught her and held her, still and trapped, rendered helpless by a wash of feeling she'd never known.

This wasn't lust, though lust was part of it. This feeling was large and terrifying. And wonderful. Being Nora, she took a deep breath and did what she always did when she reached an edge.

She plunged off it, straight ahead, no holding back. "Okay. We've got half an hour. Show me how to linger properly over a kiss."

She'd startled him. That was obvious from the way he froze for a second, his eyes widening slightly. Then he smiled and laid his hand along the side of her face. "Well, first you have to remember to proceed slowly." He pressed a kiss to her forehead, another to her cheek. "You save the best for last. That isn't as easy as it sounds." His lips hovered over hers for a second before moving to tug gently at her ear.

"Ah..." Already her blood fizzed, her breath grew shallow. "It might be hard to tell what 'the best' is. What if you—just accidentally—did something entirely wonderful?"

"Show me." His hand cupped her shoulder and slid slowly down her arm, his grip firm, as if he were molding her flesh. "Show me what you mean." He took her hand in his, and waited.

Nora knew a challenge when she saw one. "Well..."

She bit her lip, looking at his face—the strong bones, the freshly-shaved skin along his cheek and jaw, the thousand possibilities for touching. Tasting. For a second she hesitated, fears fluttering up to distract her, but dissolving before they quite formed into doubts.

Half an hour. That's how long they had to play this game. And fifty feet away, on the other side of the canvas wall of his tent, the others were at work. The two of them couldn't go too far. Those limits made this—almost—safe.

His mouth drew her, but that was supposed to be last, wasn't it? His short hair left his nape deliciously bare, and that was where her fingers went. "This, for example."

He had a tiny dent in his chin, less than a dimple. More of a suggestion. She took that suggestion, kissing him lightly there, feeling all tight and happy. Free to touch, to kiss—but within limits.

Then there was his neck, so strong, yet somehow vulnerable, especially where the pulse beat. A temptation, yes, and one she gave in to easily, tasting him with her mouth slightly open.

She heard his breath hitch. His hand tightened on hers.

Oh, yes. This going slowly was marvelously difficult. She wanted to press her body to his. Instead, she straightened. "I think I'm getting the idea."

His slow smile was a masterpiece of suggestion. "I'm getting some ideas, too. My turn to show you."

This time his lips followed the line of her jaw. She kept her eyes open, though it would have been easy, so easy, to close them. To lay back on the floor of the tent and forget about limits.

His black hair gleamed in the light that filtered through the mesh opening of the tent. His breath was warm on her skin. He still held her hand with one of his, while his other hand lifted, drifted, fingertips trailing along her throat...and down.

When he stroked the side of her breast her breath caught. "Are you...still going slowly?"

"Oh, yes." His mouth was at her ear now, his words barely a whisper against her skin. His fingers drifted up, and back down. Up and down along the side of her breast, teasing. "I'm definitely saving the best for later. But later...is getting very close." His fingers slid inward, almost touching her nipple. "Closer all the time."

All at once the game was over. His mouth came down on hers—hard and hot and demanding. His hand closed over her breast, firm and possessive. And she opened her mouth to him, opened her self, meeting his demand with her own.

When the earth shook beneath her, it seemed no more than right. The distant *boom* was almost lost in the rush of blood in her ears, the dizzy certainty of being found and lost all at once.

Almost. A tremor of uncertainty shook her as, belatedly, her mind absorbed and processed what she had heard.

An explosion?

She jerked her head up. For a moment all was silent. Then she heard the cries from outside the tent, and the world was back with her. And Alex's hand was still on her breast. His face was oddly blank.

She pulled away, scrambling to her feet. "My God. What was that?"

He sighed. "I think something just blew up."

Chapter 8

"Pipe bomb," Nora said flatly. She rose to her feet, dusting off her hands in a gesture more symbolic than necessary.

"Oh, my God."

"But who would do such a thing?"

"Let me have a look, Nora. With the mess things are in, I don't see how you can tell."

She glanced at Tim. "Sure. Look away. But that piece of pipe embedded in the pump housing didn't get there by accident." She moved away, feeling angry and out of her depth.

The pump, of course, was a complete loss. The damage to the well was less severe—it could be cleared, but that would take time and money. And her shower—oh, her shower was a mess. It was stupid to feel that one minor loss so keenly, but she did. Jagged pieces of metal from the pump housing had flown out when the motor exploded, slicing the canvas walls.

Damn, damn, damn. She knew how to deal with bureaucracies on both sides of the ocean. She could lecture to seventy bored freshmen or survive an academic tea without making too many enemies. Most of all, she knew the painstaking care involved in excavation and the leaps of intuition that made interpretation so exhilarating.

But pipe bombs? What did she know about pipe bombs, or people who blew things up to make a point?

Yet she was supposed to be in charge. She would have to figure out how to handle this—and quickly, too. Her people were shaken. Ahmed looked pale beneath the bronze pigment of his skin. Gamal was speaking loudly and gesturing broadly to Lisa, who hugged her arms to her chest and didn't speak. DeLaney had followed Tim to the well, where they both crouched, inspecting the twisted metal of the pump housing.

Alex stood slightly apart. Instinctively Nora moved toward him.

He glanced her way. His expression puzzled her, mainly because there was no expression on his lean face. If he had a reaction to the newest disaster, he was hiding it.

"You're going to have to report this," he said when she reached him.

"I know. I was going to talk to Ibrahim anyway." She sighed, dreading it. "Something tells me it will not be a fun conversation."

"I meant that you'll have to report it to the authorities."

"It's going a little far to call this a terrorist act, isn't it?" That came from Tim. He looked upset, but already he was recovering—and ready to argue with anything Alex said.

Nora was in no mood for his antagonism. "Enough, Tim. What else can we call a bomb?"

"Especially considering the note someone left us," Alex said, and nodded at the back of the main tent.

Startled, Nora looked in the direction he'd indicated. Arabic letters staggered in splotches of blue paint across the canvas.

"What does it say?" DeLaney asked in a small voice.

"'Power to the people.'"

Tim scowled. "That's semantically all but meaningless."

"Oh, it has meaning," Alex said. "It means that this was a political act."

"Or that someone wants us to think so."

Nora's temper hitched a notch higher. Finding that trite slogan on the tent meant that some of her decisions were already made, and she *hated* having her hand forced.

"Enough," she said sharply. "Whether this was a genuine act of political terrorism or not, we have to behave as if it was. I'm going to drive into Tor to report it. Tim, you'll be in charge while I'm gone."

He nodded. "You may as well bring more water back with you. We're going to need extra, now that the well is gone."

No more showers, she thought, and stifled a sigh. It was a minor loss when so much else was wrong. "Ahmed and Gamal, you need to strike your own tents, then start helping pack everything else up. Lisa and DeLaney, I want you to pack your things. Gamal and Ahmed will strike the main tent and set it up again in the quarry, but I'm afraid the two of you won't be using it for a while."

"What?"

"Nora, you can't mean you're going to pack us off like children, while the *men* stay here!"

"Your gender has nothing to do with it. The university's policy doesn't give me much choice. Students are not allowed to work in areas where political unrest puts them in danger. Until we have some idea why we've been targeted and how much danger is involved in continuing our work here, you and Lisa will have to stay in Tor. Or maybe Cairo."

DeLaney tried to protest again, but Nora was in no mood to argue or placate. "Not now. Get your things together. I want to leave as soon as you're packed." DeLaney moved off, still complaining, but to Lisa.

"Alex..."

"Yes?"

"I'd like you to ride into Tor with me. You know the area and the language much better than I do, and you're the right gender. Whatever bureaucrat I end up talking to will undoubtedly be more comfortable dealing with a man."

He nodded slowly. "I'd recommend talking directly to whomever is in charge of the army garrison."

"I'll definitely need you, then. They won't want to talk to a woman." She fell silent, the muscles in her jaw tight. "Do you think that some of our other problems—the thefts, the sabotage to the ladder—were caused by the same people who did this?"

"It seems possible."

"*Damn* them. Whoever they are."

Something passed over his face, a subtle change she couldn't read. She thought he was going to say something more, but Tim broke in with a question. "If you're taking the Jeep into Tor, how are we going to move everything to the quarry?"

She frowned. Some of the equipment, like the generator, was pretty heavy. "Gamal!" she called, but he'd moved out of sight, no doubt already striking his tent. "Tim, go get him. Tell him we need him to get word to his cousin in Feiron."

Tim sighed and moved off.

She looked at Alex. "The radio phone isn't always reliable. Would you mind if we used your phone to arrange things? Gamal's cousin owns camels. With them and a sledge, I think Tim and the others will be able to get camp moved."

"Of course. Does this cousin also have a phone?"

"No, but I'm sure Gamal knows someone who does, and he'll know someone who knows someone who can get word to his cousin."

"One more question. Will we be coming back today or tomorrow?"

"I don't want to stay away overnight, but I'm not sure how long everything will take. I need to figure how much water to get, and work out some costs. Maybe leave word for Mahmoud that we'll need more frequent supply runs." She frowned, thinking quickly. "You might want to take a change of clothes, just in case. And I'd better get my stuff ready to be moved, and throw a few things in a tote."

He nodded and started to turn. Impulsively, she reached out and touched his arm. The muscles beneath the cotton cloth of his shirt were so tense she was startled. "Alex?"

He was looking at her, waiting for her to speak, but she had no idea what she wanted to say. *I wish this hadn't happened. I wish you would kiss me again. I wish...* "I'm glad you're here. Thanks."

There was a grim, tight look to his mouth. He nodded once, then moved off.

Thank God for Alex, Nora thought as she headed for her tent. How many men would have waited quietly, ready to support her, without trying to take over? Especially when his experience of the area was so much greater than her own.

Her movements were jerky as she stripped the bedclothes from her cot. Might as well visit a laundry while she was in Tor, she decided, and crammed the sheets into the plastic garbage bag that held her dirty clothes.

Until now, they'd been able to wash things up by hand in one of the big tubs they'd bought for that purpose. Now she'd have to schedule regular trips into Feiron just so they would have clean clothes. Without the well, a number of things would change.

Who could have done such a thing? And why? Was there some group who hated all Americans, and had targeted them because they were isolated?

The muscles in Nora's neck and shoulders were tight with anger as she tossed clean underwear and toiletries into her backpack. If there was fear mixed in with that anger, she preferred to ignore it. And if there was another feeling—a faint, pervasive tingle of excitement at the idea of spending time alone with Alex—she did her best to ignore that, too.

She'd made things so damned easy for him. Alex stared out the windshield of the Jeep and congratulated himself bitterly on having manipulated Nora and the situation so well.

They'd managed to complete their business in Tor in one day, but they were returning late. The moon was up. It hung in the eastern quarter of the sky, a misshapen blob several days past full. Its borrowed glow turned the flat stretch of land to the left of the highway a murky gray. Beyond that, the land humped itself up in tumbled hills to reach the dark, uneven bulk of the western horizon.

To the left was a strip of beach, silver in the moonlight,

and the dark, vast water of the Gulf of Suez. Alex watched the moving lights of boats making their way along one of the most important waterways in the world. That miles-wide strip of ocean was a good deal busier than this road he and Nora traveled. He hadn't seen another pair of headlights for some time.

Behind him lay the small city of Tor, where an unhappy DeLaney and Lisa had been banished. Twenty miles ahead was the turn-off. For another ten miles or so he'd have a road of sorts, then he'd have to leave it behind, and head up the wadi to camp.

Earlier, this road would have been busier. Cars, tankers, produce trucks, semis—virtually everything that traveled from northern to southern Sinai, whether goods or people, used one of the two coastal highways. Including the army. The squad that had been dispatched to investigate the bombing would have taken this road. They had probably already set up camp near the quarry.

Beside him sat Nora, silent and dimly visible in the glow from the dash lights. She'd changed into a long-sleeved blue shirt and khaki slacks before they left, covering far too much of that slim, luscious body for Alex's taste. But it had been the proper thing to do, of course. Bare skin would have shocked those she'd had to deal with.

She had hardly spoken since they left Tor.

Alex hadn't even had to hint that she should let him help her deal with the authorities. No, Nora was too sensible. She had realized immediately it would be better to let a man talk to the men in charge in this profoundly patriarchal society. She'd asked him to handle things at the army garrison, and it had been easy to make sure the captain there responded the way Alex wanted him to. Between the current bombing, the thefts earlier, and the sabotaged ladder, it was obvious someone had targeted the archaeologists.

The slogan Farid's son had painted on their tent before setting off the bomb hinted at who that might be.

He glanced at the silent woman beside him. She'd looked wrung out by the time she climbed into the Jeep. Tired enough that she hadn't protested when he suggested he drive.

It wasn't as if losing the well would put a stop to work altogether, Alex reminded himself. It would delay things, yes. The army would scout around for a few days, finding nothing but forcing El Hawy to lie low with their presence. While the army was there, Jawhar wouldn't be able to bring the arms to the base, giving Farid a better chance of finding the shipment.

And the excavation expert he'd promised to find her wouldn't show up. Not until the threat of further terrorism seemed resolved—which might not be until he found El Hawy's base, and shut it and them down. Permanently.

Alex shook his head. Guilt, like regret, was a dangerous indulgence. It could make a man hesitate when hesitation might prove fatal. He set it aside—for the fourth or fifth time that day.

"Are you getting tired?" Nora asked.

She'd seen him trying to shake off his doubts, and thought he was trying to stay awake. "A little stiff, that's all. Does the radio work?"

"Sometimes. When you're close enough to a broadcast source, and the gods of electronics are smiling. The tape player is more reliable, but I don't think...wait a minute." She opened the glove compartment—which fastened with a loop of wire, the lock being sprung—and pulled out a couple of tapes. "Here they are!"

"Yours?"

She nodded. "They may have melted," she said, holding one up to the moonlight. "I shouldn't have left them in the glove compartment. But the cases don't look warped."

"Stick one in and see." He glanced at her. "You don't seem up to conversation. Maybe some music will help."

She sighed and pushed a tape in. "Sorry. I'm trying not to give in to depression. I always feel down after indulging in a good mad. Takes some of the fun out of getting angry."

He stole another look at her. The old Jeep did have seat belts, but lacked the shoulder harnesses that were standard back in the States. Nora had scooted around in the seat so that her shoulder rested against the door. Her eyes were dark in the dim light. Something about the set of her head, the slight slump in her shoulders, made her look soft and sad.

He faced the road again. "This is just another delay. Not the end of the line. You're still going to get to clear your tunnel."

"I hope so. Your friend isn't going to send his assistant out now, though. Not while things are so...uncertain."

"That's why this is a setback, not a disaster. Rashi's assistant wasn't going to be able to clear his schedule for a week or so, anyway. By then, the army may have found something, or determined that there really isn't anyone out there to be found."

"The army captain mentioned an organization called El Hawy."

His fingers tightened on the steering wheel. He made them relax. "Yes, the similarity between their usual slogans and the one written on the tent was what made him take this seriously. But El Hawy is a major-league bunch of fanatics. They aren't likely to interest themselves in you and your crew. Most likely it was an individual with a grudge.''

She shivered. ''That doesn't make me feel better.''

It should. But, of course, she didn't know what she might have been facing if Alex hadn't asked Farid's son to blow up her well. ''If it's an individual rather than an organized terrorist group who has been sabotaging the dig, the army will either find him or scare him off. Then Rashi's assistant will head out here, and you can finish exploring your tunnel.''

''And if it isn't an individual?''

''He'll probably come anyway. People in this part of the world have had to come to terms with the possibility of violence erupting in their everyday lives.''

''I suppose so. Kind of like living in the projects back in Houston.''

''That must have been difficult for you.''

''Yeah.''

He waited, hoping she'd confide in him, but she was silent.

For the first time he noticed the music that was playing—an old sixties' song about a ''surfing safari.'' He smiled. Listening to the Beach Boys here, while driving alongside a vastly different beach from the California sand they sang about, appealed to his sense of the absurd. ''This doesn't sound like one of DeLaney's tapes.''

She chuckled. ''It's mine. The tape is, anyway. The music's really my mother's. I grew up hearing the Beach Boys, Elvis, the Rolling Stones...it's funny. She's been gone for several years now, but when I found out I was coming here, I went out and bought some tapes featuring hits from that time. They're sort of a musical teddy bear, I guess, to make me feel less lonesome in a strange land.''

''Nothing wrong with that. You could call my copy of

Omar Khayyám's poems a comfort read, for the same reasons."

"A comfort read in Arabic." Amusement was strong in her voice.

"Works for me." He hesitated. "You left the tapes here in the Jeep, though."

"I got tired of competing with DeLaney's boom box every night. Besides, after a while I didn't need the sounds from home as much. The desert has its own sort of night music, as full of silence as sound. Once I got used to it, I liked it."

He used to like it, too. Alex's jaw tightened around a quick bite of feelings, tangled, complex feelings that tasted more important than fear, less critical than regret.

The song changed from the cheerful male harmony to a ballad featuring a female singer who wanted to know if the man she'd given herself to would still love her tomorrow. "I don't recognize this one. What is it?"

"You've never heard the Shirelles?" She shook her head. "And here some people might think I was the one with an underprivileged childhood. I suppose you grew up listening to Bach."

He smiled. "You don't like Bach?"

"You know what I mean. We're...very different."

The idea seemed to make her sad. He wanted to argue with her, but that was difficult when he knew they were even more different than she realized. He was shadows and lies, weary and old in a way that had nothing to do with his actual age. She was sunlight and dreams and innocence. He shrugged, wanting to drop the subject.

But she wasn't ready to let it go. "I suppose you went to private schools."

"Boarding schools, sometimes. The embassy school in Cairo at times. I didn't have what you could call a stable, early academic career. I guess you had a more typical high school experience—passing notes, going to football games, dating, the senior prom."

"Football games, yes. I never went to the prom, though."

That surprised him. "It couldn't have been because you didn't have a date. Did you get sick?"

"I came down with a bad case of pride." She chuckled. "No one, but no one, is as touchy about her dignity as a teenage girl. I wouldn't go because I couldn't have a new dress. We couldn't afford one, of course. At least, not the sort of dress I wanted. So I didn't go. Isn't that silly?"

It didn't sound silly to him. He wished, with sudden, blinding illogic, that he could go back in time and buy her whatever dress she'd yearned for. Pride, yes—she'd had it then, and she had it now. Enough for any three normal people. It went with that independent streak of hers that was a few miles wider than the gulf that glittered darkly on their right.

"Did you have a dress all picked out?" he asked, speaking lightly so as not to bruise that stubborn pride. "Something glamorous and inappropriate?"

She chuckled. "How did you guess? It was black, all sequins and slink. Nothing a seventeen-year-old girl should wear, and everything she wants. My mom offered to make me a dress, and my sister—my second-oldest sister, Mary—said I could wear her old prom dress. But all I wanted was that glittery, impossible dress. I didn't want to make them feel bad," she added. "So I pretended I just didn't want to go."

"Surely they didn't believe that."

"Oh, but I was a very studious sort of teenager. Very serious and driven. It used to worry my mom." She shook her head, smiling. "She lectured me gently sometimes on the need to have a little fun."

She was making his heart hurt. "If I'd known you then, I would have asked you to the prom, and I wouldn't have taken no for an answer. I would have bought you one of those great, huge, ridiculous corsages that look like someone pillaged an entire flower garden, and I would have picked you up in a limo."

"A white stretch limo," she said, getting into it. "And we would have gone out to eat first in some terribly posh restaurant with a maître d'. Someplace where I couldn't read the menu."

"But I, being young and self-important, would have shown off by ordering for you."

"And I wouldn't have been able to eat more than a bite or two because I was too worried about spilling something on my sequins."

"Then, when I'd impressed you sufficiently with my class, we would have gone on to the prom. Where was it held? In the high school gym?"

"Of course. All fancied up with strobe lights and paper flowers."

"Okay," he said, and started braking. "Let's do it."

"What?" Her head swiveled toward him. "What are you talking about?"

The sand alongside the road was firm enough for him to pull off. He put the vehicle in park and shut off the headlights, but he left the motor running. Then he turned to face her, his voice low and coaxing. "We've just arrived at the gym. You're wearing your sequins, and I'm in—what? Would a tux have been too much?"

She chuckled. "Maybe not, if you left off the cummerbund."

"Okay, I'm in my tux, but no cummerbund." He

opened his door. "I do have on one of those silly little bow ties, though. I insist on that."

"What are you *doing?*" Amusement quivered in her voice.

"Coming around to open your door, of course." He got out, leaving his own door open, spilling light out onto the sand. The air was still and sharp. He began rolling down the sleeves he'd shoved up earlier.

"Alex, this is ridiculous," she said as he rounded the hood.

"Now, don't get out. Teenage boys are very big on dignity, too, and you'll fluster me if you don't let me do this right." He buttoned the cuffs on his shirt, then opened her door with a flourish.

With the overhead light on, he could see her expression clearly now. Her lips were turned up, but her eyes had forgotten their part of the smile. They were wide and uncertain. "But what are we supposed to do when we get out?"

"Dance, of course. Turn up the tape player. We'll need some music." He held out his hand, and waited.

She hesitated, but only for a moment. The she reached out quickly and turned the volume all the way up. The song was just changing; the last few words of "It's My Party" were belting out at full volume, then Bobby Darin started singing "Mack the Knife."

This one Alex knew. He grinned. "Come on, they're playing our song."

She put her hand in his and let him help her out. He tucked her hand into the crook of his arm and escorted her around the front of the Jeep. "What color is my tux?"

"Black, of course. You look very sexy and mysterious." Nerves, amusement, and something else fought for control of her voice. Her hand tightened on his arm. "Are you a dancer or a hugger?"

"What's a hugger? A guy with twelve hands?"

"Sometimes. Mostly, though, a hugger was just a boy who didn't really know how to dance. He'd avoid the fast dances, then, when a slow dance came on, he'd drape himself all over his partner and shuffle his feet around."

"Sounds like you did make it to some of the school dances."

"A few. The ones I went to were pretty casual, with everyone in jeans."

They'd reached the firm sand alongside the road. He held out his hand at the correct angle. "But tonight you're in sequins," he said softly. "Sequins and slink."

She smiled shyly and put her hand in his. He drew her closer—but not too close. They were in the high school gym, after all, and the music was lively. But he could definitely sympathize with all those "huggers" she'd mentioned. He wanted nothing more than to snuggle her up against him and drape his body all over hers.

But he didn't. This is for Nora, he told himself, even as his heartbeat picked up and the faint lilac scent of her drifted into his nostrils. She moved with him smoothly, easily, one of her hands on his shoulder, the other clasped warmly in his.

Of course, a woman who could race him down the slippery bank of a quarry and win—by a second or two—would have to have good coordination. He smiled at the thought.

"You're good at this," she said after a moment.

"My father taught me how to dance when I was thirteen. There's a strong spark of romanticism lurking behind those thick glasses of his, and he insisted I'd thank him for it later. He was right, but it was a good ten years before I was ready to admit it.''

''My sister Mary taught me how to slow dance.'' She shook her head, her eyes smiling at the memory. ''We must have made a funny-looking couple. She was seven months pregnant.''

He chuckled. ''I'll bet my dad and I made an even odder couple. I was half a head taller than him by then.'' Her hand had started out properly on his shoulder. It was on his neck now, though, and her fingertips stroked the skin there in small movements in time to their steps. Alex wasn't sure she was even aware of what she was doing.

He sure was, though.

''You know,'' she said after a moment, ''I would have figured you'd learned to dance at a country club. Or maybe a preppie private school.''

''I did go to a thoroughly stuffy prep school for a couple of years,'' he confessed, ''until I got tossed out.''

A spurt of laughter escaped her. ''Were you a trouble-maker?''

''I wouldn't say that I actually *made* trouble, but I did manage to find it rather often.'' It was getting harder to pay attention to his steps. Harder not to pull her up against him. And very hard to remember they were supposed to be in a gym swathed with crepe-paper streamers and crowded with a hundred other couples, not dancing alone on a beach. Alone beneath a stark, black sky ablaze with stars.

The song changed then. Instead of the jazzy ''Mack the Knife,'' the slow, dreamy sound of Elvis crooning ''Love Me Tender'' floated out from the tape player, soothing the night with its slow, simple melody.

Alex's steps slowed. His arms tightened slightly in spite

of all his resolves...and she drifted up against him. Sweet, pliant, welcoming.

Not that she was pressed to him tightly. No, she was just close enough that her body brushed against his as they moved—slower now, their feet shifting through sand to mark out the low, throbbing rhythm.

"One more thing." He tried to speak lightly, but his voice betrayed him, turning husky. "When I asked you to the prom, I made a special request."

She tilted her head back, her eyes meeting his. He saw dreams there...and desire. "What was that?"

"I asked you to wear your hair down for me." He kept his eyes on her face and one hand at her waist, continuing to guide her, though they were both moving very slowly now.

With his other hand, he reached for her braid. He pulled it over her shoulder and eased the covered band off. Taking his time. Savoring the moment, the woman, the cool slide of her hair through his fingers as he worked the braid loose.

His hand began to tremble and his heart pounded. He felt as callow and shaken as the boy he was pretending to be. And as deeply aroused as the man he was.

"Like this," he whispered, when her hair spilled loosely over her shoulder, a fall of silk as black as the night around them. "This is how I asked you to wear your hair. For me."

No male, boy or man, could resist what he saw in her eyes then. Alex didn't try. He slid his fingers into her hair, cupping her head firmly. And bent.

She didn't stiffen or pull back. *Oh, Nora, you should,* he thought as her eyes drifted closed. *You should run as far and as fast as you can.* But she pressed against him instead, her lips parting, welcoming his. Heat flared, a heady rush just this side of need, as he brushed her mouth with his once, then again.

It was hard to pull back, but he managed. Then he made another mistake. Instead of tossing out some teasing comment, turning the unsteady moment to playfulness, he looked into her eyes.

He saw welcome there, and warmth. And something more. Something that made his chest tight and his head light, while his own lips turned up in a smile to match hers.

Alex reminded himself that he wasn't going to seduce her. He wouldn't take this too far.

Then he kissed her again.

Chapter 9

This was right. The stars, the music...the man. When Alex's lips nibbled at hers, when his hands urged her closer to him, and closer still, Nora's blood turned to champagne. Fizzy, dizzy bubbles rose to pop-pop-pop in her brain like a dozen tiny surprises happening all at once.

Her gasp was equal parts pleasure and astonishment.

He took quick advantage of her open mouth, his tongue sweeping in to set off another round of bubbles—but they happened everywhere now, all over her body.

She had never dreamed that her first experience of love might happen on a beach thousands of miles away from everything she knew. A romantic setting, yes—in a movie. In reality, there was all that sand. The practical side of her nature was very aware of the way sand tended to creep into the most uncomfortable places.

She didn't care. What if bliss was mixed with grit? After a lifetime of waiting, she had found the right man. Her heart and her body agreed, even as her mind fogged and slowed.

Nora had always dreamed of tenderness. She felt that now, in the way his hands smoothed over her, soothing her confusion even as they gently urged her hormones to riot. He was careful of her, and she loved that.

She loved *him.* She was sure of it, though she didn't understand. This wasn't the way she'd thought love happened. How could she love when she scarcely knew? Surely love, like trust, had to be built over time—earned with constancy, courted with slowly growing intimacy.

This feeling was intimate enough. It was also huge and reckless, and it seemed to demand...everything.

His hand closed over her breast, warm and gentle and very sure.

Uncertainty fluttered through Nora, but instead of cooling her blood, it made her restless. She moved against him, and the ache deepened. So she moved again, locking her hands behind his neck, and opened her mouth wider to his inquiring tongue.

His careful hands paused. And when he accepted her silent invitation, there was something decidedly ungentle about his kiss. Something raw and a little wild about the way his mouth sucked, licked and teased, and then, with his tongue, penetrated.

Shivers of discovery traveled over Nora, and she learned that she craved the wildness at least as much as the tenderness. When he tugged at her shirt, pulling it out of her slacks, stopping didn't occur to her. When his hand touched the bare skin of her stomach, the muscles there contracted sharply in pleasure.

And when his hand traveled up, pausing between her breasts to unfasten her bra so he could touch her bare breast, she moaned.

He was murmuring against her lips—soft words in English and Arabic, words her dazed mind wouldn't string together into sense. Something about her skin, and her warmth. Something about need.

Yes, she needed. Needed him, more of him. Her hands became hasty then, pushing under his shirt, finding the smooth muscles of his chest. His skin was hot and it danced under her touch, the muscles clenching. His reaction thrilled her, and when he plucked at her nipple, she touched his.

He groaned and urged her down onto the sand, and if part of her insisted this was too much, too fast, that they had spoken no words of love and she'd heard not a scrap of a promise from him, the rest of her didn't care. What were promises compared to the feel of his hand on her skin, the taste of him on her tongue, the heady urgency rushing her onward to a new, unknown destination?

The sand was smooth and firm beneath her, Alex was rock-solid and hot on top of her, and hunger clenched in her belly, tight and demanding. "Yes," she whispered when his mouth closed over her nipple. Her hands fisted in his hair, hugging him to her.

"Alex," she said or sighed. "Alex."

He suckled her, and it was sweet and wonderful and perfect, so lovely that it was almost enough. Somewhere, on the other side of him, away from his hard, wonderful body, the world waited. But she didn't see it, or care. She saw only the stars, points of brilliance in the black vault above them, as sharp and bright as the sensations he roused in her.

She almost told him. The words were there, singing in her blood, pushing at her mind—but so was another voice, a quiet, doubting, practical voice.

It was so soon. So sudden. And Alex was a wanderer.

He'd warned her of that. He wouldn't be ready to say the words back to her, and she didn't think she could bear to say them and have him turn away. Or listen while he tried to let her down lightly.

But he should know that this was her first time.

She touched his cheek, the roughness of his beard making her fingertips tingle. She felt his muscles move as he sucked, and went dizzy with love and lust. But she should speak. She had to speak.

"Alex," she said again, but this time her voice was different. She stroked her fingers along his jaw, wanting him to look up, to look at her. If he would just look at her, make that close, unspoken connection, she could get past this sudden shyness.

He lifted his head. Met her eyes. For a second the words hung there between them—all the words she wasn't going to speak, along with the ones she had to say.

His own eyes widened. "My God. Have I lost my mind?" And rolled off of her.

She lay on her back, staring in disbelief at nothing, the air suddenly, shockingly cold on her bare skin.

"I'm sorry," he said. His voice was muffled. She turned her head and saw that he'd thrown his arm over his face. "I'm so sorry, Nora. I never meant to take things this far."

She was dizzy. Aching. Humiliated. "What do you mean?"

"It's not fair to you to pretend I...that I have anything more to offer you than a little fun. A little play. But you aren't the sort of woman who plays at romance. I was wrong to kiss you, wrong to...I'm sorry."

Wrong? How could he say that, when she had felt as if everything was finally right? Her hands shook as she gathered her shirt and her dignity around her. She sat up slowly and fumbled with her bra. Her hair hung loose, hiding her face as she bent her head and tackled the buttons she didn't remember him unfastening.

When she had her clothing put back together she spoke, picking her words out carefully, one at a time. "You want to know how to make a woman really, really angry?"

He didn't move, not even to take his arm off his face. "I suspect you're going to tell me."

"Turn her down. And tell her you did it for her own good." She stood.

Her legs held her up admirably, considering the way they trembled when she started walking. They carried her back to where yellow light from the Jeep washed the sand.

The tape hadn't finished playing yet, but it was on the last song—Elvis Presley singing "Heartbreak Hotel." Nora smiled without a trace of humor, and climbed in.

This time, however, she sat in the driver's seat. And waited. It would have been deeply satisfying to put the Jeep in gear and drive away while he lay there on the sand, preoccupied with his hormones or his stupid ideas about what was fair. In a better-ordered world she could have done just that, leaving Alex and humiliation both behind.

But she couldn't do it. And if she told herself that her reluctance was because she still needed his help to get an engineer out to the dig, that was true enough. Even if it wasn't the whole truth.

After a moment he came up to the Jeep. He stood near the still-open door on the driver's side. She could feel him looking at her and stared straight ahead, willing him not to speak.

Quietly he went around to the passenger's side and got in.

She slammed her door, put the vehicle in gear and punched the accelerator. The tires shot up a spume of sand, the front wheels lurched onto the pavement, and the rear of the vehicle fishtailed slightly before grabbing hold.

He didn't say a word. But then, he'd already said too many words, and all of them the wrong ones.

The army had set up camp a couple of miles west of the quarry. Alex and Nora had to identify themselves to the sentry before they were allowed to proceed to the quarry.

It was late, nearly midnight, when Nora pulled up near the footpath that led to the quarry. Through his window Alex could see Orion the Hunter, his bow perpetually cocked and ready, his three-starred girdle shining brightly in the southern sky.

Through the windshield, he could see a faint glow from the other side of the low hill that separated the quarry from the wadi. No doubt Tim had left a lamp burning. Maybe he was waiting up for Nora—like a faithful hound, Alex thought, and wanted to put his fist through something.

But a faithful hound like Tim would undoubtedly be better for Nora than Alex had been, or could be.

Nora shut the motor off and opened her door. "Get the flashlight out of the glove compartment, will you?"

They were the first words she'd spoken to him since they left the beach. Alex grabbed the flashlight and got out, slamming the door harder than necessary. Nora had moved to the front of the vehicle and waited there for him, looking up at the slight hill they had to cross to reach the quarry.

He switched on the flashlight. "Nora, I know you're angry. For God's sake, why don't you yell at me? You've every right to. I acted like a fool."

"One of us was certainly a fool." Her voice was cool and distant. "I think we'd better take the path this time.

It's too dark to go scrambling around without following one." She made a little gesture for him to precede her.

Instead, he handed her the flashlight and took her arm because he had to touch her. Then had to tense against the urge to touch more than her arm—or to shake her, make her drop this pretense of courtesy. "I don't want to leave things like this between us."

"You won't be happy until I say it, will you?" She jerked her arm away and, at last, looked at him. The moonlight fell full on her face, catching the sheen of tears in her eyes, but her voice was entirely steady. She held her head high as she met his gaze. "You were right, Alex. Exactly right. I wasn't playing at romance. You were, so you were smart to put a stop to things. I'm sorry I got carried away and embarrassed us both."

His throat ached. "Not embarrassed, Nora. Not that."

She gave a quick, angry little shrug. "Whatever. We won't speak of it again." She started for the path.

Alex followed. He wanted, badly, to take her in his arms and comfort her. Or maybe it was himself he wanted to comfort, little as he deserved it.

Because he'd lied to her. Again. He hadn't stopped for her sake, but for his own.

Tim confronted Alex the next day.

They were alone in the first cave, the one that long-dead Egyptians had used as quarters for the slaves and overseers who worked the quarry. Nora had announced that morning that she, Ahmed and Gamal would finish sifting the fill from the tunnel, while Alex and Tim were to continue the original work of the dig.

It was a reasonable decision, professionally. It was also a damned convenient decision, Alex thought. It would keep her away from him for the next few days.

This cave was quite different from the one with the tunnel. It consisted of a single, vaulted chamber that opened directly onto the quarry through a wide entrance that let in plenty of light. The remains of postholes at the entry indicated that there had once been a wooden wall across it, but in this wood-hungry land those posts and planks had long since vanished.

Much of the floor of the cave had been gridded with string tied to small stakes; several of the sections marked off this way were already fully excavated. Tim was sitting in one of the remaining sections, scraping away the soil a few centimeters at a time.

Alex worked at the front of the cave, doing his own scraping. Above him was an open fissure, the rock around it discolored from the smoke of fires that had gone to ash centuries ago. With careful excavation, he expected to establish the existence of a fire pit.

It was exactly the sort of slow, painstaking archaeological work that used to make him crazy when he was young. For some reason it didn't bother him today.

No, what bothered him was Nora's determination to keep him at a distance—physically, and every other way. That, and the memory of her, hot and willing, in his arms. And the moment when she'd said his name and he'd lifted his head, looked into her eyes…and known himself for the worst sort of bastard.

She hadn't been playing last night.

But it hadn't been her feelings or his faulty sense of honor that had made Alex pull away so quickly. It had been terror. Though it made his teeth clench to admit it, he knew he'd better be honest with himself, however little he had been with her.

He hadn't been playing, either. And realizing that had scared him as badly as the nightmares that still rode his sleep, the haunts of darkness and cold left over from his near-death in the Negev.

What was wrong with him?

"You and Nora got in pretty late last night."

Alex grimaced. He'd been so busy brooding, he'd almost forgotten that Tim was around. "We did well to get everything done in one day."

"I suppose so. Nora mentioned wanting to get some laundry done while she was there. And a bath. The two of you checked into a hotel for a couple of hours, I understand. So you could, ah, take advantage of the plumbing."

Alex looked up, his eyes narrowing. "Yes, we both wanted to enjoy the wonders of hot and cold running water while we had the chance. Sorry you missed out on that."

"I'm not worried." Tim didn't look up, and his hands didn't pause in their steady, careful digging. "I'll get my chance soon enough. You won't be around that much longer, will you, Bok?"

The reminder scraped at Alex's already raw temper. "You know, Gaines, I get the impression you consider yourself a friend of Nora's."

"I *am* her friend. There's no 'consider' about it."

"For a friend, you're remarkably ready to jump to conclusions. Unless I'm wrong. Maybe you weren't implying that Nora and I checked into that hotel so we could wrestle around in bed for a couple of hours of hot, mindless sex."

Tim stopped working. His complexion turned ruddy with rage—not embarrassment. "You've got a damned nasty tongue, Bok. It's a wonder no one ever pulled it out."

Alex's mouth quirked up, though the humor didn't make it to his eyes. That was one of the few things no one had tried to do to him. "And you've got a damned suspicious mind. You ought to know Nora isn't interested in a one-night stand. Or even a quick affair."

"I knew it. I didn't think you did." The angry color faded from Tim's face, and a speculative gleam entered his eyes. "Very few virgins are."

Alex sucked in a breath. Gaines was lying. He had to be. Nora was thirty years old. She wasn't—surely she couldn't be—a virgin at her age. Could she?

"You don't know what you're talking about," he said roughly.

"Oh, but I do. It seems I know a few things about Nora that you don't." Tim returned to his scraping. "I won't pretend I'm not relieved as hell you haven't learned that particular fact for yourself."

Alex wanted to believe Gaines was lying. He couldn't. The man's satisfaction was all too evident—he believed what he'd said. "I suppose she told you all about it."

"As a matter of fact, she did. We used to sit up and talk about all sorts of things before you showed up." He gave Alex a hard look. "Like I said, we're friends. That may be hard for someone like you to understand, but—"

"Give it a rest, Gaines. You aren't as pure as you like to pretend. Not unless you told Nora, while you were exchanging all these confidences, that you were hoping like hell to be more than a friend to her."

The other man scowled and said nothing.

Alex let the silence stand and put his hands back to work at their task, though his mind wasn't on it.

Maybe Gaines had misunderstood Nora. The man might be wrong, after all. If Alex could get him to reveal exactly what Nora had told him...and, of course, he could do that. It was part of his stock-in-trade, the ability to extract facts from people who had no idea how much they were revealing. By pushing the right emotional buttons, he could find out exactly what he wanted to know.

But he wouldn't. Not this time. Not about Nora.

Damn her. Nora should have told him herself. *If* it was true. Maybe it wasn't. Why hadn't she said something last night, when he'd taken them both halfway to heaven? Wouldn't she have told him then, if…oh, hell.

Why was he working so hard to convince himself Nora wasn't a virgin? It fit. In some screwy, unthinking way Alex felt, but didn't understand, it fit what he knew of her.

Why did it matter so much?

Why, indeed, unless it made him feel like even more of a heel.

Nora was innocent. It was one of the things that drew him to her, that purity of soul that was so unexpected in someone with her background. Innocence wasn't the same thing as virginity, of course. But with Nora…with Nora, he feared the two were very much linked.

Alex didn't need to trick anything more out of Tim. He *knew*. Part of that knowing came from pure intuition, but he knew more about her than she had any idea of. She had watched her mother, then her sisters, pick the wrong men time after time, messing up their lives—and hers. She must have decided at a very young age to avoid their mistakes.

And what Nora decided, she did.

She was a stubborn woman, infuriatingly so at times. She came across as being deeply practical, and she was, in many ways. But she was also a dreamer. She'd needed the stubbornness, every ounce of it, to pull herself out of the abyss of poverty.

But she'd needed the dreams, too.

Learning that Nora had never been with a man might not have been enough to make Alex leave her alone, but understanding why she'd made such a choice made it impossible for him to do anything else.

If he took her to bed, he wouldn't be taking her virginity. He'd be taking her dreams. Alex knew, deep in his heart, that Nora was waiting. Waiting for the right man, the one who would never leave her, never break her heart...never lie to her. A man who would work with her, play with her, stay with her.

Not a man who would show up from time to time, when he was between assignments—if he lived through those assignments.

Not Alex Bok.

He should be thanking God he'd stopped them from going too far, but he wasn't that noble. He would keep his hands off of her, he thought savagely, but he sure as hell wasn't going to like it.

In the next week, one year ended and the next began, according to the Bedouin's ancient calendar, if not the Muslim calendar in official use. Fall came to the Sinai—Assfari, the rainy season. To the Americans at the quarry, the change was slight, but welcome. Daytime temperatures were becoming bearable even in the afternoon, while the nights grew chilly. Now and then clouds floated in the high blue overhead, but so far they were wispy and white. No thunderhead. No rain.

During the week following their dance in the moonlight, Nora was pleasant to Alex. Oh, yes, he thought, as he pulled his T-shirt on, then reached for the belt that held his holster. She was invariably pleasant, willing to discuss professional matters...and only professional matters. There were no more confidences, no mention of anything remotely personal. Certainly no kisses. They were colleagues. And nothing more.

It was driving him crazy.

He knew this was the way things had to be. He had no business wanting more, pressing for more. So he let her set the tone and kept his hands to himself.

The tunnel waited. Alex knew Nora was longing to get back to it. But she would have to wait a little longer—just over two weeks, according to the arrangements Alex had made with Rashi. The great man's assistant would arrive the week before the Muslim holy month of Ramadan began.

By then, this region should be as safe as it ever was. By then, Alex would either have finished his business here…or he'd be dead. Alex's lips were tight as he slid his SIG Sauer into the holster at the small of his back. He grabbed a windbreaker to hide the gun.

Either way, he would be gone. Which was why he had to let Nora keep her defenses and her distance. He knew that. Honor might be cold comfort, but it was all the comfort he had.

His days were compounded equally of frustration and the dullest sort of excavation work. His nights were hell.

He had the mornings, though, he thought, as he tugged on his running shoes. At least he had the mornings to look forward to.

Though the nights weren't pleasant, they had at last been productive. He'd found the base.

Three nights ago, he'd spotted a thin plume of smoke, and tracked it to a fissure in the ground—a smoke hole, like the one above the fire pit he'd worked on. He'd known that he stood above a cave like the ones whose secrets Nora was determined to expose. But this cave was occupied.

He hadn't yet found the entrance. He could stand directly above where the base must be located, but he couldn't get inside it. Still, from that vantage point he could watch. And so he had, for the last three nights. Sooner or later he would spot someone coming or going from the base. El Hawy was running out of time. They would have to bring in the arms soon.

Alex hadn't heard from Farid for several days. He hoped like hell the man had found the arms. If not, everything would depend upon Alex spotting them when they were brought to the base.

It was a good thing he could function on very little sleep, he thought as he left his tent in the gray light before dawn. Between nightmares, guilt and a constant ache, what little sleep he did manage to snatch didn't do him much good.

But still he got up early every morning—to run. Nora wasn't willing to let a little thing like a bombing keep her from her morning runs. Since Alex knew she was actually safer now than she had been before, he hadn't tried to change her mind.

And she hadn't tried to change his. She'd kept her promise not to leave the camp without him. Probably that was just common sense on her part. He had no real reason to think otherwise.

He rounded his tent and saw her stretching as she waited for him.

She wore a lightweight jacket with a black T-shirt and wrinkled running shorts that left her beautiful legs bare. Her braid hung over her shoulder, and it swung forward when she bent in one of her stretches.

Such a sensible braid. Twice now he'd seen her hair down. Once when she'd spread it over him like a blanket and saved his life. Another time when she'd let him loosen it himself, using his fingers to set it free while they danced in the moonlight.

Alex looked at her and ached. And when he walked up to her, this professional liar and manipulator, who always knew what words to use to create the effect he wanted, said only, "Chilly this morning."

"We'll warm up as we get moving. Ready?"

"Sure. Let's go."

She wouldn't talk much while they ran. He didn't expect it. Mostly, she would avoid looking at him, too. But when they ran together, he felt as if they really *were* together, as if in silence and motion they found a connection that talk would spoil.

Maybe that was no more than a pretty illusion he'd sold himself. Maybe she waited for him every morning because that was the sensible thing to do. But for once, Alex didn't care if he was fooling himself. For once, he'd take the illusion, if that was all he could have.

A bead of sweat ran down the side of Nora's face. She was winded. Her calves and quads twitched.

The man beside her ran easily, effortlessly. He never seemed to tire, damn him. Nor was he ever cross or unpleasant, no matter how tedious the work she assigned him. And he had never tried, not once in the past week, to get past the wall she'd put up between them.

She wondered just how much of a fool she was.

They'd nearly reached the narrow place in the wadi where she always ran. Just ahead was the huge boulder she'd been passing the day Alex had surprised her on her run. She remembered the expression on his face that morning—still and taut and somehow savage.

He'd frightened her then. He still did, but for different reasons.

She had tried to put a stop to the longing, the dreams, the ache. Nora didn't fail often, but so far she'd failed spectacularly at doing that. ‘‘Slow down...time...for me.’’ Her words came out between breaths.

He immediately dropped into a slow jog. ‘‘You going to join us in the cave today?’’

Her chest heaved as she slowed, gratefully, to match his pace. ‘‘You...can still...talk,’’ she said accusingly.

He grinned. Out of the corner of her eyes, she saw the way his grin flashed out, as if she’d said something wonderful. ‘‘Have you been trying to run me into the ground? If I’d known, I would have warned you it wouldn’t be easy.’’

That was almost a reference to their dance on the beach. Closer than either of them had come in the last seven days to referring to it, anyway. Her heart managed to beat even faster. She thought she ought to turn the conversation back to the dig, but couldn’t make herself do it. ‘‘You said...you liked running.’’ She paused to breathe. ‘‘You didn’t say anything about marathons.’’

‘‘I’m not competitive enough for a marathon. Unlike you.’’ He chuckled. ‘‘If I offered to race you right now, I’ll bet—’’

She was never to know what Alex would have bet. One second he was jogging along beside her, easy and relaxed. The next, he hurled himself at her, knocking her to the ground just as a loud, booming noise sounded, then another, the doubled sounds echoing eerily in the rocky banks.

Chapter 10

They were rolling almost before they hit the ground, Alex's big body compelling hers to move with it. Nora hit the side of her head on something and cried out as they rolled over and over, ending up beside an enormous boulder of dull red stone.

He didn't pause, grabbing her bodily and shoving her into a niche between the boulder and the wall of the wadi, thrusting himself in with her, just as another loud *crack!* sounded.

She landed on her butt, wedged into the narrowest part of the niche, her heart drumming frantically. She felt all akimbo—arms, legs, brains, no part of her knew what to do.

Alex did. He'd placed himself between her and the wadi, crouched, facing out, crowded up against her. She saw his hand flash behind him, reach under his jacket, and come out with a small, businesslike gun. It was black, the barrel short and stubby. He aimed that gun outwards, his head tilted as he scanned above them for whoever had shot at them.

Her mouth was open, panting for air. It had been a long time, a very long time, since she'd heard sounds like the ones that still rang in her ears.

But a woman who had spent her early childhood in the projects knew gunshots when she heard them.

"Dear God," she breathed.

"Keep down." He was terse, cool, his voice so low she had to strain to hear.

"Someone is shooting at us!"

"There are two of them. One to the south, near that scraggly bush at the top of the bank. I caught a gleam from the barrel of his rifle before he fired. I don't know exactly where the other one is—north of us, of course. I think he's on the other side of the wadi, too."

He'd seen the gleam from a rifle barrel and, in a split-second, known what it was. He hadn't even had to think about it—he'd acted so fast. It had been instinct that sent him crashing into her, forcing her ahead of him into the dubious safety of this rocky crevice. "How do you know there are two of them? And that one of them is—is north of us?"

"The second shot came from behind us," he said absently. "He'll probably stay where he is—he's in a good position to pick us off if we stir out from behind this boulder. The first one, though…duck."

"What?"

In answer, he turned and pushed her head down in her lap—firmly, but not roughly. "Sorry. You're in the way."

She couldn't see him with her head in her lap, but she heard him and felt him. Some part of him brushed her right leg, which was bent up near her head.

"The first man may try to make his way closer, so he

can shoot down at us here..." A small grunt of effort. "Can't do that without changing his position."

He was pushing himself up the boulder, she realized. She managed to twist her head around without raising it.

She had an odd view—mostly legs, covered in gray sweatpants. Running shoes, one of them planted on the boulder. She couldn't see his other foot, but the angle of his leg made her think that it, with his back, was pressed against the bank of the wadi, which was nearly vertical here.

"God, Alex, they'll see you," she whispered urgently when he inched a little higher.

"The idea is to see them—or him. I just need to keep him from—" He straightened his arm, and fired.

The noise was even louder from this close. Her ears rang.

There was a second shot—from a rifle, not Alex's snub-nosed pistol. She bit her lip to keep from crying out.

"They'll hear that." He sounded satisfied.

At least his body hadn't come crashing down on her. She supposed that meant he hadn't been hit. "Who will hear? What's going on?"

"If I can keep the first man from getting any closer, we'll be okay." He snapped off another shot. "Gunshots carry like crazy out here. They'll hear the shots back at camp, and the army's still in the area. Someone will be along soon. I've spotted the first man," he added, as if to reassure her. "He doesn't have a clear shot at us, and can't get closer without giving me a target."

She hated this, hated sitting scrunched over, trapped in a small space. Hated the sound of gunshots, and the fear. She couldn't even straighten—Alex's body was in the way.

Right between her and anyone who shot down at them from above.

Claustrophobia hit her. She was trapped here, trapped beneath Alex, who had placed his body as a shield between her and whoever wanted to kill them. If they shot him, his body would fall on her, bloody and damaged—like he had been when she first saw him, when she had found him half-dead in the desert.

All at once she couldn't seem to get enough air. She was gulping it down too fast. No, no. She knew better, dammit, knew that when that trapped feeling hit, she would hyperventilate if she wasn't careful. She fought to control the frantic grab for air, to breath slower, deeper.

It helped. Her pulse steadied and her head cleared slightly. She was still frightened, but not terrified. Not as terrified as she probably should have been. Sheer disbelief, she thought, must be numbing some of the panic.

Alex knew what to do, knew what their attackers were doing, too. His competence both reassured her and frightened her.

Maybe he'd been in the army. Yes, she thought, her cheek pressed to her bent knee, her pulse drumming in her ears, that made sense. He must have learned this sort of thing in the army, or maybe one of the other services, and—

Another exchange of shots. She flinched.

Where had he gotten the gun, though? He'd had it with him, tucked against the small of his back. She had the odd, disjointed thought that it should have fallen down his pants—sweatpants surely wouldn't hold up a gun, even a small one.

That prompted an image of the ugly black gun sliding down his pants to bump at his ankles, bumping along there as they ran, and she bit her lip hard to keep a hysterical giggle from climbing out of her throat.

He must have a holster beneath his jacket.

A holster. A gun. Who was he? What was he?

Alex shifted position slightly, sending a little rain of dirt down on Nora. "How—" her voice wobbled, and she paused to steady it "—how long do you think it will take for someone to show up?" Another frightening thought occurred to her. "Alex, what if Tim and the others come out here instead of calling the army?"

"If they do, these two will probably leave."

"Probably?" Panic began beating against the edges of her mind. She fought it back. "We have to do something!"

"Nothing we can do, except try to keep them from killing us while we're waiting. I doubt they'll hang around long. They must know—"

There was another quick exchange of shots.

Her position was rapidly growing more uncomfortable, and her cheek was throbbing. She remembered hitting it on something when he tackled her. Gingerly, she touched the sore place. There was blood, her damp fingertips told her, but not very much.

A scrape, she thought, nothing major. But her hand was shaking. "You know why they're shooting at us, don't you?"

"Shooting at me, I suspect. Not you." He was grim. "Not that you're safe because of that. I'm sorry, Nora."

She tried to think, tried to reason out what that meant, but her mind wouldn't cooperate. Physical sensations absorbed her—the scent of dust in her nostrils. The way her cheek throbbed. Another little rain of dirt falling on her when Alex shifted. The sour taste in her mouth. Her pulse, beating much too fast.

For the first time in her life, Nora wanted a gun. If she

had one, she could do something other than cower here, scrunched into a small, useless ball.

There was a single shot—not Alex. One of the rifles. She thought she heard someone cry out—a sound almost lost in the reverberation of the gunshot.

Not Alex. Someone else, from farther up the wadi. "Alex?" She lifted her head slightly.

A man's voice shouted in Arabic—*one is left,* she thought he cried.

"Thank God," Alex said, suddenly cheerful. "The cavalry is here."

"The army?" She wanted badly to move. "The army is here?"

"Someone who will help. Hang on. It won't be long now."

She waited, tense, silent. Her legs threatened to cramp in their uncomfortable position. She wanted to stretch. To run. She couldn't. She could only huddle there while questions pressed against her, the weight of them trapping her mind as surely as the gunshots had trapped her body.

Finally she heard another voice—no, more than one voice, coming from the other direction, from down the wadi. From camp.

"Alex." She squirmed around so she could touch his leg. "They're coming from camp. We have to warn them."

"I think—I hope—there's nothing to warn them about. The second man is dead. The first man has probably cleared out by now."

Dead? How did he know? "I want to know what's going on!"

Instead of answering, he moved, pushing off from his awkward perch to land on the other side of her. Out in the open.

"Alex!" Instinctively she grabbed for him—a quick, unthinking move. She needed to keep him with her, keep him safe. But he'd landed too far away. Her fingers barely brushed his pants.

"Stay down." He didn't look at her, but he looked everywhere else, scanning the upper banks of the wadi.

No gunshots came. After a moment he straightened and tucked his gun behind his back again.

A holster. Yes. She saw it this time, a small black holster at the small of his back, fastened to a leather belt he wore beneath his shirt.

He turned and reached for her. "You can stand up now, but stay where you are. Just in case."

She didn't take his outstretched hands. But when she tried to stand, she nearly fell. One of her legs had gone to sleep, and it buckled beneath her. Alex caught her, his hands steadying her.

"I'm okay," she said, stamping her foot, feeling circulation return in a thousand fiery nips.

"Your cheek." He lifted his hand and touched the side of her head next to the scrape.

"I—I scraped it. When you knocked me down."

Some strong emotion tightened his jaw—guilt, pain, anger—she couldn't tell. "Nora." His grip tightened on her shoulder. "Don't tell them about my gun. Follow my lead."

"What? Why not?"

"I can't explain now. The others will be here any second." She heard their rescuers approaching even as he spoke—running feet, Gamal's voice calling out something in Arabic. "It's best if the authorities don't know about my gun."

A chill washed through her, drying her mouth and making her stomach clench. "Best for whom?"

He hesitated. "For me, obviously. For others as well, but I can't tell you why."

She stared up into his eyes, looking for something—some clue, some hint of which direction truth lay. Lying was wrong. Lying to the authorities was unthinkable. Yet she *was* thinking about it, seriously considering covering up the truth for a man with amber eyes, simply because he'd asked her to.

He'd put his body between her and the people shooting at them.

He had a gun he didn't want the authorities to know about. An illegal gun.

She licked her dry lips. "You think the second man is dead. Who shot him?"

"Someone who's too good a marksman to have missed." He smiled crookedly. "You do know the right questions to ask. Stock-in-trade of a good scientist, I suppose."

"And you dodge my questions like someone who's used to avoiding the truth."

But it was too late for answers—at least, answers from Alex. More questions had arrived, shouted at them in Arabic by Gamal, who was running flat out, an ancient-looking rifle gripped in one hand. Tim was several yards behind him, unarmed and seriously out of breath.

"We're okay!" Alex called out to them.

"What happened?" Tim puffed the question out between pants as he slowed. "We heard shots."

"Did you call the army?" Nora asked.

"Ahmed is doing that. What's going on?"

Alex answered before Nora could. "I think they're gone—ran off when they heard you coming. Thank God you showed up when you did."

"But who was it? Why were they shooting?"

"I don't know. We got caught in a crossfire." Alex shook his head. "It was wild. There were two of them, maybe more, shooting at each other across the wadi. Nora and I showed up just as they opened fire."

"Good God!" Tim's accent was more British than usual. "You're all right, though?"

Nora was staring at Alex. He looked shaken. Not hard and cold and shockingly capable of dealing with an ambush. No, now he looked just like anyone would expect him to look. "I think someone was hit," he said. "I heard him cry out. But not us. We're fine."

"Nora?" Tim said, coming up to her. Anxiety wrinkled his forehead. "You all right? The side of your face is all bloody."

"I...scraped it." She couldn't look at Alex. "Alex knocked me down to—to get me out of the crossfire." She hadn't known, until she said it, that she was going to go along with his story. Lie for him.

Just like her mother used to lie for Stan when the bill collectors called. Like her sister had done for a couple of her unsavory boyfriends. She felt sick.

"Nora's pretty shook up," Alex said. "Maybe you should take her back to camp, Tim, and wait there for the army to show up."

"And you? What will you be doing?"

"I'd better see if I was right about someone being hit. He might need medical attention."

Not if he was dead. And Alex had seemed pretty sure of that.

"You do that," she told him, making her voice as cool and authoritative as she could. "But I'd better stay here. If someone is wounded, I've had some first aid training."

Tim shuddered. "Grisly." He put an arm around her

shoulders. "Come on, then. You can at least sit down. You look like hell."

She felt a strong, irrational urge to throw off his comforting arm, but fought it back and let him lead her back to the huge, reddish boulder where she and Alex had found shelter.

Alex spoke to Gamal, and the two of them moved off—looking for a wounded man, or a dead one. Nora sat in the dust, leaning against the side of the boulder.

Tim sank down beside her. "This is crazy," he said, shaking his head. "Crazy. First the bomb, now people shooting at each other."

"Yes." And she'd lied and said that they'd been caught in the crossfire. She hadn't mentioned Alex's gun.

Was she going to lie to the Egyptian army, too?

Nora licked her lips again and realized she was desperately thirsty. When she reached for the water bottle that should have hung at her waist, though, it was missing. "I don't suppose you brought any water with you?"

"Didn't have time. But I see your bottle—must have fallen off when Bok knocked you down."

She saw what he was looking at, but the plastic bottle lying in the sand a few feet away was green, not blue. "That's Alex's bottle. I don't see mine." She started to rise.

Tim's hand on her shoulder stopped her. "For God's sake, sit still. I'll get it." He heaved to his feet and went to get the bottle. But when he picked it up he just stood there, staring at the plain green bottle with the most peculiar expression on his face.

"If you're thirsty," she said impatiently, "you can have a drink, too, but don't be greedy. I'm really dry, and I expect Alex is, too."

"It's, ah—it's empty." He held it out, and she saw why.

There were two neat holes in the water bottle—entry and exit holes, one on each side. As if the bullet had punched through while Alex was still wearing it.

By the time Alex was able to slip away from camp that afternoon, the sky was piled high with clouds, a dirty white ceiling that stretched from one horizon to the other.

Rain clouds. He hoped like hell they wandered farther inland before dumping their burden on the dry land below. It would be just his luck for the Sinai to see one of its rare storms on the one night of the year he needed clear weather.

Something was going to happen tonight. He didn't know what. He could guess, but guessing wasn't good enough—which was why he was out here now, scrambling up one of the small hills near the quarry. He needed to talk to the man who had come to their rescue that morning, then vanished.

Alex had recognized the voice, of course. He and Farid's son had set up a couple of possible meeting places earlier. It was to one of these that Alex headed now.

The ambush that morning had been hastily planned. If they'd had more time to arrange his execution, they would have had silenced weapons. They'd been rushed. Something must have happened to make Alex's death vital.

He expected to learn from Farid's son what that was.

But it had not been a clumsy attempt. No, it had very nearly succeeded. They'd used the very spot he'd noted as being an excellent setting for an ambush…the place where he'd once tried to frighten Nora into staying in camp.

Nora. Cold slithered down his spine. She had nearly been killed that morning. Because of him.

Well, he wouldn't be around to put her in danger much longer. A day, maybe two. Things were coming to a head quickly. After that...with an effort, he shoved aside any thought of the future he might not have.

He didn't pause at the top of the hill, but moved automatically so as not to present his silhouette against the sky as an inviting target. Guilt rode him as he made his way to a sheltered spot halfway down the hill, where he would be able to see any who approached. He took his cellular phone out of the pocket of his jacket, punched in a number, and waited.

His thoughts were not good company.

If he hadn't seen the sunlight glinting on a rifle barrel this morning—or if Farid's son hadn't come looking for him—dammit, he had to stop this. He knew better than to brood over might-have-beens. But standing there in the cloud-dimmed light of afternoon, knowing how close he'd come to costing Nora her life, he couldn't put the guilt or the chill behind him.

A series of clicks sounded in his ear. He punched in the numbers that would route the call directly to Jonah, paused until a low tone sounded, then said his name and hung up. Word would be sent to Jonah that Alex needed to talk to him. There might be a wait. Jonah might be anywhere in the world, and unable to respond right away.

Alex had learned one important thing from the attempt on his life—or, rather, from the consequences of having survived it. The Egyptian captain had shown up promptly in response to Ahmed's call; he'd questioned Alex and Nora; had the body taken away; and sent his men to look over the ambush site. All in all, he'd behaved promptly and efficiently...for a fool.

Or a man in the pay of El Hawy.

The captain's troops should have searched for, and found, the spent bullets, which ought to have raised some pretty strong questions. Some of the bullets would have been from Alex's gun, and the locations of the others would have made it clear that the snipers had been firing at Alex and Nora, not at each other. Alex had been prepared for a second, less friendly round of questioning, ready to be shocked at the idea that he and Nora had been the targets.

Instead, the captain had thanked Nora and Alex for their cooperation, assured them that he would pursue the investigation rigorously, and left the camp.

Maybe the man was simply incompetent. Maybe, but Alex didn't believe it. No, he thought El Hawy's leader had bought himself an army captain. With the officer in his pocket, Jawhar didn't have to worry about the army's presence in the area.

It introduced another variable into a game already too complex. The captain might have been told simply to slant his investigation a certain way. He might have been instructed to pull his troops out of the area. Or he might have been told that Alex was a criminal who was attempting to move illegal arms, which was what Jawhar himself believed, and that if he found Alex Bok wandering the area at night, El Hawy and the Egyptian government would both be pleased to hear that he had been killed while "evading arrest."

It also meant that Alex wouldn't be able to call in local troops to clean out the base, once he found it. He had the authority to summon one of SPEAR's elite attack squads, but that was a last resort. SPEAR kept a low profile, and relations between the U.S. and Egypt were too uneasy to risk an incident in any but the most extreme circumstances.

That was why he was reporting in now.

There was a single ring. Alex pushed the "talk" button and held the phone to his ear. "Bok here." A cool, familiar voice said simply, "Code Yellow."

Alex froze for a split second. "Code Yellow" was a warning that the communications channel being used might not be secure. It should have been impossible. No one except Jonah should have been able to receive this call, but Jonah had just told him that was no longer certain.

He chose his words carefully. "The local congregation is full of hypocrites. I'd rather attend services with my friends. Is Merrick around?" Dale Merrick was Alex's backup on this mission. He and a hand-picked squad stood ready to parachute in—but only if the mission was already shot to hell. Egypt did not look kindly on having its air space violated.

A pause. "Do you know when that will be? Has the preacher arrived?"

Damn. If Jonah was asking him whether the traitor had shown up, that meant he'd learned nothing more about the man. "I don't know, but the congregation seems ready to welcome him at any moment."

"Merrick and your friends will be standing by. Call one-two-three if you want to talk to him."

Alex thumbed the disconnect and stood quietly, the phone still in his hand, while he assimilated this latest development.

On a practical level, the possible breach of security didn't change his plans greatly. He wouldn't be able to keep Jonah informed of the details of the situation here, and that lack of information might affect future SPEAR operations if Alex didn't survive to report in full afterward. But it shouldn't affect what Alex did in the next twenty-four hours.

It occurred to him that he was contemplating his possible death as coolly as he ever had when going into a particularly hairy situation. He frowned. Why was that? He *was* afraid. In some wordless corner of his soul the fear crouched, shivering, a half-frozen beast that might yet leap out and try to consume him.

But...was it really death that he feared?

By three o'clock that afternoon, the army captain was long gone, Ahmed and Gamal were standing guard over the camp, Nora and Tim were barely speaking to each other, and Alex was missing.

The unhappy silence between her and Tim was mostly her fault. Nora knew and regretted that, but she didn't know what else she could have done.

In fact, she knew all too little. That was the problem.

Sometime after lunch, Nora had realized Alex was gone. She'd been furious and frightened and in no mood for the easygoing Tim to turn mulish on her. Tim hadn't wanted to work on the dig. No, he'd wanted to go looking for Alex, or to call the army captain back and have him hunt for Alex. Not because he was worried about him, but because "there's something damned havey-cavey going on, and Bok's at the bottom of it. And if you're too dazzled to see that, I'm bloody well not!"

One word had led to another, most of them unnecessary. In the end, Nora had threatened to pack Tim off to Tor with DeLaney and Lisa if he refused to accept her authority and get to work.

A despicable way to win the argument, she knew, and as unfair as it was high-handed. Tim cared about her. He wouldn't leave her out here with only two hired workers for protection...and Alex Bok.

Especially since he considered Alex the biggest danger.

He might be right about that. Though it made her heart hurt, she faced that possibility.

Nora's conscience ached along with her heart as she scraped at the dirt in her section. She didn't like herself very much right now. She'd used Tim's feelings for her to keep him from looking for Alex, afraid of the consequences if someone blundered into whatever Alex was doing—afraid, mostly, for Alex. But some of her fear had been for Tim. Only that morning, she had nearly been killed just for being with Alex, and she didn't even know why.

And Tim thought she was dazzled by him still.

Maybe she was. Nora emptied her scrapings carefully into a plastic bag and sealed it. If getting shot at hadn't opened her eyes, nothing would. Try as she might to look at the situation clearly, all she could think about was that one of the snipers had gotten away and might even now be aiming his rifle at Alex again.

The damned fool. What was he doing out there alone?

Thoughts of drugs and smuggling and other unsavory activities kept pushing into her mind. Nora wanted to be reasonable and sensible, to consider all the possibilities, but her heart was so very sure of him. It was dragging the rest of her along willy-nilly into confusion.

When she heard Gamal calling out something, she dropped the digging tool and sprang to her feet. Then she realized what he'd said.

Alex was back.

Tim stood, too. "I'm going with you."

His jaw had that mulish look. For some reason—maybe because she was no longer wondering if Alex's body was lying in some gully, bloody and unliving—his stubbornness made her blink back tears this time.

"Tim," she said gently, "I appreciate you. I really do, and I'm sorry I let my temper get away from me earlier. But I have to talk to him myself."

He didn't speak for a long moment, then nodded stiffly.

She turned, her own jaw tightening grimly. Alex had some explaining to do.

The wind was up. It hissed and moaned through the rocks, reaching the bottom of the quarry in unsteady gusts that set the sand to dancing. It made the canvas walls of the tents shudder, tore at the loose wisps of hair around Nora's face, and left grit in Alex's mouth as he watched her coming toward him.

Maybe the wind would push the heavy clouds away, and the skies would be clear tonight. He hoped so. He was going to need all the luck he could find.

Ahmed and Gamal were getting the worst of the wind, up on the rim of the quarry. Alex stood near the main tent, sheltered somewhat by the walls of the quarry, and wondered what on earth he was going to say to Nora.

She was upset. He could tell by the way she moved, quick and stiff as an offended cat. Her expression was tight, hard to read, so that he couldn't tell whether it was fear or fury that moved her.

Her first words upon reaching him gave him a clue. "Where the *hell* have you been?"

"I needed to get away."

Her eyes narrowed. "From camp? Or just from me?"

All at once, it hit Alex. What was left of this day was all the time he would ever have with Nora. Why that knowledge came as a shock, he had no idea. Hadn't he always known it would come to this? A few more lies, maybe a half-truth or two, then an ending that didn't even allow him to say goodbye.

"Well?" she demanded. "Were you traipsing around out there because you wanted to give your enemies another chance to shoot you? Or were you avoiding me? You must know you've got a lot of questions to answer."

He didn't want questions. Questions meant finding the energy, somehow, to manipulate this woman, for her own good as well as his. But there was one question he could answer, one she didn't know to ask. "I'll be leaving soon," he said quietly. "Very soon."

The angry color faded from her cheeks. She took a deep, shaky breath and looked away. "That doesn't answer my questions."

So stubborn. He had to smile. "What do you want to know first?"

"Okay. Where did you go this afternoon, and why?"

"Not far. My reasons for needing to get away from camp were…personal and pressing."

"Pressing enough to make you risk your life?"

"Yes."

That shocked her. Her eyes widened, then narrowed, as if she steadied herself by remembering her anger. "Why? And why do people want to kill you, and who came along in the nick of time and shot one of them? Why do you have a gun that you don't want the authorities to know about?"

"All very good questions." The wind had tugged loose one long strand of hair, and was whipping it in her face. Tenderly he tucked it behind her ear. "Thank you for not telling the captain about my gun."

Her breath caught. "Don't do this, Alex. Don't dodge my questions and then touch me so that I'll forget that I need answers."

"I touched you because I wanted to." He saw too much in her eyes. Wariness. Hurt. Hope that flickered in spite of everything. And a raw longing to match his own. "Don't press me for answers, Nora."

"Why not?"

"Because you won't like what you hear." And because

he was tired, bone-tired of parceling out the truth in small doses, mixing it with lies. He felt cold and small, as if he were vanishing.

"Try me."

For one wild moment he thought about telling her, just telling her everything—who he worked for, why he was here, and that he probably wouldn't live out the night. The impulse shocked him. Aside from what such rashness might do to his mission, what would it do to Nora? What would she do if she knew?

Nothing predictable, he thought. Very possibly something dangerous. And for no reason he could understand, that thought made him smile. "Would it help if I told you I'm one of the good guys?"

"Not unless you tell me what that means to you. The people who shot at us this morning probably believed *they* were the good guys."

Undoubtedly they had. Terrorists tended to be stuffed full of the rightness of their cause—so full of their one, righteous priority, there was no room in their hearts or minds for any ordinary virtues.

Kind of like him. "All right. I don't know why they tried to kill me. I have some guesses, but I don't know. The person who saved us by shooting one of the snipers is a business acquaintance. And I have a gun for the same reason most people would—self-protection."

"That tells me nothing. Dammit, Alex, don't I deserve to know what's going on? I lied for you today!"

"You deserve a great many things I can't give you."

She turned away, took three quick steps, then stopped and hugged her arms to her body. "Oh, yes. You've made that clear—that night on the beach, and all week long."

She was hurting. He heard it in her voice, the acid-raw edge of self-doubt, and he couldn't stand it. "Don't fool yourself. I've stayed away from you because you made it clear that was how you wanted it. I'd much rather have been in your bed every night."

Nora was braver than he was. She proved it then, turning completely to face Alex and looking at him with her level, straight-ahead gaze. "You could have changed my mind with very little effort. I'm sure you knew that."

He could change her mind now. That was what she meant, and oh, God, he wanted to. He wanted to drag her over to his tent and spend a couple of hours changing her mind—then spend the rest of the day buried inside her. But sometimes conscience has claws. Remembered shreds of honor caught him on their sharp talons, pinning him in place.

Barely. "Along with Kipling and poetry, my parents filled me with all sorts of inconvenient ideas about right and wrong. I didn't want to seduce you. I wanted you to come to me. To choose me, in spite of everything." He stopped, afraid the yearning was there, all too clear, in his eyes. *Come to me. Touch me. Make me feel warm again, real again.*

Her eyes widened—and, at last, he saw fear there.

Alex didn't intend to say anything more, but the rest of it slipped out, raw and unwise. "I still do."

"How?" she whispered. "When you tell me you're leaving soon—when you tell me nothing *except* that you are leaving—how can I do that?"

He swallowed, afraid he was going to beg. How stupid, how very stupid and selfish he was.... "Of course you can't," he said gently.

Without another word, she turned and walked away.

Chapter 11

The yip-yipping of jackals drifted through the canvas of Nora's tent, faint and far-off. Gamal had once told her that was the sound they made to summon the rest of the pack when one of them found carrion.

Somewhere out there, something had died.

She shivered and huddled deeper into her sleeping bag and wondered how far the temperature had dropped tonight. Her cheeks felt cold.

She was cold. In spite of the warmth of her sleeping bag, a chill had settled deep inside. She kept remembering the look on Alex's face when he'd said he wanted her to come to him.

Lost. So lost, and so desperately alone.

How could she go to him? He was leaving—soon, he'd said, though he'd told her nothing more. Nothing. In the face of his silence, logic spoke loudly. It said there were only two possible explanations for the mysteries surrounding Alex: either he was some sort of spy, or he was a criminal.

What would an American spy be doing in the Sinai, on an archaeological dig? But a criminal—a smuggler, like his friend Farid was said to be—oh, yes, she could think of several possibilities, all of them ugly.

Drugs were the likeliest. The Sinai was a major drug-smuggling route, as Alex himself had once pointed out.

There was no comfort to be found on her narrow cot tonight. Restless, she rolled over and stared at the glowing dial on her travel alarm. Eleven forty-nine. She'd been trying to sleep for over an hour, but she was wider awake now than she'd been when she first lay down.

Her muscles ached, as if from some slight fever. Or grief.

It reminded her of how she'd felt when her mother died—the sluggish pain, so deep in her soul she'd felt it physically. The cold that went even deeper. As if she'd lost something precious and necessary, something that would never come again.

Tension, she told herself, flopping over on her back. It was tension that had her muscles so tight they ached. She felt like an unaimed bow, drawn taut by opposing needs, as if the slightest touch might send her springing off in some unknown direction.

She thought of her mother—a strong woman, in so many ways. Clever and sensible...most of the time. But where men had been concerned—oh, she had wanted someone to love so badly. Over and over, she'd lavished her love on the wrong men. Needy men. Men who had little or nothing to give back to her. The wrong men.

Had her mom felt like this every time? Had her heart cried out that this time it was right, this man was the right one, the one she would love forever?

How could Nora be in love with a man she couldn't trust?

But Alex wasn't like any of the men who had broken her mother's heart. When had he acted selfishly? He wanted her. He could have had her, and they both knew it. He wouldn't have had to lie or promise more than he intended to give. All he would have had to do was look at her, laugh with her...touch her.

I wanted you to come to me. To choose me, in spite of everything.

Nora had spent the last seven days telling herself that he'd held back because he hadn't really wanted her all that much. That would have been true of any number of her mother's boyfriends. It wasn't true of Alex. And deep down, she'd known that.

He'd stayed away because he was an honorable man. Because he hadn't wanted to take more from her than she was willing to give.

Because he wasn't anything like the men who had hurt her mother—and her—when she was a little girl. Sometimes she'd liked them, and wanted them to stay because she'd wanted a father so badly. They never had. After a while, she stopped caring, and couldn't understand why her mother did care, why she went on hoping.

None of the "uncles" her mother had brought home had been bad men, not really. Not cruel or abusive. Just weak, inconstant, undependable. They'd all left, sooner or later.

Just as Alex was going to leave.

Her breath caught on a sudden stab of understanding. That was the only thing Alex really had in common with the men who had waltzed in and out of her life when she was small. Just like them, Alex wasn't going to stay.

For so many years—forever, it seemed—Nora had held

tight to a dream. The dream of the one man, the right man. The one who would never leave her.

Staring up at the blank darkness in her tent, Nora faced the truth. She would never have more than half her dream. Because she'd found the man, the one man, the man she loved with everything in her. And she was going to have to let him go.

But she didn't have to let him go tonight.

Nora's hands shook when she unzipped her sleeping bag. Her legs felt too unsteady to hold her up, but they did. Without lighting her lamp, she reached for the clothes she'd taken off before lying down.

Ahmed would be out there, on guard. She'd decided they needed to keep watch at night, though Alex had said he didn't think it was necessary.

Possibly he knew what he was talking about. Oh, undoubtedly he knew a great deal more than she did about what was going on, but she'd asked Gamal and Ahmed to take turns at sentry duty anyway. So she fumbled for her clothes in the dark, not wanting Ahmed to see a light—and then see her sneaking out of her tent to go to Alex.

He wouldn't turn her away, would he?

Fear balled up in her stomach, making her hesitate.

Let him try, she thought, filled with a sudden, fiery determination, the same surge of courage or recklessness that always sent her straight at whatever goal she'd set. He might try to send her away for her own good. She wouldn't go. He wanted her, maybe even needed her. And she wanted him—oh, how she wanted him!

Tonight. Tomorrow he might leave, but she would have had half of her dream, anyway. She would have had the man she loved, if only for one night.

Nora found her shoes, thumped them automatically, and

crammed them on her feet without taking the time to hunt up a pair of socks. Then she felt for her jacket.

There would be no rain tonight. Alex thanked God for that piece of luck as he slipped out of his tent, and for the wind that had hurried most of the clouds on their way. He hadn't had everything his way, though. Nora had decided to post sentries. Ahmed was to stand watch for the first part of the night.

It was a reasonable decision, from her viewpoint. A damned nuisance, from his. He was almost sure he could slip out of camp without Ahmed seeing him, but almost wasn't good enough. Not when there was a strong chance that Ahmed reported to El Hawy.

The night was brighter out here than it had been in his tent, so his eyes were well-adjusted. What remained of the moon was playing tag with scattered threads of clouds. Not great light, but it would do. He waited, motionless, in the shadows at the front of his tent, his backpack sitting in the dirt beside him, until he spotted Ahmed.

Instead of walking the perimeter, as he should have been doing, Ahmed sat at the big table in front of the main tent ten yards away. Playing cards, for God's sake. He'd even lit a lantern, though the wick must be lowered because the light was dim.

Alex hesitated. No soldier of El Hawy's training would make himself such a perfect target.

But Ahmed might be a sympathizer rather than a soldier, or in it for the money. Alex couldn't take a chance on the man's innocence. He made sure the tiny hypodermic was fitted snugly into his palm and stepped openly out of the shadows.

Ahmed's head came up when Alex had closed half the

distance between them. His muffled exclamation was in Arabic.

Alex made a hushing sound, smiling as he came up to the man, who stood hastily. "I couldn't sleep," he said in a voice that wouldn't carry beyond the empty tent behind them. He glanced at the cards. "It must be boring, standing around out here for hours."

"Pardon—my English is not so good."

Alex repeated his comment in Arabic, adding that he wouldn't mind playing a hand or two of cards himself.

It was all too easy. A quick slap on the arm when Ahmed agreed, a single, bright look of alarm on the young man's face—Alex's hand clapped over the man's mouth to stop his outcry, his other arm going around him. Ahmed struggled, but the drug was strong, and fast-acting. Alex had little trouble restraining him for the scant seconds it took before he swayed, then slumped, a dead weight.

Alex eased him back onto the bench where he'd been sitting, turning him, with some difficulty, so that his head and shoulders rested on his cards, as if he'd fallen asleep—which, in an entirely involuntary sense, was what had happened.

A quick glance around the camp assured Alex that no one had been awakened by their brief struggle, and he set off.

Standing unseen in the shadowed interior of her tent, one hand on the flap of the door, Nora watched Alex cross to Ahmed. She saw him greet the other man, clap him on the back—and then slap his hand over Ahmed's mouth. She saw the sudden, brief struggle, and the careful way Alex arranged the limp body at the table.

Her eyes wide with horror, her hand over her own mouth, Nora watched Alex head back to his tent. He didn't go in—he wasn't there long enough. Then he started across the quarry, heading east.

What had he done? Dear God, what had he done to Ahmed, and why?

Where was he going?

Irresistibly, her gaze followed the man she'd fallen in love with. He was leaving. After knocking out the guard she'd posted to keep them safe, he was leaving camp.

He wasn't coming back. There was no reason to be so sure of that, yet she was stubbornly, overwhelmingly certain Alex didn't intend to return.

She hesitated for only a second. Then she followed him.

Nora's ankles were cold. Her feet were okay, even without socks, but her ankles felt all the chill of the desert night. She leaned against a boulder and breathed in slowly through her mouth, fighting not to gulp air down loudly. That last hill had been a mad scramble after fading hope, and her heart was thudding miserably.

She'd lost him.

Maybe she'd managed to lose herself, too. She'd had to let Alex stay well ahead, far enough that he couldn't hear her following, so it wasn't surprising that she'd lost sight of him twice. The first time, she'd continued on what seemed the likeliest route, and been rewarded by catching a glimpse of him moving, silent as a shadow, up the next hill.

This time she hadn't been so lucky. She straightened, her breathing back to normal, and looked around.

She wasn't sure where she was now. East of camp, certainly. Maybe about two miles away, measured horizontally—but there was precious little horizontal about the route Alex had taken.

But the land looked vastly different at night, all dark

shapes and unseen obstacles. Had the moon been full she might have been able to see a landmark to orient herself by, but it wasn't. It was well up, hanging almost directly overhead like a fat, cartoon grin someone had stood on end, but clouds kept drifting across its diminished face.

What was she doing out here? Was she crazy?

Nora's lips tightened. Maybe. But the impulse that had pulled her out of camp, sending her scrambling in Alex's wake, remained strong.

She had to *know*. That was all.

It was enough.

The moon slipped coyly out from behind its veil of clouds. Good. She pushed both her fatigue and her dismay away. With the increased light, maybe she could spot Alex again.

Nora stepped back from the boulder, tilting her head back to study it. If she could figure a way to climb it, she should be able to clamber higher onto the rough bulk of the hill that loomed behind it. From there, she might spot Alex—or at least figure out how to get back to camp.

The night darkened once more. She glanced up, frowning, to see that another finger of cloud had drifted in front of the moon. Dammit, if she could just see better…

What was that? Some sound, so faint—

Before she could turn, a hand clamped over her mouth. An arm circled her chest, yanking her backwards, off balance, to land against a hard male body. She tried to wrench free, the sudden energy of terror lending her strength.

The hand on her mouth forced her head back firmly against a hard shoulder. She couldn't pry her jaws open to bite it, but managed to yank one arm free. She drove her elbow back into his middle.

His foot swept her feet out from under her. She fell. He came down on top of her, still gripping her mouth with one hand, and used his weight to pin her. Terrified, she tried to buck him off, but he was too big, too strong, too quick. In seconds he had her motionless, his legs trapping hers, his other hand holding both of hers over her head.

Between fear and the weight of him, pressing down on her, she could hardly breath.

Then he lowered his head. She felt his breath on her cheek when he spoke, softer than a whisper. "Not a sound."

Alex. Oh, thank God. She went limp. When he didn't remove his hand, she realized he was waiting for her agreement. She managed a tiny nod.

He leaned back, taking some of his weight off her, and she drew in air gratefully. He did something with his shirt, or his belt—she couldn't see what. It was too dark, and she was too dizzy with relief. Questions pressed at the back of her throat, but she swallowed them, obedient to the need for silence.

Then he pulled her hands down in front of her. With a brisk, businesslike motion, he wrapped cord around her wrists—binding her.

Tying her up.

Nora went a little crazy. She fought. Silent still, not from obedience but because it didn't occur to her to cry out, she gave the brief battle everything she had. And lost.

Endless terrifying seconds later she lay, bound and gagged, on the ground. Tears of rage and fear stung her eyes. Alex lifted her, laid her over his shoulder and stood. She struggled still, her head hanging down and dizzy, but the cord around her ankles dug into her skin painfully when she tried to kick him.

A few steps. The sensation of falling, his arms controlling that fall. Then she was sitting almost upright in a small ditch or gully, her back against the slanting earth, her legs wedged up close to her body.

His fingers smoothed over her face in a shocking imitation of tenderness. She didn't notice the tears on her cheeks until his fingers wiped them gently—then she felt the dampness, cool and distinct on her skin when his hand withdrew.

He bent closer. "I'm sorry," he whispered so softly she couldn't tell if anything lay behind the words except air.

Then he straightened. And left her.

The ground was cold, and grew colder. So did Nora as she huddled into herself, her mouth dried by the rag stuffed in it, her arms aching, her pulse thudding in her throat. Moment drifted into moment as the tears dried on her cheeks.

Then she heard voices, several yards away, somewhere on the other side of the lump of earth and rock he'd dumped her behind. Alex supplied one of those voices. He was speaking Arabic, greeting someone...oh, yes, she knew that voice, too. Farid Ibn Kareem.

She strained to hear, to understand, but they kept their voices low. Alex, especially. Most of what snatches she heard was spoken in Farid's raspy baritone. She wasn't fluent enough to understand all of it, but she understood enough.

They were talking about guns.

Guns, arms, ammunition—a shipment Farid had found? Stolen? He'd done something with those guns, and that was why someone wanted to kill Alex.

Because Farid was acting on Alex's orders.

There was more—something about a man Farid wanted to see, a man he thought Alex knew. She couldn't hear Alex's reply. The rest jumbled up together in her head—danger, an argument, money. A great deal of money. And there was a third voice, lighter in pitch, but definitely male. He wanted to kill someone.

Nora shuddered. And began to think, really think, for the first time since Alex's hand had closed over her mouth.

Chapter 12

Alex watched the clouds sifting across the black dish of the sky, and waited. And tried not to think of what Nora was thinking and feeling with her hands and feet bound, her mouth foul and dry from the gag he'd stuffed there.

She would have heard him talking to Farid and his son—parts of it, anyway. There hadn't been time to hide her very far from the appointed meeting spot. She would have heard Alex leave, too. By now she must be thinking he wasn't coming back.

He swallowed bile and checked his watch. Five more minutes, he told himself. Only ten minutes had passed since he'd parted from Farid, though it seemed much longer. He had to give the others time to be well away from here. Everything he'd done—the bindings, the gag—no, he wasn't going to think about it. It had been necessary, but it would end up a useless cruelty if Farid or his son saw Alex go back and untie Nora.

Would she believe him? When he explained, would she

agree to keep silent over tonight's events? Dear God, let her believe. Not for his sake. He knew what he'd done would not be forgiven. But for her sake, for the sake of what he still had to do—or try to do—he prayed that she would accept the truth, once she heard it.

Alex waited out the five minutes, then slipped silently from his hiding place, his backpack gripped in one hand.

It took him less than a minute to reach Nora. The sight of her, a small dark mass curled in on herself for warmth, made him hasty. He abandoned silence for speed, sending dirt flying as he half-slid, half-ran down the side of the hill that had separated them for the last fifteen minutes.

She lifted her head. Her face was a pale oval in the darkness, her expression blurred by the poor light. He crouched beside her. The gag first—but his fingers strayed for a second, testing the skin of her cheek.

Dry. Gratitude fluttered inside him, frantic and unspoken. He reached behind her head and worked at the knot.

Damn this cord. It was too narrow. It would have dug into her wrists and her ankles. There, he had it loose.

The gag fell out. She made a disgusted sound. "I *hated* having that thing in my mouth. I thought you were never going to get here."

His hands froze for a second, then went to her wrists. "You knew I was coming back?"

"Of course." She was hoarse. "I hope you've got some water in that backpack."

The knot loosened and the cord fell free. He chafed her wrists gently. The skin seemed unbroken, at least.

How could she have known he would return for her? After what he'd done—what she must have heard. He didn't understand. A confusion of feeling, vast and unsteady, made him drop her hands and turn to reach for his backpack.

He handed her his water bottle and bent to tackle the cord on her ankles. "I never meant to hurt you."

"Just untie me. And don't *ever* do such a thing again."

For some unholy reason, that brought a glimmer of a grin. "I, ah, think I can promise not to. I'm not all that fond of tying women up."

"I am not in the mood for stupid innuendoes. Do you have any idea how much you scared me?"

"Better scared than dead. Farid might not have killed you out of hand if he'd seen you spying on us, but I didn't want to count on that. The best-case scenario was that I would have had time to draw on him and stop him." More likely, Alex would have had to shoot Farid and try to shoot his son, too, before the younger man dropped him. That would have put an end to any chance of accomplishing his mission.

And left him with the death of a man who had been something of a friend on his conscience. "It was less risky to immobilize you." Damn, he couldn't get the tight knot unfastened, and there wasn't enough slack to get his knife under the cord and cut it.

"I figured that out." She put down his water bottle and started rubbing her wrists. "Pleasant people you hang out with."

His fingers stopped moving. "You figured it out?"

"Sure. I admit it took me a while. I was too scared to think at first, but once I did it seemed obvious. What I don't understand is why you thought tying me up made me safe. What if I'd stayed in a panic? I might have tried to attract Farid's attention. I could have, you know, even with the gag in my mouth."

Oh, he'd known that, all right. The fear that she might move around, grunt, do anything to let Farid know she was nearby, had ridden him hard the whole time he was talking with the man.

But she said she'd figured that out. How? How could she have known he meant her no harm—that he was, in fact, doing everything he could to keep her safe? "I was hoping you'd be too scared to say or do anything to draw his attention. If you had, I would have told him the truth."

"Which truth would that be?" she asked dryly.

"That you followed me, I caught you, tied you up and left you nearby, so I could deal with you later myself."

"And that would have made him less likely to shoot me?"

"Of course it would. You wouldn't have been an immediate threat, and I would have had a chance to persuade him that we had other options." Not that Farid would have shot her. A gun was too loud. A knife was just as sure, in the hands of one who knew how to use it—and Farid did. "Dammit, why did you come out here without socks?"

"I was in a hurry."

At last the cord yielded to his fingers. She flinched slightly when he drew it away. He bent to rub her ankles. "So you tied me up so Farid wouldn't feel threatened, panic, and shoot me."

"There's a difference between panic and reflex. He would have killed you because that was a reasonable response, under the circumstances. You have no idea what kind of situation you've pushed your way into, Nora."

"You could have told me."

He was silent as he stowed his water bottle in his pack.

"You didn't have to tie me up and—and all the rest of it. If you'd just told me to keep still and quiet when you caught me—"

He made a derisive sound. "And you would have done whatever I asked? Right. You didn't follow me out here because you trusted me implicitly.'' She had no reason to trust him at all.

''You might have trusted *me* a little bit. I did have the sense to keep quiet when Farid was talking to you.''

''And if you'd been free while we were talking, you would have tried to get closer so you could hear better. And if Farid had heard you...''

''Ah—good point.'' She shivered.

''You need to get up. The ground is cold.'' He held out his hand. Belatedly it occurred to him that she might not want to touch him.

She wiggled her feet, stretched and grimaced. ''I'm sore all over. Have you ever been tied up for an hour and left on the cold ground?''

Yes, he had. Or something along those lines, anyway. ''It wasn't a full hour, but it is getting late. We need to get moving.''

She eyed him. ''You *are* going to answer my questions, you know.''

''Yes.'' It didn't matter now. He'd already compromised his mission by choosing her safety over what he should have done tonight. And there wasn't much point in trying to keep her out of it anymore. She'd made that impossible.

He left his hand outstretched, waiting to see if she would take it.

She did. He felt a little tremor go through her when he pulled her to her feet, and didn't know if it was fear of him or a reaction to everything else that caused it.

He wanted to ask, wanted to know what she was thinking, feeling, why she didn't seem more afraid of him. He did understand why Nora pushed and pushed against anything she feared, the way she had in the cave with her claustrophobia.

But this time, she should have accepted fear as the reasonable response. If she had feared him more, she would have stayed in camp.

She pulled her hand away and straightened her shoulders. "So—who's Farid, and why are you meeting secretly with him about some kind of weapons shipment?"

He went still. "So you did hear that much. If you think I'm involved in selling illegal arms, it would be very stupid of you to ask me that."

"You're not. Not in a criminal way, at least."

"How do you know?" Her answer mattered, he discovered. It mattered a great deal.

"You go first. I've been waiting for answers longer than you have."

"All right. But we'd better start moving while we talk." He turned and headed for a small cut between two rocky mounds. "Farid is just what you heard—a smuggler, among other things. Who told you that, by the way?"

"Ahmed," she admitted. "Is he—did you—"

"So you saw that. He's all right," Alex said curtly. He was moving more slowly than he had on the way out. There was no hurry; nothing waited back at camp but complications. He wanted to keep moving because Nora needed to get warmed up, and he didn't think she would let him do that the way he would have liked.

"What did you do to him?"

Moving forward was easier than looking at her, too. "I drugged him."

It sounded like she was moving easily enough behind him. "Are your feet okay? You don't have blisters from going without socks?"

"I'm fine. Why didn't you just drug me when you wanted to keep me quiet?"

"I didn't bring another dose with me. And if I had, I

wouldn't have used it. You would have been unconscious too long."

"This is a very weird conversation, you know," she said after a moment, moving up to walk abreast of him.

"It's been a strange night." He didn't see why she was so ready to go with him. To trust him. "Why in heaven's name did you follow me?"

"I had to know. You wouldn't tell me anything, and I had to know what was going on."

"It didn't occur to you that it might be dangerous? That *I* might be dangerous?"

"Of course it did. Stop changing the subject and tell me about Farid."

He had to smile. Stubborn, single-track woman.

So, as they moved over the dim, night-shrouded landscape, Alex told her the truth, or most of it. He didn't mention SPEAR by name, and he didn't say anything about a traitor, but told her he worked for a secret agency that was dedicated to fighting terrorism. He admitted his part in blowing up the well, and explained about El Hawy—their base, the arms they were bringing in and Farid's part in intercepting those arms.

"So Farid really is a criminal, but he's working for you."

"With me," he corrected. "He thinks I'm every bit as big a crook as he is, of course, connected to an international criminal organization. So does the leader of El Hawy, and several other people in this part of the world. I've encouraged them to think so. Some of the things I've done," he added deliberately, "*have* been criminal. In every sense of the word."

"I suppose a spy would have to break the law at times."

"I'm not talking about telling a few white lies, Nora. I've killed people."

She was silent a moment. "I get the feeling you're trying to persuade me that you're as black as the people you're hunting."

"I'm not. But the lines can blur between hunted and hunter. After a while...a man who has stolen and lied and used people can lose touch with his own humanity." He forgets how to sleep at night. After a while, he grows cold. So cold. "I don't want you romanticizing what I've done, seeing me as some glamorous Hollywood version of a spy."

"Oh, sure. You've knocked me down, tied me up and stuffed a horrid gag in my mouth. Really glamorous. Was it El Hawy who shot at us this morning?"

"Yes." Her matter-of-fact reaction had him off balance again.

"Who came to our rescue this morning? Someone from this agency of yours?"

"No, I'm on my own here for now. One of Farid's sons shot the sniper."

"Why did El Hawy try to kill you? Because they think you're after this arms shipment of theirs? It seems like they'd try to kill Farid, not you, since he's the one who's supposed to intercept it."

He hesitated. "This afternoon when I was away from camp, I learned that Farid had taken possession of the arms. That changed my idea about what happened this morning. I think they intended to wound me, not kill me. I'm more useful to them as a prisoner than I would be dead." He was counting on that.

"They wanted to make you tell them where the arms are."

"Yes. Watch your footing on this next part," he said as he started up a rocky slope. "It's tricky in the dark."

The moon was hiding again, but they were close to camp now. They wouldn't have far to travel in the darkness.

She was silent while they scrambled up the short hill. When they reached the top, she put her hand on his arm. "Alex, why were you meeting with Farid tonight? Did I mess things up badly by following you?"

He'd expected that question, and had a lie ready. "I wanted him to bring the arms closer—close enough to draw some of El Hawy's soldiers out of hiding. While they tried to take the shipment back, I could find their base."

"Is that what you were arguing about?"

"In part. My turn for questions now." He wished the moon would come out again. Her face was no more than a pale blur in the darkness, but her hand was still on his arm, warm and steady. "How did you happen to see me leaving camp?"

"I couldn't sleep. I got up and got dressed and...and I saw you do something to Ahmed."

"And that made you decide to come after me? Dammit, Nora, of all the crazy, impulsive, harebrained—" He ran a hand over the top of his head. It shook slightly. "I knew someone was following me, but I thought you were one of El Hawy's people. If I hadn't realized who you were in time—" He broke off, closing his eyes as if he could shut out the might-have-beens.

"I...." He heard her swallow. "That didn't occur to me."

"I asked this once before, but didn't get much of an answer. Why did you follow me?"

Very low, she said, "I didn't think you were coming back. I don't know why. I was just certain you wouldn't return to camp, and I—I had to see what you were doing. Why you had to leave."

There was no way she could have known that. It was

true, but she couldn't have known. He raised his hand to her face. He couldn't see her expression, but he could tell what she was feeling this way. "Were you so sure I wasn't a criminal? Or were you planning to turn me in if you found out I was up to no good?"

"I wasn't sure of anything, then," she admitted. "I thought you had to be either a spy of some sort, or a smuggler of the worst sort."

His other hand was on her face now. "What made up your mind?" Her braid had loosened, making it easy for him to thread his fingers in her hair. "Was it when I tied you up? Or later, when you heard me talking to Farid about the arms?"

He couldn't see her smile, but he felt it in the bunching of her cheeks. "You make me sound like an idiot. It was after you tied me up, and while you and Farid were talking, that I finally started thinking, not just reacting. There's something about being tied and gagged and left in a ditch," she added thoughtfully, "that gets your mind working wonderfully well."

"Does it?" How could he want her so much? It was the wrong time, the wrong place, and he was certainly the wrong man for her. And all of that wouldn't have stopped him, if he could have been sure they were safe here.

Regretfully he dropped his hands. "We're almost back at camp." Where he would tell her goodbye. Feelings knotted up tight in his chest, making him want to grab her hand and run in the other direction. Any other direction.

She glanced around. "I don't see anything familiar. Everything looks different at night."

He indulged himself by taking one of her hands in his when he started walking. "The camp is just ahead. What did you figure out once your mind started working?"

"That you couldn't be what I was afraid you were.

You're not like that. I—I couldn't care about you if you were."

Disappointment mingled with elation. She cared. He'd known that, yet it was still sweet to hear. But he was afraid she was drawn to a fantasy. "How do you know what I'm like? I've lied to you from the first day we met."

"Oh, surely not on the very first day. You were quite honestly bleeding then."

He couldn't keep from grinning. "True. Nora, I care about you, too." It sounded so weak. Wrong, somehow. Yet it was true. He cared about her so much he'd jeopardized his mission for her sake.

She glanced at him, her eyebrows raised. "That's surprising, since you think I'm a fool."

"Not that. An innocent, maybe. That's not a bad thing."

"You think I'm letting my feelings blind me. But believe me, Alex, I know the difference between a good man, one who takes responsibility for his actions, and a weak one. I learned a lot about the other sort when I was growing up. My mother had lousy taste in men."

He squeezed her hand. "You don't have to explain."

"Don't I? I get the feeling that you're arguing with me—not out loud, maybe, but somewhere inside you're insisting that I don't know what I'm talking about. That you're really not a very good person."

She stopped and moved in front of him. "There are gangsters who are good to their dog and cold-blooded killers who help old ladies across the street. Men like that are capable of some forms of kindness—but only the easy sort. Not the kind that costs. And you..." Her voice trailed off, then came back firmly. "You could have taken me to bed. We both know that. But you didn't. I didn't understand until—until you told me, earlier, that you still wanted me—but the decision to keep your distance *did* cost you, didn't it?"

More than he knew how to tell her. It was costing him now, right this minute. His hand tightened on hers. "I didn't want to hurt you."

"I know." She said that very softly.

The moon chose that moment to slip out from behind the clouds. Light fell across her upturned face—clear, colorless light. Pure. Like the feelings that shone from her when she reached up, smiling, to caress his cheek. "A man who could persuade himself it was okay to sell drugs or weapons wouldn't have thought he was responsible for my feelings. A man like that would have taken what he wanted from me. You're not that kind of man, Alex."

There was no way to answer her. No way except one. He kissed her.

Her lips were dusty, which made him smile. Her taste was sweet. Though his body was urgent, craving more, it was enough to kiss her, feel the giving pressure of her lips returning his kiss. He wanted to spend an hour like this. A day. A lifetime.

The last thought slipped in so naturally he didn't question it. Not when her arms lifted to circle him and her body pressed against him, making the world spin. Slow, dizzy circles it made, a gentle earthquake that slid the pieces of him around and around, sorting him into shapes he hadn't known he could feel.

He pulled her closer. His body ached. Gradually he realized he did need more than the simple mating of lips and tongues, and his mouth went searching for it. He found what he needed in the scent of her, behind her ear. In the swift pulse at the base of her throat. The soft feel of her breast in his hand, and the way her nipple peaked and her breath sighed out when he rubbed her there.

Need mounted, his heart raced and he could have taken her then, could have pulled her to the ground and rolled with her in the dirt, hands and hearts and bodies taking and giving joy.

But not now. Not here. It wasn't safe. He had to stop.

Shuddering, he cupped her head in one hand and cradled her against him. He rubbed his cheek against her hair and tried to understand what was happening with him.

The quick, hot burn of desire was familiar. This was different. More intense.

She was different.

"Nora." He hunted for words and found only need. "I want to see you again."

She gave her low chuckle. "Are you asking me for a date? That's one thing we haven't done."

His body throbbed, reminding him of another thing they hadn't done. "After this is over, I mean. When I'm...finished with my assignment." He had no business saying that. Not when there was every chance he wouldn't survive the assignment. But if he knew he had Nora to come back to...

He took her hand and carried it to his mouth, pressing a kiss on her palm. "A date, if you like. Time we can spend together. I want more, I won't deny that. I want to take you to bed and make love for hours, then sleep, and then do it all again...but most of all, I want to spend time with you. Afterward."

"Yes. Oh, yes."

"I can't promise anything—"

"I know that. I—"

"Shh." His head flew up and his body went on alert, adrenaline making his heart pound while his eyes searched the darkness around them, his ears straining to catch any slight noise. His hand went to the holster at the small of his back. "Get down."

He'd heard something. Some slight, wayward sound—an animal, maybe. Probably.

His gun was out and ready. Nora hadn't dropped to the ground, so he pushed her down and dropped into a crouch, started to turn...

The sound of the shot, muffled but loud in the desert stillness, reached him at the same instant as the sting in his neck—sudden and sharp, like a wasp sting. He dropped on top of Nora, covering her—but he fell badly. Awkwardly. His body wasn't *right,* and his mind was slowing.

He slapped his hand to his neck, expecting blood, thinking he'd been hit worse than he'd realized. His fingers found and identified the shape of the dart embedded there, knocking it loose even as the muffling grayness closed over him.

He might have cried out. He might have only been screaming inside, where the drug was rapidly locking him, deep inside the waves of darkness that lapped higher and higher.

He had one more clear thought before he passed out. He'd succeeded in tonight's mission, after all. He'd managed to get himself captured. But he'd failed at what he'd most wanted—to keep Nora safe.

Anguish slid with him into the waiting darkness.

Chapter 13

Darkness. It wrapped around Nora, cushioning her from other sensations. Like nausea. Fear. Both floated slightly apart from her, but waiting.

She tried to hold onto the darkness, but it was shredding, as if some unseen hand grabbed the stuffing from her pillow one fistful at a time, dropping her closer and closer to hard reality.

Reality was an aching head, an uneasy stomach, and a hard, rough bed. Warmth…her head and shoulders rested on something warm and giving. Her body felt stiff, uncomfortable, as if she'd lain too long in the same position. She needed to move, to…she shifted her legs and heard someone moan.

"It's all right, sweetheart," a voice murmured. "You're all right."

Alex. Alex was with her. He hadn't—all at once memory returned. Her eyes shot open.

It was still dark, but not completely. She saw his face,

a ruddy blur in the dimness. Her head pounded, and she swallowed a surge of nausea. "You're here." The guns—she remembered his falling on top of her, going limp. Horribly limp. She reached for his face, wanting to assure herself that he was truly alive, but her hand shook.

He caught her hand in his. "Lie still a little longer. You're feeling sick to your stomach, but it will pass quickly. It's the drug."

The drug? "I—I shot someone. Or tried to. After you collapsed, I got your gun. I saw them coming…" Dark figures emptying out of the darkness around them, coming toward her and Alex, who had lain so still on top of her. "But they shot me, too." Her voice ended on a bewildered note. She didn't *feel* shot.

"They used anesthetic darts. The effects have already worn off for me, but you have less body mass. You'll feel better in a few minutes." His voice changed, still gentle, but with a grim note entering it. "We're prisoners, Nora."

Prisoners. She sorted out the sensations she'd been feeling. She was lying on a stony floor, her head and shoulders supported by Alex's lap. There was a blanket wrapped around her legs. The air smelled damp compared to the dry desert air she'd gotten used to, and somewhat sour.

Stone. It surrounded them, she realized, looking around. They were in a small stone chamber, the walls rough, the ceiling low and sloping steeply to meet the floor at one end. On her right, an arm's-length away, was an arched entry, no more than four feet high, fitted with an odd-looking door. Wooden slats were spaced so that several inches lay between each one. The only light came from between those slats, a warm, not quite steady glow.

Oil lamps, she realized. On the other side of that door was an oil lamp, or more than one. Not electricity's bright, unwavering shine. "Where are we?"

"El Hawy's base." He hesitated. "It's in a cave, or a system of caves."

Underground. She was underground. How deep? She shuddered. But there was light. At least it wasn't completely dark.

Suddenly she needed to sit up. She felt too helpless lying there and struggled to move, but her body was clumsy, her limbs not quite ready to obey her.

"Easy, now." He put his arm behind her shoulders and helped her sit, leaning against him. "How's your head?"

"Pounding." But the nausea was already easing, just as he'd said it would.

She heard voices—male voices, speaking Arabic in low tones on the other side of the wooden-barred door. "What's out there?"

"Another chamber, bigger than this one. They use it for storage, from what I could see. Nora..." His voice caught. He bent his head, and she felt the slide of his cheek against her hair in a single caress. "I'm sorry. God, I'm so sorry. I never meant for you to be involved."

"You didn't involve me. I did that myself, when I followed you." His breath was warm against her hair—warm and unsteady, as if he were fighting for control. She turned her head and touched his cheek, seeing his eyes, shiny-bright, in the dimness. "This is not your fault, Alex. You can't take responsibility for my foolishness."

And she had been foolish, very foolish, and she wasn't done with folly yet, it seemed. Her heart still refused to regret one moment of their time together. No, the only thing she regretted was what she *hadn't* done. If only they had made love that night on the beach. If only...

Grief—for her, for him, for everything they hadn't had a chance to share—rose, choking her. She turned her head into his shoulder and fought back the tears.

"Hey." His hand was gentle on her hair. "I'm not going to let them hurt you."

He spoke so certainly, as if it were an obvious, established fact. As if he truly were in control of their situation. Oddly enough, that made her smile. The urge to cry faded. "I'm okay. My head isn't pounding so much." She lifted it. "There's a cot," she said, surprised to make out its outlines in a dark cranny well away from the door.

"Yes. It's bolted to the floor, or I would have pulled it over here."

"Why..." Her voice drifted off as she answered her own question. The rocky ceiling was very low over the cot. If Alex had lain her there she would have woken, dazed and frightened, to darkness and rock bearing down on her.

Instead, he'd chosen to sit on the floor and hold her here, near the low entry, where there was light and the ceiling wasn't so close.

Her heart had chosen well, she thought. She'd waited all her life for the right man, and he had been worth waiting for. If only...

"Listen," he said, his voice very low. "They're going to come for me soon. I don't think this place is bugged—I checked out every inch while I was waiting for you to wake up. But there are directional devices that don't require a transmitter. It's possible they could hear...there are things I can't tell you."

She nodded uncertainly. Did he want to know that she wouldn't give him away? Fear ghosted over her when she thought of what might lie ahead. "I understand."

"Probably you don't, not really, but I can't say more. I want you to remember two things, even if you don't understand: I won't let them hurt you. And I'll come back to you. I promise."

Again, she nodded—though she didn't understand, not at all. After being so careful not to offer her promises he couldn't keep, now he promised the impossible. He couldn't keep them from hurting her. And he couldn't guarantee that he would come back to her.

She laid her head against his shoulder and worked hard at living only in the moment, this moment, with Alex's heartbeat steady and comforting beneath her ear, his arms warm and solid around her.

A few minutes later, two guards, one robed and one in western clothing, came and took Alex away at gunpoint.

As soon as he stepped outside their cell, Alex pushed all thoughts of Nora from his mind. He had to. He couldn't be the person he needed to be—the criminal who had engineered the theft of the arms from El Hawy—if he let himself worry about what she was thinking and feeling and fearing.

Both guards were armed; both kept a safe distance, and held their weapons at the ready. They were being careful with him. It was a compliment of sorts, since he didn't even have shoes or a belt, much less a weapon. Their captors had taken all the extras from them—jackets, shoes, his wallet and watch, as well as the obvious things like his knife, gun and backpack. But they hadn't stripped them completely, which was something of a surprise. Nudity could be an important psychological weapon. Sooner or later, he supposed, they would use it.

His guards gestured for him to sit on a chair in the center of the room. This chamber was, as he'd told Nora, much larger than their cell; crates lining one wall had lettering in the Cyrillic alphabet, and rudely-built shelves held large rounds of cheese and other foodstuffs. He looked the room over carefully, noting the exits, the behavior of his guards, the lighting.

They tied him securely to the chair. He wasn't surprised when Jawhar walked into the room, using the nearest of the three entries.

The terrorist leader was a small man, all bone and sinew and sharp angles, as if the fires of his fanaticism had burned away his flesh. A scar bisected one of his eyebrows and ran in a straight line up into his hairline. His beard was dark, his teeth very white when he smiled at Alex. "I am pleased to meet with you, *ya beyh* Bok."

"The pleasure is all yours, I assure you. You've made it difficult to avoid accepting your hospitality."

"Ah, yes. You Americans love to make jokes of everything, do you not? But some things are not so funny. I know you are working with that dog, Farid, who has stolen something that belongs to me. Whatever part you played in that—"

"The part of a businessman. You might say that I am a rival of Simon's. I prefer that the profit on those arms be mine, not his."

The tightening around Jawhar's eyes confirmed Alex's guesses about Simon. "Businessmen must be practical. Why not save yourself a great deal of pain and tell me where the weapons are? I will pay you well for the information."

"I am not such a fool. You will kill me once you have no more use for me."

Jawhar studied his face a moment. "It is the nature of most men to cling to life. You may learn in the next few days that death can be a blessing. But we will try something else first." He gestured at the man standing next to him, who advanced on Alex and shoved up the sleeve of his shirt. He had a hypodermic.

Alex didn't allow himself to react when the man jabbed the needle in, but he felt a flicker of hope mixed with fear. This might not be as painful as he'd expected. Not this first time, at least.

SPEAR did everything possible to protect its agents. He was conditioned to resist the effects of some drugs; whether he would be proof against this one he wouldn't know until it took effect.

If he wasn't, he and Nora would be dead within the hour.

Coolness spread under his skin as the drug seeped into his system. "I am surprised that a good Muslim such as yourself would make such frequent use of drugs."

Jawhar shrugged. "Allah is merciful, and so must his followers be. There are many ways to make a man talk, but I do not approve of cruelty for its own sake. This is the easiest way to learn what I need to know, and will cause you less pain."

Whatever they'd stuck him with, it acted fast. Already Alex felt woozy, disconnected. At the same time, his senses sharpened. He smelled the oil burning in the lamps, the musty scent of underground, the sweat on the bodies of his captors.

Jawhar's pores were very large, he noticed. Large and dirty. "You need a bath," he observed, blinking. The lights seemed very bright.

Jawhar nodded, satisfied rather than offended. "He rambles. The drug is working. Tell me now about the arms Farid Ibn Kareem stole from us, Alex Bok."

"Arms..." In a fragmenting world, Alex's mind floated, disconnected, his senses as keen as his brain was fuzzy. His senses, yes, that was the key, drift in that direction, not the other...he smelled something....

"The arms. Where are they?"

"Arms. Shoulders...arm*pits*," he said firmly. "You smell bad."

That was the first time they hit him. But not the last.

Nora heard it all. She sat on the cold stone near the slatted door and listened. Though they'd taken Alex out of her range of vision, they hadn't gone far. She was able to hear every question asked, every rambling response. Every blow.

She heard them bringing him back after what seemed a very long time. Somewhere out of sight, a man complained in Arabic too idiomatic for her to follow. *"It can't be helped,"* another voice said. *"First they talk, then they sleep. He will have to..."* She couldn't make out the rest of it.

The guards stopped in front of the door and commanded her to get back. She obeyed. They unlocked the door and pushed Alex inside.

He had to bend over to make it through the low doorway. One of the guards gave him another shove and he stumbled, nearly falling, then straightened with a groan.

She hurried to him. He was shaking.

"Alex," she said, putting her arms around him, steadying him. "Come sit down."

"'S'all right. Can't talk right, though. My mind's all...the drug."

"I know. Do you hurt anywhere? They hit you."

"Not bad." A hard shiver traveled up him. "Cold, though. Cold in here to you, Nora?"

"Come lie down." She urged him toward the cot. "You'll have to duck your head."

He set his feet and refused to move, though he swayed like a sapling in a high wind. "You don't like it there. Too...little."

"I'll like it fine if you're there." Cajoling him, tugging on him, she got Alex over to the cot, where he lay down with a sigh of relief. She started to turn, bent awkwardly to avoid the low ceiling. They would need the one blanket their captors had spared them, and it was near the door.

His hand closed on her wrist with surprising strength. "You're going away."

"No, I'm not." She smoothed his forehead. "I'm going to get the blanket, then I'll be back."

"Lie down with me."

"Yes." She blinked back tears. "I'll lie with you."

When she came back to spread the blanket over him, he'd managed to roll onto his side, leaving her a narrow space beside him. His eyes were closed, but as soon as she lay down, his arm went around her and cuddled her close.

"Warm," he murmured, "very warm, Nora."

She closed her eyes and tried to sleep, but she was tense and not at all sleepy. After all, she'd slept for several hours under the influence of the drug they'd shot her with.

Her eyes came open again.

Nora was brave enough, ordinarily. But this situation was far from ordinary. They were in the hands of people who put no limits on what they would do for their cause. She couldn't keep herself from wondering, there in the smothering dark, whether they would take her into the other room and tie her up, too. And drug her. And hit her.

Nora tried to push all the possibilities from her mind. She tried to think about the dig. What would Tim do when he discovered she was missing?

But that subject was little better, for it led her mind back to the idea that she would never see Tim again, never finish excavating her tunnel. Maybe never see the stars again, or run in the dust and gravel of a wadi's twisting bed while the sun eased up over a jagged horizon, painting the sky in the bright, clear colors of morning.

Alex had promised he would come back to her, and he had. He'd also promised he wouldn't let them hurt her. She thought it was a lie, one given for the best of reasons, to ease her fear. But maybe not. Maybe they wouldn't hurt her. She didn't know anything, and in their eyes she was only a woman, of little importance.

They would hurt *him,* though.

She'd heard their questions, heard the smack of flesh against flesh when they hit him. He'd rambled, sounding incoherent much of the time, but he'd never given himself away as being other than they thought him—a man who trafficked in illegal arms. Somehow, he'd withheld the information they wanted. After a while, the drug had made him sleepy and they'd had to stop. But they would come for him again. And again. Until he told them where the arms shipment was.

And then, she supposed, they would kill him.

She shivered and eased a tiny bit closer to him.

The rocky ceiling seemed to be pressing down on her. She made herself close her eyes again and concentrate on how warm her back felt, with Alex's body pressed all along hers. His arm was warm, too, and heavy where it was draped over her waist. He was breathing slowly, easily. She tried to match her breathing to his, courting the peace of sleep.

It was a long time before she found that elusive escape, however.

Dreams stirred Nora's sleep, a jumble of images that broke and changed and changed again, until one image held.

She was lost, wandering alone in a strange land of rock

and darkness—lost, but searching for something. For Alex. Something terrible followed her. Killers, she realized. She had to find Alex. She ran, but they ran, too, getting closer, closer—

Caught! Trapped because she couldn't see which way to go when the darkness suddenly thickened and swirled around her, tripping her. Terror. She fought, but hands grabbed her and moved her and put her beneath a stone, a huge, heavy stone pressing down on her, crushing her, driving the breath from her lungs—

"Nora. Nora, it's all right. Wake up."

Her eyes flew open—to darkness. Complete and smothering, like the darkness in her dream, like the stone. Stone above her, unseen in the crushing darkness but she knew it was there, pressing down on her, stealing her breath.

"Shh, sweetheart, it's all right."

Alex's voice. His hands, stroking her face, her hair, turning her toward him. "You were dreaming," he murmured. "Just a dream."

He was warm and solid and she clung to him. But she couldn't see him, not the dimmest outline of his shape. Nothing. And the dream was real—pursuit and capture and stone pressing down on her, terrible men who would hurt Alex, who would... Nora bit back a whimper, ashamed of her terror, unable to shut it off. "I can't see."

"They put out the lamps in the other room. That's all. I heard some of them talking—it's night now."

Of course it was dark—black as it only can be underground, shut away from every source of light. Nora squeezed her eyes closed, trying to pretend the darkness was of her own making. But it continued to press against her eyelids like a weight, like the weight of all that stone above her.

She trembled. "I'm sorry. I—I can't seem to stop."

"You're scared." He stroked her hair again. "Of course you're scared. How could you not be?"

"You aren't."

"Sure I am. I've had more practice at hiding it, that's all."

Her heart still pounded madly, but her breathing was steadying. "I don't *like* being underground."

"I know." He pressed a kiss to her cheek. His breath was warm and moist. "You'll be okay in a minute."

"Are *you* okay? The drug..." She touched his cheek, finding beard stubble. "They hit you."

"They weren't serious about it. Just a few slaps to get my attention."

As her panic eased, she became aware of other things. The way his legs and hers were tangled together. The warmth that came from his body, like the heat of a stove, only better. A human heat. The beat of his heart—a little rapid, like hers.

How close his lips were, only a breath away from hers in the darkness.

Without thinking, she closed that distance.

Alex froze when Nora's lips brushed his. *Comfort,* he thought. She wants comfort. He would give her what she needed, but...

But her lips were so soft, and he ached so badly. He'd woken from his drugged sleep some time ago and lain awake, his fears every bit as strong as hers. Not fear of the dark, no, but of failure. Of the pain that he knew was coming.

Of loss. He'd had her such a short time. To lose her so soon...but she was here now, warm and alive. Her fingers were tender on the nape of his neck, drawing little circles, and she sighed with pleasure when he returned her kiss.

Though he'd thought the drug gone from his system, his

mind still wasn't working right. He could think only of Nora—the scent of her, the softness of her cheek when he skimmed his lips across it. When she arched against him, pressing her breasts to his chest, the shock of desire made his hand fist in her loosened hair.

He had to stop now, while he could.

He buried his face against her neck. Her breath was hurried, like his. He tasted the rapid pulse of her throat once, just once, then turned his head resolutely aside. "I can't...Nora, I can't just kiss you. Not now."

"I don't want just a kiss."

Need burned in his belly. "This is the wrong time, the wrong place, but dear God, how I wish it wasn't."

"The only time we ever have is now." Her hands clenched in his shirt. "I want you *now,* Alex."

He should ask her if she was sure. He should wait, hold her, give her a chance to get over the nightmare that had driven her from sleep and bore all too close a resemblance to reality.

He couldn't. He needed her too much.

Gently, then, he kissed her again, pressing a kiss to each eyelid, closing them so the darkness wouldn't weigh on her. How he wished for light so he could see her face, her body. But as she'd said, they had only now, this moment.

It was enough. More than enough.

He raised himself up on one elbow, making room for her to shift onto her back. Somehow he knew, even before his lips met hers once more, that she was smiling. *Sweet Nora, smiling for me in the midst of darkness...*

He lifted his head, his heart pounding out a primitive rhythm, and cupped her breast. Her T-shirt was little enough barrier between his palm and the soft swell he held.

"I would very much like to get you naked," he whispered, nuzzling her neck. "But you might not want to do that...here. They're shorthanded, from what I overheard, so there's no guard posted in the storeroom at night.'' Nor any need for one. The door was crude but sturdy, and the lock on it worked all too well. ''But—''

She interrupted him silently and firmly. He felt her reach for the hem of her T-shirt and tug it off over her head. Then her hands pulled at his shirt

''Naked is good,'' she whispered. ''As long as you are, too.''

They undressed—themselves, each other, their hands distracting and becoming distracted by every new inch of flesh uncovered. Then they were skin to skin, sigh to sigh. She was curious. Though she hadn't told him how new this was to her, he knew. But even if he hadn't, he might have guessed from the eager, uncertain explorations of her hands and mouth.

He lavished attention on her breasts, savoring her low moan when he licked and sucked there, telling her with lips and tongue how perfect she was. How right.

Heat built quickly, a rising, rushing tide of delight that carried Alex into a place where past and future alike vanished. There was only passion. Only now. Only Nora.

The cot was narrow, the ceiling close and the air chilly. It didn't matter. She was beneath him, her taste in his mouth, her hands urgent and her breath breaking as he slid his hand between her legs and found her heat.

Her body responded instantly, but her voice was soft and shy. ''Alex, I—I don't have much experience. Well—none, actually. Not with this.''

Now she mentioned it. He smiled. ''I hope you don't think I'm going to be noble and stop.''

Her laugh was unsteady. He felt its vibrations in the flesh he caressed. ''Don't you dare.''

He kissed her long and deep, and while his tongue was in her mouth he positioned himself. And pushed inside.

Nora was an active, athletic woman. There was no barrier.

Hot velvet closing around him as he eased into her. He groaned. She laced her fingers into his hair and said his name, and said yes, *yes, Alex, yes.*

Yes. With one firm thrust, he seated himself fully. And stopped, overwhelmed by feelings strong and shimmering and new.

Warmth. It flooded him, reaching every part of him, body and soul. He was inside Nora, yet she was in him, too. Part of him. "Nora," he gasped, but he had no words for what he was feeling. "Nora!"

"I'm here." She ran her hands along his back, soothing him. As if she *knew*. He should have been comforting her, but she was the one to offer comfort.

And more. "I'm right here, Alex," she whispered, her fingers making magic on his skin. "I love you."

He shuddered. And began to move. Physical need took over, the ancient, compelling rhythm. He tried to be careful of her, fought not to let his own need master him. He moved in her gently, touched and caressed her, aching to bring her as much pleasure as she was giving him. And he had his reward when she cried out, her body arching beneath him just before climax grabbed him and shook him in its delirious fist, then set him free.

Nora lay smiling in the darkness, cradled in her lover's arms. Alex's chest rose and fell beneath her head, and his fingers stirred her hair idly. "What are you thinking about?" he asked softly.

"Thunder," she said drowsily. "And stars going nova."

He ran his hand down her spine, raising slow, sleepy

tingles. "Make that supernova, for me. Nora—" he hesitated "—I don't have the words. I'm all jumbled up inside."

She knew which words she wanted to hear. Yet she was oddly content, even without them. Maybe he didn't know how to say it, but she *felt* loved. Wholly, truly loved. "Is it a good jumble?"

"A very happy jumble."

"That's all right, then."

He didn't answer right away, but he kept touching her—her arm, her back, her hair. "I've made a mess of your braid," he said after a moment. "It's come loose."

He sounded pleased with himself. She smiled. "I guess I'll forgive you this time."

He sighed. "We should get dressed."

She nestled closer. "Not yet," she whispered. She didn't want to think about where they were, or why they needed to be dressed. She didn't want to lose the glow of happiness that covered her more warmly than the blanket he'd drawn up over them.

"We don't want to fall asleep like this."

No, they didn't. She didn't know what to expect of the coming day, but it wouldn't be good, and she didn't want to start it by being found naked by their captors. Nora made herself sit up and reach under the cot, where they'd stashed their clothes. Not that it had occurred to her in the fever of the moment to be careful of where her things landed when she pulled them off, but he had thought of it.

They dressed in the darkness, then lay down with him spooned around her so they would both fit on the narrow cot.

It occurred to her that she wasn't afraid. Oh, a little bit, yes, but she was getting better at not letting the future, short and terrible as it was likely to be, intrude on the present moment. But this moment included the same total darkness and cramped space that had panicked her earlier.

It didn't bother her now. Not anymore. Alex had filled the darkness so full of him, the terror was gone. With a sigh, she closed her eyes.

Sleep came easily, and without dreams.

Chapter 14

They came for him the next morning.

At least, Nora assumed it was morning. First there was a light—a single oil lamp, she thought, carried by one of the guards into the room outside their cell, its flickering beam reaching them only as a slight lessening of the darkness. Then she heard voices, and more lamps were lit, their light stealing between the slats of the door to build a murky half-light in the cell.

Soon after that, the same two guards who had taken Alex to be questioned last night brought them bread and hard cheese and water.

Some time later they returned and took Alex away at gunpoint.

They didn't bother with drugs this time. This time, they beat him.

After a while she covered her ears, but that was worse somehow. Nora sat on the stony ground near the door with tears running down her cheeks, feeling more helpless than she ever had in her life, while they hurt him and hurt him.

Again he told them nothing, though he made sounds sometimes—harsh, ugly sounds of pain. He said something once, when one of them told him to make it easy on himself, about not being eager to die, and Nora understood then. They would kill Alex—and her, too, she supposed—once they learned what they wanted.

What would they do if he never told them anything? How much more would they hurt him?

She shuddered and pushed that thought away.

At last she heard one of their captors—the one who seemed to be in charge—say impatiently to take him back to the cell. She hurriedly wiped her eyes and cheeks dry and moved away from the door.

This time, when they shoved him into the cell he fell. And stayed down.

She was at his side immediately. "Oh, God. Alex." She brushed his hair out of his face and saw a cut lip and another cut over his cheekbone, but in the poor light couldn't tell how bad they were, or where else he'd been injured. "I don't want to touch the wrong place."

"Mostly my feet. They have—" he winced as he rolled over. She helped him sit. "There are a lot of nerve endings in the feet."

She glanced down at his feet and gasped. They were bare and bloody. The soles were the worst, with the flesh raw and oozing, lacerated by dozens of blows from something thin and hard. Welts and cuts crisscrossed the top of his feet, too.

How had he walked on them at all? She swallowed bile. "Maybe you'd better crawl to the cot. I don't think you should walk on them at all. I can—"

"I don't want to lie down, Nora. Let's sit together over by the door."

"I don't mind the closeness of the rock over there anymore, Alex. Truly."

"I'd rather sit up."

She got the blanket and they sat on it by the door, leaning against the rocky wall, close to each other. She tore one of the sleeves off her T-shirt and used that and some of the water their captors had left them to clean his wounds as well as she could.

They talked. All that morning—if it was morning—they talked.

He wanted to hear about Houston, her sisters, her college days—everything she could think of to tell him about her life until now. And he told her things, too. Though he couldn't say much about his life the last few years, he shared a lot of stories about his childhood.

He told her what had happened when he was fifteen—a terrorist attack on a small village near the Palestine border. He'd been staying there with his best friend for a few weeks before school started again back in the States.

"You probably don't remember the situation in Beirut, the massacre there—that had the world's attention at the time. A minor attack on a small village no one had ever heard of, with no one killed—it didn't make any headlines."

"No one was killed?"

"Five people were injured." He glanced at her, his eyes hard. "Like I said, a very minor incident."

It hadn't been minor to Alex. "Were you hurt?"

"No." He leaned his head against the rock behind them. "My friend was. The bullet lodged near his spine. He was—and is—paralyzed from the waist down." He sighed. "I'd spent so much time in this part of the world. You'd think I would have been aware of the endless, ongoing tragedies wrought by violence, but I wasn't. Not really."

"We don't feel things deeply until they affect us personally, I guess. Especially not at fifteen."

"Everything changed for me after that. My parents didn't understand. I was so angry...I think they'd absorbed some of the fatalism of the Muslim attitude. *Inshallah Allah.* These things happen. It is very sad, but we must go on." He paused. "I couldn't just go on."

"You went on, but in a different direction. Not one your folks understood, maybe?"

"No. Until then, I'd been as fascinated as they were with digging up stories from the past. Well...almost as fascinated." He grinned. "I was fifteen. Other things took priority at times, like girls. But after that...I couldn't make archaeology my life's work the way they had."

Instead he'd grown up into a young man who wanted to put a stop to terrorism, and had eventually been recruited into this mysterious agency of his. She wished she could ask him about that—how he'd become involved, what it was like, and whether his work for that agency was still the most important thing in the world to him. But she couldn't. Not when their captors might overhear.

She squeezed his hand instead. "You found your own direction. Or made it."

"I—" He turned his head, then held up a hand for silence.

She heard the others' voices now, too. Two of El Hawy's members had come into the storeroom to get something. They were joking and complaining the way, she supposed, soldiers do everywhere.

At first she assumed Alex didn't want the men to hear what he and she were saying. Then she realized he was listening intently. Nora listened, too, but heard nothing startling or useful until they were leaving. One of them complained about the American *ziboon,* which Nora thought meant customer or client. The other told him harshly to shut up—they weren't to mention that one, ever.

The two of them finished their task silently and left.

Nora looked questioningly at Alex. He shook his head slightly and asked her something about her oldest sister, and she took the hint and started talking again.

He grew quieter after a while, and she knew the pain must be dragging at him. But he seemed to want her to keep talking, so she did. It was an odd place to find intimacy, but that day was every bit as intimate, in its way, as their lovemaking had been the night before. As they sat in their cell awaiting pain or death, they built another world to spend those hours in. A shared world of memories.

When voices grew hoarse and memories faltered, they simply sat there, shoulders touching, holding hands. Together.

Alex lay awake in the silent darkness and tried not to think about the pain. It was an impossible task, of course. The pain was bad. He wondered if there was an infection setting into some of the cuts.

He'd almost been able to forget for a while, though, when he and Nora made love again. He smiled slightly, and lifted a hand to stroke her hair—lightly, so he wouldn't awaken her. She'd been hesitant, fearing to hurt him, until he explained that when he was loving her he could push everything else aside. Then she'd been tender, and eager, and beautifully giving.

She shifted slightly in her sleep and Alex tensed, then relaxed when her foot didn't touch his. Ah, God, but they hurt.

How much longer? How long would he have to hold out? Today's beating had been bad. His feet were swollen, impossible to walk on, exquisitely painful.

Tomorrow's session would be worse.

Alex wasn't guessing about that. Jawhar had explained it to him. He supposed he was lucky the terrorist leader was so rigid about his peculiar morality: torture was acceptable for the cause, but only in the degree required to accomplish a necessary end. Alex wasn't to be hurt more than was needed to break him. The pain, the amount of sheer physical damage, would increase in severity every day, until he broke—or Jawhar ran out of time.

Which would happen when the mysterious Simon arrived.

Simon had to be the one, Alex thought. The traitor he was here to find, and stop. Alex had learned a surprising amount by eavesdropping on his guards. They were shorthanded because most of Jawhar's soldiers were out searching for the missing arms. The men seemed nervous, even scared, of the American who would be arriving soon. Of the consequences if they didn't have the arms that the man had bought.

Alex hoped Simon would arrive soon. He couldn't act until then. Until then, he would have to live with beatings and pain and Nora's anxious grief.

She'd tried to hide her tears from him, but even in the poor light he'd seen the dampness on her cheeks and the pain on her face. He hated that. But otherwise—otherwise, in spite of the pain, in a strange way he was happy. Or content, at least, with moments of real joy. And peace.

Because of Nora. Because he could lie here with the sweet weight of her curled up half on top of him, sharing the tiny cot and the warmth of their bodies. Lie here and listen to her slow, even breathing, and remember the perfection of their lovemaking.

Funny. He'd thought it was death he feared. Only now, with Nora's warmth beside him, inside him, did he understand. With understanding came peace.

He'd been cold for years. So cold, and so alone. And so unaware, because both conditions had gradually become normal.

He hadn't feared dying but dying *alone.* A cold fate, yes, but not the worst, since in a sense everyone died alone. And even that wasn't all of it. The fear that had broken into his sleep as nightmares and dogged his waking hours had come from his memory of giving up. With death pulling at him, his body in shock and his mind sucked down into a cold, helpless place, dying alone had seemed no more terrible than continuing to live alone.

But now—

What was that? Light, faint but gradually brightening. Growing nearer. It couldn't be morning yet, but they were about to receive visitors. At least, he was. Random brutality was more effective than questioning that took place at predictable times. A prisoner broke faster if he never had a space of time when he felt safe.

He tensed against the ordeal to come.

But what came was worse, far worse, than he'd expected. He was sitting up, ready to try to walk on feet that were raw and bloody, when the door to their cell opened.

"Both of you will come out now," Jawhar said.

And Alex knew he'd run out of time.

The flood of pure, physical fear Nora felt when the terrorist leader insisted that she, too, was to leave the cell shamed her. Alex's arm tightened around her. "Remember what I said," he told her urgently, then called out in Arabic, "I'm afraid our conversation earlier has left me unable to walk. You'll have to send someone to carry me out."

"I am not such a fool. If you cannot walk, then crawl. But both of you must come, and quickly, or Mohammed will shoot the woman."

Alex looked at her, his expression unreadable. "I'd rather go out upright," he said. "If you'd help me—?"

So she put her arms around him and took as much of his weight as she could, and the two of them moved slowly, haltingly, to the door. His breath caught with every step he was forced to take.

The lights in the other room seemed very bright, after so long in dimness. The terrorist leader—for so he must be, Nora thought, from the way the others deferred to him—came as a surprise. He looked small and insignificant…until she saw his eyes.

They burned with something like madness. "You will take me to where the arms are hidden now. Tonight," he said brusquely in Arabic. "You will take me there, or your woman will watch while you are questioned. Then you will watch while my men do to her everything that is done to you. And then she will die."

"You make war on women now, Jawhar?" Alex's voice was grim.

"You force me to it."

The two men stared at each other for a long moment. Nora's heart was pounding so hard she thought they must be able to hear it. She was terrified of the coming pain. And of failing Alex. They mustn't know he was an agent. If she spoke at all, she might give away what had to remain unsaid. She would have to be silent, utterly silent, but dear God, she didn't know if she could do it.

Hearing them hurt him had been bad enough. Watching them do it—

"All right," Alex said suddenly. "I will tell you, but—"

"Alex, no!"

He smiled at her—an achingly sweet, real smile. "It's all right, Nora." He faced Jawhar again. "I have conditions."

"You are in no position to bargain."

Alex's eyebrow went up. "Am I not? You are suddenly in a great hurry. If you must find the arms soon, then I do have something to bargain with."

Jawhar's narrow face tightened further. "What conditions?"

"Well, first I'd like to sit down."

The man laughed. "Very well. Bring the chair," he told one of his men. "And? Your other condition?"

"The woman goes free. Unharmed, and free."

"No. That is not possible. I will agree not to kill her." He shrugged. "I prefer not to kill women, even shameless western women. And there is a market for such beauty as hers."

A market? Slavery? Nora wasn't sure if she'd understood. Some of the words were strange to her, and her head felt so light, as if she weren't entirely there....

"She goes free, or we don't deal."

"You would have me believe you'd rather see her bloody and broken than sold to some old man who will likely use her kindly once she learns her place?" Jawhar shook his head. "Enough. Bring the ropes, Gamal, and ready your blade."

Gamal? Nora's eyes widened. She hadn't noticed the other men, but, oh, God, Gamal was there. He was one of them. Simple, talkative Gamal. It added another note of horror to a situation already steeped in it.

"Wouldn't you?" Alex said coolly. "If she were your woman, would you not prefer to see her dead than so shamed?"

"You have not the wisdom to understand this."

"I've lived in Egypt half my life. Don't tell me what I understand. If the woman doesn't go free, we have no deal. And you know I can hold out," he added conversationally. "Not forever, but perhaps longer than you can afford to wait."

Jawhar scowled. He turned half-around, paced away two steps, turned back. "She will summon the army."

"What, so that your tame captain can shoot me instead of you?" Alex turned to Nora, still speaking Arabic. "You aren't to call the army. Do you understand? I am serious, Nora. This is important."

Confused, aching, she nodded.

"Very well," Jawhar said. "We have a deal."

Alex made them treat his feet. He would be walking a lot, he said, and the pain would make him slow. So one of them used a syringe to inject painkiller under what remained of the skin on his soles, over and over, the way the doctor had done when Nora was twelve and had to have stitches in her forearm. They gave him bandages, too, and sandals.

Then they blindfolded her. They didn't blindfold Alex, and she knew what that meant—they weren't afraid of his learning the location of their base because they intended to kill him.

Her heart was breaking. "Alex," she said when he took her arm. "Please, there has to be some other way. You can't give up the arms, and I—" *I can't bear for you to die. Oh, my love, don't make me leave you to die.*

One of the terrorists growled at her to shut up.

"Shh." Alex squeezed her hand. "Trust me. Remember what I promised, Nora. Remember."

That he wouldn't let them hurt her? *Oh, Alex, better that hurt than this one.* But she didn't speak again as he led her, blind and terrified of what was going to happen to him, in the wake of their captors.

They walked for what seemed a long time, trending gradually upwards, turning now and then. She thought they remained in the caves. There was no dirt beneath her sock-clad feet, none of the scraps of vegetation she would have stepped on outside. Finally Alex stopped her.

"This is it," he said, his voice very low.

"Quickly," one of the others said—Jawhar, she thought.

"I will say goodbye," Alex told him in Arabic, then switched to English. "Listen. I don't think he understands English, and Gamal isn't close enough to hear me. When you get to camp—"

"Is—is that where we are?"

"Speak Arabic," Jawhar commanded.

Alex switched to that language. "I'll see you safely in camp before I lead them anywhere. When you get there, I want you to call my parents."

"Your parents?" Disbelief made her forget to speak Arabic. She was rewarded with a slap from one of the guards on the back of her head.

Alex's fingers tightened on her arm. "Yes. Their number is in memory on my cellular phone." He had to use the English words for that; there was no Arabic equivalent. "1-2-3. That's all you have to remember. Punch in 1-2-3 and tell my parents what has happened to me. Tell them about the preacher not showing up on time to marry us. Tell them everything."

The preacher? Her head spun. "A-all right, but—"

"Nora." She felt his hand on her cheek beneath the blindfold. "I love you."

Her heart stumbled. "I love you. Alex—" But hands, hard, strange hands, tore her out of his grasp and propelled her forward. She was pushed around some unseen corner and forced to move forward by those hands.

Then, his voice fainter with distance, he called out one more thing. "Remember my promise, Nora!"

There wasn't a wisp of cloud in the sky tonight. Thousands of stars blazed overhead as Alex watched Nora leave her captors behind.

He stood, flanked by men with guns trained on him, very near the entrance to El Hawy's base that he'd searched for, for so long. It was a tall, narrow fissure in a rocky cut near the spot where he and Nora had been shot with anesthetic darts. The entrance was even better camouflaged by the surrounding rock than the one to Nora's cave. He'd walked past it on one of his nighttime excursions.

It was also chillingly close to Nora's camp. From where he stood, he could see the main tent, glowing with artificial light. He watched until he saw Nora stumble into that welcoming light.

Tim was there—he would take care of her now. Alex had done all he could. Nora was safe, and though he saw no way now to capture the traitor, he still hoped to complete part of his mission.

He turned to Jawhar. "Very well. You have kept your part of the deal. I will take you to the arms now."

Nora was running by the time she reached the tents. Ahmed saw her and shouted something, and Tim came running out of the main tent. He grabbed her and hugged her. "My God, Nora, I've been so worried. First you and Bok disappeared, then Gamal, and that bloody fool of a captain doesn't seem to be doing anything—where have you been? Are you okay?"

She pushed him aside. "Later. I'll explain later. I've got to get Alex's phone."

"What?"

There was no light in Alex's tent, of course. She shivered as she shoved the flap back, finding the emptiness of his quarters ominous. Tim was right on her heels, questions tripping over themselves as he tried to find out what she was doing, where she'd been, where Alex was, if she knew why Gamal had disappeared.

"Not now," she said again. She prayed she'd understood what Alex wanted—and that it would make a difference. That there was some chance he could keep his promise. The second promise.

I'll come back to you.

His phone was easy to find, even in the darkness—right on the small table by his cot. She grabbed it and carried it at a run back towards the main tent, where there was light enough to read the dial.

One. Two. Three. She punched the numbers in, and waited.

Surely this wasn't really his parents' number. Surely he'd told her to call for some other reason than to tell the Boks their son was about to be killed. Surely—

"Yes?"

The crisp male voice was unfamiliar. "Is this Franklin Bok?"

"Who is this?" he snapped.

"Nora. Nora Lowe. Alex told me to call. He said to

punch 1-2-3 into his cell phone and—and tell you everything. Are you—"

"Never mind who I am. Where's Alex Bok?"

Please, God, let this be one of his agency's people. "The terrorists have him. El Hawy. They hurt him. They were going to hurt me, too, and he—" She stopped, not wanting to say the rest. But Alex had said to tell everything. He'd asked her to trust him. "He said to tell you that the preacher never arrived. And he—he's leading the terrorists to where the arms are stashed."

Alex hadn't lied about having a lot of walking to do. Moving on feet he couldn't feel was a clumsy business, but better by far than trying to walk without the drug-induced numbness.

Fortunately, the painkiller had lasted until they reached their present vantage point—a rise overlooking a Quonset hut in the middle of nowhere. But the numbness was almost gone now. Alex lay on the ground beside the terrorist leader and wondered if he'd be able to stand on his feet, much less move quickly, when the time came.

Jawhar was no fool. Once Alex had led them to the hut, he'd settled his men and himself to wait and watch while the rest of his men, those who had been out searching for the arms, converged on the spot. He was confident that, even if there was a trap, he would prevail.

He had reason for his confidence. Jawhar knew Farid for his enemy, and he knew his enemies well; he knew how many men Farid commanded, and it was far less than he himself would hurl at those in the hut. He would lose some of his people in retaking the weapons, but that troubled him not at all. Soldiers who died in such a glorious cause would surely be taken directly to paradise.

The waiting was hard for Alex. Had Nora called the

number he gave her? Had Merrick believed her? Alex had delayed their arrival here as long as he could without making Jawhar suspicious, but had it been long enough?

One of Jawhar's men ghosted up and reported in a low voice. All but those who had been too far away to assemble quickly were in place now.

The terrorist leader's exultation was obvious even in the darkness. Jawhar might talk a good story about not giving unnecessary pain, but the truth was he lived for this. The fighting. The killing. He would enjoy massacring his enemies, and praise himself for a godly man while he did it.

"And now," Jawhar murmured, "you will play your part, Bok."

"I am not eager for it." Jawhar wanted Alex to cross the open expanse between the rise where they waited and the hut, drawing attention away from the bulk of El Hawy's soldiers who were massed behind the hut, waiting for their leader's signal to attack.

"But you will do it, hoping to alert those inside the hut, perhaps even to save yourself."

Yes, he would. It was the only chance he would have. Even if everything had gone right, Alex's chances for survival were poor.

He didn't want to die.

The thought brought fierce determination, however, not fear. He wanted to live. Nora was waiting for him to fulfill his promise.

"Up," Jawhar said, prodding Alex with the muzzle of his rifle.

"The medicine has worn off. I don't know if I can stand."

"Then I will shoot you here."

Since Jawhar intended to shoot him anyway—it would be the signal to the rest of his men—Alex wasn't much impressed with the threat. But between being shot now and being shot later, he chose later. Even if it was only a matter of moments.

He pushed painfully to his feet, then swayed at the sudden onslaught of pain.

Jawhar gestured with his rifle again. "Move."

Alex took a single step.

"*Inshallah Allah!*" cried Farid's voice—from behind them.

Jawhar swung half-around as a shot blasted the stillness. Alex caught a split-second glimpse of the terrorist's wide, surprised eyes and the hole drilled neatly between them even as more shots rang out.

A slug tore through his leg as he fell and rolled. He grabbed Jawhar's rifle from dead hands and sought a target while the night exploded with gunfire, tracer rounds lighting up the darkness like macabre fireworks—rounds coming from *behind* the terrorists.

Nora had made the call. And Merrick and his friends had, indeed, been standing by, just as Jonah had promised.

Alex got one of the terrorists in his sights and squeezed off a shot, then another—but though they were spread out, awaiting the signal to attack below, there were so many of them, all around him.

Too many.

Another bullet struck him high in the back. He felt it as a blow. He kept firing, but his hands quickly grew weak, and the starry night no longer gave enough light.

Then the pain hit—huge, mastering, overwhelming. His rifle slipped from limp hands. The darkness spun up, swift and swirling, grabbing at him even more fiercely than it had that night in the Negev.

This time, though, he fought it.

* * *

"Dr. Lowe?"

Nora started. The man had melted out of the darkness—one moment no one was there, the next he stood a few yards away. He was dressed all in black. Even his face was blackened—a hard face, his striking blue eyes the only lightness in either color or expression. He carried a rifle slung over his shoulder.

She stood, slowly, every muscle taut from the long hours of waiting—three full hours, counted off second by painful second. "Yes," she said slowly, "I'm Nora Lowe."

Tim rose with her, scowling furiously. He'd waited with her, sitting at the picnic table in front of the main tent. "Who the bloody hell are you?"

"A friend of Alex's." The man responded, flicking Tim a glance. He then addressed Nora. "It's best if we speak privately."

"If you like." Fear churned sickly in her stomach. "But I'm afraid Tim overheard me when I called that number, so he knows something of what's been happening." And she'd had the devil of a time keeping Tim from calling the Egyptian army. In the end, she'd disabled the radio phone to keep him from doing the logical thing.

"Very well. I'm sorry you've had to wait. Things have been...busy. Alex had arranged for some of our people to join Farid Ibn Kareem's men once they received his signal—which you gave us. They arrived in time to catch the terrorists in a pincer movement. There was a stiff firefight, but it didn't last long. Our people are good."

"But what about Alex? Is he all right?" *Why wasn't he here, telling her this himself?*

"He was hit," the man said gently. "In his leg, and in the back."

The world spun. She grabbed at something to steady

herself—Tim's arm, she realized. "He isn't dead." She said that furiously, as if challenging him to argue with her.

"No, he's not. But he's been airlifted out. I'm afraid he's in critical condition."

Oh, God. Oh, God. "I'll go to him." She let go of Tim and moved closer to the man. "You'll see that I'm taken to him, wherever he is."

"I'm sorry, Dr. Lowe." His voice was very gentle now. "He was conscious until shortly before they took him out in the medevac copter. He was in pain, of course, but he managed to make his wishes clear. He wanted you to know what had happened to him, but you were not to be told where he was, or allowed to see him." He paused. "He said something about a promise, too, but I couldn't make it out. He was...pretty blurry by then."

I won't let them hurt you.

I'll come back to you.

Nora's legs were shaky when she sank onto the bench by the picnic table. The hand she raised to push her hair out of her eyes trembled, too. But her voice was entirely steady. "Then I'll wait for him. He'll be back."

Epilogue

The Sinai, February 27

The sky was messy with stars. Nora tilted her head back and absorbed the peace of that distant splendor, along with the silence and solitude of the night.

She needed both the peace and the solitude. Her days were busy. The tunnel had been cleared over two months ago, revealing a surprising treasure trove—archeological treasure, that is. There had been little gold found, but many rich clues to the past.

Her crew now numbered twelve. Nora had had little trouble extending her leave from the university under the circumstances. Lisa was still part of that crew, but DeLaney was gone, back in class. Just yesterday they'd finished stabilizing the second sarcophagus; it would be shipped to the museum in Cairo tomorrow.

She had a great deal to be thankful for, she reminded

herself. Her life, first of all. Alex had bought that, very nearly at the cost of his own. She had work that mattered. And...her hand curved protectively over her stomach.

And she had the future to look forward to, and dream on.

She had everything except the man she loved.

It had been four months, almost to the day. Four months. She knew he was alive; the reports had come in regularly over the phone. Always the same voice—cool, unaccented, masculine. First she'd been told that Alex was in surgery. Then he was out of surgery and doing "as well as could be expected." That call had been a painful blessing. She'd learned that he was alive, but she'd also heard the extent of his injuries for the first time.

His survival was a miracle, nothing less.

The calls had slowed after that, reporting his progress in terse sentences. Finally, she'd been told that he had been released from the hospital.

That was over two months ago. He hadn't called. She'd tried to find him, even nerving herself to contact his parents, but if they knew where he was, they wouldn't tell her.

He hadn't come to her.

"You shouldn't be out here alone."

She turned, shaking her head ruefully. Tim had grown ridiculously protective ever since she told him about the baby. "There aren't any monsters lurking in the dark, waiting to grab me." Though she'd been afraid, horribly afraid, the first time she'd left the circle of light near the tents.

Once, there had been monsters. Human monsters. And they had grabbed her...and Alex. But Nora had had no intention of letting the fear win. And the voice on the phone had told her she was safe, that she could and should resume a normal life.

Normal. And alone. In spite of her family and her friends, the friends who assured her gently but firmly that she had to stop hoping, she was alone.

"You know I worry about you," Tim said, moving up beside her. "After what happened...I nearly lost you."

She sighed unhappily. Tim had made it clear he didn't believe she would ever see Alex again. Yesterday, he had said he wanted to take Alex's place—in her life, if not her heart. He'd asked her to marry him. "I can't live my life afraid of the shadows."

"You aren't living your life at all. You're waiting for *him.*" Tim put his hands on her shoulders. "It's time to look to the future."

"I am. I do." She looked up at his craggy, earnest face, and wished he didn't care so much, when she could give so little back. Friendship was all she would ever be able to offer him. He insisted that was enough, but she knew better. "I also need a little time alone, now and then," she said gently.

"I hope you're using your time alone to think about what I asked you."

She felt a pang. "Tim, I gave you your answer then. It's not going to change."

"He's not coming back, Nora. You have to stop clinging to this idea—"

"He said he would."

"How can you still believe in a promise made by a professional liar? Maybe Bok meant it for the best. He thought he'd be dead within hours when he told you that. He said what he knew you needed to hear, and maybe that was a kindness at the time. But he's had months to make his promise good—if he was going to."

Nora shook her head. There was no way to explain the nonsense and certainty of her heart to this gentle, reasonable man. Alex had told her to remember his promise. It had been the last thing he'd said. "I'm sorry, Tim," she said, helpless to ease his hurt.

"Well—" he straightened his sagging shoulders "—I'm not giving up, you know. But even if you have the poor sense to keep turning me down, I'll be there for you."

On an impulse, she leaned forward and kissed his cheek. "I know. But you have a life to live, too. I hope you can find someone else you want to spend it with."

He grimaced. "Right. Well—I'll see you in the morning."

"Good night."

She was glad when he left, and felt guilty for her gladness. But it was so good to be alone for a few minutes. Here, with none but the stars to witness, she could dream.

Of Alex. Always of Alex.

He came to her out of the darkness. It was so like her dreams that for a moment she thought she'd slipped wholly into fantasy, and her sudden step backward came from the fear that she'd lost her mind.

He stopped. It was too dark to see his face, and he'd moved awkwardly, not with Alex's sure grace.

Whoever he was, he wasn't Alex. Maybe her nightmares had come true instead of her dreams. She fell back another step, ready to run.

"Nora."

"Alex?" It was his voice—she couldn't be wrong about that. Her own voice sounded distant and lost.

"I was waiting for Gaines to leave. I thought that if you didn't want to see me, it would be easier this way. If you want me to go away..."

Alex. She didn't stop to think, to answer. With a glad cry, she ran to him.

His arms closed around her, steady and sure. "Nora—oh God, I was so afraid. I didn't think you'd want to see me, to listen...careful," he said, when she hugged him tighter. "We could wind up sitting in the dirt rather suddenly." His low chuckle was unsteady. "My leg tends to buckle on me sometimes."

"Your leg." Her fingers went to his face, tracing the lines she knew well. "He said—the man who called—that there was permanent damage."

"Some. I won't need the cane forever, though."

The cane? She hadn't noticed—but there it lay on the sand beside them, silver-bright in the starlight.

That's why he'd moved so awkwardly. "You're all right, though." Her hands traveled over his shoulders, his chest, assuring herself of his reality. "You were so badly hurt—"

"Hey, I'll be running with you again before a year is out. You may find it easier to keep up with me, though, since my leg—well, I lost a fair amount of muscle tissue in the thigh. Of course," he added carefully, "that's assuming you want to run with me."

"I want to kill you!" But she was laughing when she said it. And crying. "I knew you'd come, but—"

"Did you?" His hands tightened on her arms. "Did you believe in me all this time, in spite of everything?"

"Yes."

He kissed her then, and made the stars disappear and re-form inside her. Giddy, whirling stars of passion and joy. "Oh, Alex," she said at last, her head resting on his shoulder, his arms as tight around her as hers were around him. "How could you stay away, and not *tell* me anything?"

"I had to." He said it quietly. "I had to wait until we were sure every member of El Hawy had been accounted for. My cover was blown to hell and gone, and some of them might have wanted revenge. I couldn't be a part of your life unless I was sure I wouldn't bring danger into it."

"Then you do want to be part of my life?" she asked, suddenly shy.

"You're part of mine," he said simply. "Forever."

Happiness shimmered inside her, but it still seemed fragile, more dream than reality after the long months of waiting. "You said you wouldn't have come back, though. Not if you hadn't been sure it was safe."

"Alex Bok couldn't have come to you if every member of El Hawy hadn't been accounted for," he corrected her gently. "Another man—one who looked somewhat like him, but with a different name and a slightly different face—would have. I promised."

Starlight was heady stuff, growing and glowing inside her. But she thought about the baby resting snugly in her womb, and about Alex's job, and the glow dimmed. She would tell him about the baby. Soon. But first she needed to know… "I guess you won't be going on any missions for a while. Not until you finish healing."

"Not ever."

"But…" She lifted her head to search his face. "Because of your cover being blown?"

"No, though that started me thinking. I've done a lot of that, Nora, the last four months, and I've realized that I'm finished with that part of my life. Oh, I might do a favor for a friend now and then. But not often. Working for the agency was the right thing for me for a lot of years, but it isn't right anymore."

He took a deep breath. "I came back because I had a

promise to keep. I want to stay, if you'll let me, because I have some promises still to make.''

''Yes,'' she said. And ''Oh, yes, Alex,'' she said again, just before he kissed her.

* * * * *

Look for Eileen Wilks's exciting new trilogy about three wealthy bachelors who have to get married—Coming in Silhouette Desire in 2001.

And now, here's a sneak preview of HER SECRET WEAPON by Beverly Barton, the next exciting book in A YEAR OF LOVING DANGEROUSLY, available in Intimate Moments next month!

Chapter 1

As an operative for the top-secret SPEAR agency, Burke Lonigan's life was only partially his own. Lonigan's Imports and Exports had been funded by SPEAR and even though Burke's expertise helped maintain the company's extraordinary success, his job required far more from him than simply acting the part of a rich London businessman.

SPEAR's head honcho, a man known only as Jonah, had telephoned Burke late last night, both using cellular phones that possessed special scrambling security frequencies. He'd been up until dawn putting into action a preliminary plan for his latest assignment. Making use of all his contacts, he had sent out word that a certain arms shipment, very much wanted by a deadly traitor named Simon, had, by a circuitous route, made its way into Burke Lonigan's control. Being known the world over by certain people as an illegal arms dealer placed Burke in the perfect position to carry out this latest job for the agency. Now, all he had to do was wait. Wait for the notorious Simon to make the next move. But until that happened, it would be business as usual for Lonigan's Imports and Exports.

A soft knock sounded on the outer door. Burke lifted his head just in time to lock gazes with his personal assistant. The lovely, elusive and very-disturbing-to-a-man's-libido Callie Severin breezed into his office, a tentative smile on her face.

"Good morning, Mr. Lonigan. Or should I say good afternoon?" Callie sat in the chair across from Burke's desk, crossed her ankles and folded her hands in her lap.

Had he heard just a hint of censure in her voice? Burke wondered. What had her in a snit? "It is noon, isn't it?" He chuckled pleasantly. "Are you upset with me for some reason?"

"No, of course not. Why should I be? What you do in your personal life is none of my concern."

"My personal life?" He grinned broadly. "Ah, I see. You assume my tardiness is due to my having spent the night in some fair damsel's boudoir, making mad passionate love until dawn."

He liked the way Callie blushed. Few women blushed these days. But then she had the complexion for it. Pale and creamy, without a hint of a freckle despite her dark auburn hair and smoky gray eyes.

"As I said, it's none of my—"

"None of your concern," he said, finishing her sentence.

She nodded agreement.

"I'm afraid I must impose on you to help me get an important dinner party planned, and then I must ask an enormous favor of you. I need a hostess for this affair."

"Isn't there someone else more suited than I am to serve as your hostess?" she asked, nervously rubbing her hands together. "I'm sure Lady Ashley or Mrs. Odum-Hyde would—"

"Lady Ashley is in Paris visiting her sister and Mrs. Odum-Hyde has landed herself a Brussel's diamond broker and is now wearing a ring the size of an apple."

Callie giggled. Burke liked her giggles, too. Girlish, yet throaty and seductive. If he was totally honest with himself, he'd have to admit that he liked everything about Callie. She was more than competent at her job. Actually she was the best PA he'd ever had.

But something about her bothered him. Not that he didn't trust her. He did. Implicitly. Her background check had given him every reason to think highly of her—as a PA and as a person. She was a bright, hardworking young lady, with an impeccable work record. He knew she was unmarried and yet was the mother of a small child. If he remembered correctly, the child was almost two. Although he had never questioned her about anything remotely personal, he couldn't help wondering about her child's father. What sort of man could have walked away from a woman such as Callie and deserted his own child?

Not much of a man, Burke thought.

I've never been with a real man, only a self-centered boy. The words echoed inside Burke's mind, but he had no idea who had said them or when. Had some woman he had made love to spoken those words? If so, why couldn't he remember the woman or the incident? Could it have been that night two years ago? He vaguely remembered drowning his sorrows at the Princess Inn after he'd been told his father had died and the family had turned him away. And occasionally, through the fog of his subconscious, he could almost make out the face of the woman who had gone home with him that night.

"Is something wrong?" Callie asked. "You had a most peculiar look on your face, as if you were in pain."

"You can alleviate any pain I might be experiencing, if you agree to act as my hostess next week."

"Of course, I'd be delighted to act as your hostess."

"Good, then that's settled."

When he rose from his desk chair, Callie stood. She was only a wisp of a girl—no, not a girl, he thought. A woman. She was twenty-seven and a mother. Hardly a girl. Size-wise, she was just shy of being petite. Short, small-boned, fragile. Round in all the right places, with a slender waist.

Although he had more sophisticated, more elegant women at his disposal, Burke fancied Callie and had since the first day she had walked into his office. However, he couldn't understand why he was so attracted to her, more so than to any woman he'd ever met....

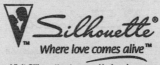

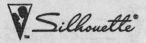

COMING NEXT MONTH

#1033 WHO DO YOU LOVE?
***Two original stories in one outstanding volume**
"Two Hearts" by Maggie Shayne
If police officer Jack McCain hadn't been in the right place at the right time, he never would have met—and ultimately married—beautiful heiress Grace Phelps. But both had secrets they had yet to reveal—secrets that could change the state of their marriage, for better *or* for worse....
"A Little Bit Dangerous" by Marilyn Pappano
It had been eight years since undercover agent Chance Reynard had walked away from Mary Katherine Monroe, leaving her with nothing but a broken heart. Now, face-to-face once again, neither was prepared for the feelings that still existed—or for the truth that lurked just beneath the surface.
#1034 HER SECRET WEAPON—Beverly Barton
A Year of Loving Dangerously
SPEAR agent Burke Lonigan couldn't deny the fierce attraction he felt toward his personal assistant, Callie Severin. So when a dangerous villain threatened both their lives, Burke proposed a marriage of convenience in order to keep Callie safe. But Callie had a secret that would drastically change Burke's life—and unite their hearts forever.
#1035 A THANKSGIVING TO REMEMBER—Margaret Watson
36 Hours
For 36 hours, an elusive killer held Tina White hostage—and FBI agent Tom Flynt was doing all he could to help the woman he loved. She'd nursed him back to health when he needed her most, and now it was up to Tom to return the favor. Would he get to Tina before her time ran out?
#1036 THE RETURN OF LUKE McGUIRE—Justine Davis
The return of Luke McGuire had the town of Santiago Beach talking—and Amelia Blair's lonely heart pounding. He'd come home to help his troubled brother, and, with Amelia's help, the boy had definitely improved. But could Amelia forget Luke's infamous past and look forward to sharing his future?
#1037 THE LAWMAN MEETS HIS BRIDE—Meagan McKinney
Matched In Montana
Wrongly accused lawman Quinn Loudon knew he was at the end of his rope the moment he kidnapped Connie Adams and convinced her to help clear his name. The unsuspecting beauty was skeptical, but Quinn's proof was irrefutable—as was the desire she saw whenever she looked in his eyes.
#1038 THE VIRGIN BEAUTY—Claire King
Brooding rancher Daniel Cash hadn't expected veterinarian Grace McKenna to be good with animals *and* with his own wounded heart. But when someone began sabotaging his livelihood, searching for the culprit put *both* their lives at risk. Now Daniel was determined to protect his ranch—and the woman he hoped to share it with.

CMN0900